TALES OF THE BALD EAGLE MOUNTAINS

McETHATTAN GAP AND OLD QUIGGLE HOMESTEAD
Photo by H. W. Swope, Lock Haven, Pa.

TALES OF THE BALD EAGLE MOUNTAINS

HENRY W. SHOEMAKER

CATAMOUNT
PRESS

an imprint of Sunbury Press, Inc.
Mechanicsburg, PA USA

CATAMOUNT
PRESS

an imprint of Sunbury Press, Inc.
Mechanicsburg, PA USA

For information about special discounts for bulk purchases, please contact Sunbury Press Orders Dept. at (855) 338-8359 or orders@sunburypress.com.

To request one of our authors for speaking engagements or book signings, please contact Sunbury Press Publicity Dept. at publicity@sunburypress.com.

FIRST CATAMOUNT PRESS EDITION: December 2022

Set in Adobe Garamond | Interior design by Crystal Devine | Cover by Katharine H. McCormick and Lawrence Knorr | Edited by Lawrence Knorr | Headpiece and tailpiece by Katharine H. McCormick, Philadelphia, Pa.

Publisher's Cataloging-in-Publication Data
Names: Shoemaker, Henry W., author.
Title: Tales of the Bald Eagle Mountains / Henry W. Shoemaker.
Description: First trade paperback edition. | Mechanicsburg, PA : Catamount Press, 2022.
Summary: Henry Shoemaker compiled these legendary tales set in the Bald Eagle Mountains of central Pennsylvania. Shoemaker's tales recall the transition of the landscape from forest to industrial logging and the decline of the native peoples as the European settlers advanced westward. This collection of tales has been modernized for 21st-century audiences but maintains the charm, wit, and suspense of the originals.
Identifiers: ISBN : 979-8-88819-029-6 (softcover) | 979-8-88819-030-2 (ePub).
Subjects: FICTION / Fairy Tales, Folk Tales, Legends & Mythology | FICTION / Cultural Heritage | FICTION / Small Town & Rural | FICTION / Short Stories.

Product of the United States of America
0 1 1 2 3 5 8 13 21 34 55

Continue the Enlightenment!

BY THE SAME AUTHOR:

Wild Life in Central Pennsylvania (1903)
Pennsylvania Mountain Stories (1907)
More Pennsylvania Mountain Stories (1912)
The Indian Steps (1912)
In the Seven Mountains (1913)
Susquehanna Legends (1913)

* * *

Immaterial Verses (1898)
Random Thoughts (1899)
Pennsylvania Mountain Verses (1907)
Elizabethan Days (1912)

* * *

Legend of Penn's Cave (pamphlet) (1907)
Story of the Sulphur Spring (pamphlet) (1912)
Stories of Pennsylvania Animals (pamphlet) (1913)
Stories of Great Pennsylvania Hunters (pamphlet) (1913)

CONTENTS

Foreword by Lawrence Knorr   ix

Argument   xii

CHAPTERS

I.	Birth of the Bald Eagles	1
II.	The Siren	10
III.	The Red Fox	20
IV.	The View Tree	31
V.	The Brown Bear	40
VI.	Old Philippe	48
VII.	King Wi-daagh's Spell	58
VIII.	Caves of the Bald Eagles	67
IX.	Pathfinder's Child	75
X.	Conrad's Broom	84
XI.	The Giantess	93
XII.	Mary Goes Over the Mountain	101
XIII.	The Fate of Atoka	110
XIV.	For the Glory of Indian Summer	120
XV.	The Lost Chord	131
XVI.	Bald Eagle's Nest	143
XVII.	The Running Race	154
XVIII.	Two Roses	165
XIX.	The Sorceress	176
XX.	Unrequited	187
XXI.	Before the Fire	197
XXII.	Simpler's Joy	208
XXIII.	Ironcutter's Cabin	220

ILLUSTRATIONS

The Gap at McElhattan   (Frontispiece)

The New Bridge near McElhattan   13

A Bald Eagle Mountain Landscape   29

The Golden Hour at the Camp   53

The River and the Round Top   77

The Meeting of the Waters   111

A Distant View of the Bald Eagles   125

A Picnic in the Woods   147

The Flight of the Wild Pigeons   171

Among the Giant Pines   193

Pennsylvania Pine Forest   209

FOREWORD

HENRY WHARTON SHOEMAKER (1880-1958) was born into a wealthy Manhattan family at the peak of the Gilded Era. As a young man, he attended Columbia College and dabbled in investing with his brother. But his true love was the hills, forests, and rivers of north-central Pennsylvania. Shoemaker's grandparents owned thousands of acres of woodlands and a rustic house at McElhattan he dubbed Restless Oaks after expanding it. Shoemaker spent many months and years there, claiming he traveled among the hills and valleys collecting folk tales from the locals. However, it is more likely Shoemaker spent most of his time with pen and pad inventing short stories set in the region.

This book is another such work. The places are real, but most of the people and certainly the natives who are named are all fictional. However, these stories are literary gems. Shoemaker was not only a gifted storyteller; he was also a gifted writer. If he were better known, he might be declared the "Mark Twain of Pennsylvania" for his clever tales and alluring characters. However, unlike Twain, Shoemaker was born into privilege and often inserted social class as a divider between people and their expectations. Shoemaker also seemed to be a hopeless romantic. Many of his stories describe young women with whom a particular young man is enamored but usually unable to meet or marry. Often mishaps prevent a successful relationship. Many of the stories are melancholy.

When Shoemaker published this book in 1912, he was 32 years old and recently divorced. His first marriage had been brief, and his wife left with their son for the West Coast. Thus, the stories of lost love and the constant observation of women can be explained by this brief interlude of bachelorhood until he was engaged again in 1913.

One story, "The Lost Chord," reads like a Victorian *Twilight Zone* tale. It captures Shoemaker's cultured upbringing and his European travels. In the story, the protagonist falls in love with a girl on a train and later discovers a doll in an antique shop resembling her. Here is a taste of Shoemaker's writing from a scene on the train:

> But now, the brakes were being thrown on, and the cumbersome steel cars were coming to a halt beneath the murky shed. The sweet, graceful little creature got up, satchel in hand, and started for the door. I did not know what to do—should I follow or remain where I was? Pursuit, that most primitive of masculine instincts got the upper hand for an instant. Perhaps she would be getting on another train; I might ride in it to find out where she lived. I ran through the empty car and out on the station platform; I got there just in time to see her dainty figure ascending the iron stairway leading to the waiting room and street. I hated to follow her; she might lose any good opinion she had of me—and stamp me as a 'masher.'

Masher or not, Henry Shoemaker married again and then had a lengthy affair with another woman. Over 350 letters from this affair were preserved and are in this publisher's possession. Also in the collection are letters from many other women from various times in Shoemaker's life. It seems he was always a hopeless romantic, always intrigued by the girl on the train or the girl at the inn, but always held back by his social class. While he might frolic with a "commoner," he was to marry within his class.

A founder of the Pennsylvania Folklore Society, he also served as the Commonwealth's first state folklorist from 1946 to 1958. Henry Wharton Shoemaker was a larger-than-life figure who sought to promote Pennsylvania but did so by inventing a history of the inland forests that were mostly figments of his imagination. Fortunately, he was also one of Pennsylvania's best writers. I leave you with this passage from the story "The Sorceress," where Shoemaker describes a cemetery in winter:

A cemetery, especially one on high ground, always is at its best when high winds shake the Norway spruces and bend the arborvitaes almost double; when the distant mountains are a purple-brown, and the sun a golden disc in the whirling mass of smoky clouds, when the gold-fish in the fountain feel too congealed to swim about freely, when dry leaves and bits of hydrangea blooms chase one another along the pebbled paths, when the old gravedigger turns up the collar of his faded military coat, when an occasional shaft of pale sunlight throws into bold relief some crumbling inscription. No cemetery was ever better fitted as the resting place of the glorious dead than the hilltop "God's acre" in old Lewisburg.

Henry Wharton Shoemaker is buried in such a cemetery, atop a hill, above Lock Haven, Pennsylvania. Guy Graybill and I visited the place in the late summer of 2022. It was windy, but had a beautiful view of the West Branch of the Susquehanna. While Shoemaker is gone, fortunately, these stories remain for your enjoyment. And, if you ever feel up to an invigorating hike, try the path behind Lock Haven University that leads up the hill to Highland Cemetery. There, near the highest point, you will find the great folklorist's grave very near Bald Eagle Mountain.

Lawrence Knorr
Boiling Springs, Pa., 2022

ARGUMENT

O N OFFERING still another volume of Pennsylvania mountain legends, the author has this to say by way of extenuation.
While his other books contained folklore gathered at random
in various sections of the central part of the commonwealth, all of these
herein were collected along the "dark and somber" range of the Bald
Eagle Mountains, the inspired origin of which is described in the first
chapter.

It has been the author's aim, as far as practicable, to give one legend
for each mountain in the chain, as far as the Juniata, where the true Bald
Eagles come to an end. Most of them have an old-time setting, and the
greater part of the personal note, which entered into some of the tales in
the other volumes, is lessened.

In *Pennsylvania Mountain Stories*, he preferred tale I, "Why the
Steiner House Patient Pulled Through," by far the best. It possessed
some, but not by any means all the eerie qualities that thrilled him when
he heard it in the hallway of the old hotel in Millheim, now alas burned
to the ground.

In the present volume, he is partial to tale X, "Conrad's Broom," yet of
all he has written, it lacks more of the marvelous succinctness and thrill it
possessed when related by a grand old gentleman whose eventful lifetime
at its close, just missed ten years of the century mark! We can only say
that the old legends may have lost in passing through our hands but have
not been added to or trifled with. As there seemed to be no one else bent
on chronicling and preserving them, the author, with a full realization of
his limitations, has "stuck at it." Chief among these "limitations" is the
fact that the time is late to have begun collecting Pennsylvania folklore

and Indian tales. This could have been done, by almost anyone, with great thoroughness a hundred and twenty-five years ago. There was a lull after all the uproar of the Revolution and Indian wars, yet romantic tales were rife. But no one thought of collecting such things then. People looked upon their individual lives as of little consequence, their deeds as simple duties. As to the Indians or their history, they were regarded with loathing or indifference. No one today would collect the annals of English sparrows or Cooper's hawks. Fifty years ago, even, was not too late, as Indians were met with from time to time, and aroused no particular attention; they were tolerated as itinerant basket weavers or harvest-hands. A few of the original frontiersmen or their sons were then living "up in eighty," as they say in the mountains, but who cared to catechize them about a troublous past? A new war between North and South was beginning to absorb everyone's attention. When the present writer came upon the scene, "all was over," but there were gleams in the embers of romance and folklore that showed that they contained life. He was able to learn the legends from a few of the old people, who were boys when there were still borderers and Indians whose talk was interesting enough for them to listen to and remember.

Incomplete and lacking the "thrill" most needed, these tales are an honest effort to preserve a period as teeming with romance as "when the world was young." They show the wealth of folklore the Indians stored up, and the first settlers brought with them from "overseas," from Scotland, the North of Ireland, France, and the Palatinate. They are worth comparing, at any rate, with the folklore of the old world. In some of them, the author thinks he was able to catch on the wing a passing phase, a time and mode of life that will come no more. Every year death has wrought havoc with the "old folks," most of them going to their graves with their reminiscences and ghost-stories unrecorded. Some of their "untold tales" were probably more startling than any here recounted and many times more numerous. Many recorded on these pages may lack vital interest, but our selection was limited. If the author has been able to perform a service, no matter how slight, to legendary history or a reader's gratification or to promote a love of all that is picturesque and best in the Central Pennsylvania mountain country, the task cannot be said to have been in vain.

But one more word, kind reader; another old friend complained that all the love-stories ended too unhappily. This is partly due to the fact that they had to be transcribed exactly as they were told to the writer; they came reeking of unhappiness. But it may be partly owing to many incidents in the author's life, which made him remember more distinctly experiences somewhat resembling his own.

A debt, an unrepayable one, is owing to the press and public for the kind reception of his previous books. The author is extremely grateful for the genial and intellectual companionship of John H. Chatham, of McElhattan, Pa., who accompanied him on many of his pilgrimages to remote spots in the mountains; to James W. Quiggle, 2nd, also of McElhattan, for valued assistance in correcting the proofs; to the Pennsylvania Forestry Department, and others, for kind permission to reproduce photographs used in the illustrations.

HENRY W. SHOEMAKER
Riverside, Connecticut
November 9, 1912

I

BIRTH OF THE BALD EAGLES

(Story of Muncy Mountain)

ON THE earliest day that Indian myth and folklore have knowledge of, the region which we now call Central Pennsylvania was a flat and fertile plain, interspersed with clumps of rich tropical-like trees and bubbling springs, and where grazed countless herds of strange-looking animals and reptiles, ancestral types of those found there upon the advent of the white men. Sometimes the bunches of luxuriant trees grew out of hillocks or knobs, and on these, the primitive forerunners of the Indian tribes had their abodes. They had come so lately from the bosom of *Getchi-Manitto* the Almighty, for the world was new, and had experienced so few of the vicissitudes now so inherent to the generations, that if they had religious belief, it would bs founded on a certainty. Things had not run contrary to their wishes; consequently, they had not found the advisability to inquire into their beginnings.

Fruits of all kinds, as well as nuts and cereals, grew at hand in abundance. A new taste, for the flesh of animals, birds and fishes had sharpened their appetites. All was easy, opulent, serene. They were beloved by their Great First Cause and grew comfortable and complacent in the very radiance of His blessing.

Wars, quarrels, strife, competition, all the emulative features of life, were lacking in their composition—their backbones had not hardened. One hour of modern life, with its upsets, backsets, and rivalries, would have exhausted their untried energies. They lacked the motive force to send a line of hardy descendants down the ages. They had not demonstrated their rights for existence. But they were fearless, in a sense, although nothing had ever happened to make them afraid. In plain words, they were spiritually "half-baked." There must be reasons why humanity was made what it is. The Christian Bible tells the origin of sin; the Indian legends repeat the beginnings of valor. The Indians never acknowledged that they sinned; perhaps they never did; the people of the Bible never laid stress on their bravery. But it was to be the fate of the Indians that they came down the ages physically and spiritually brave, and only by contamination with the Europeans did their deterioration begin. But for centuries, they lived in the broad plains of Central Pennsylvania, no better nor worse than when the Great Spirit breathed His breath into the clay; their inertia must have begun to pall on Him. Only men of action have immortal souls; the Indians had none in those days—there are no Indian ghosts dating from remote antiquity, nor are there legends of any. Perhaps their lack of individuality and progress were all a part of the deeply laid plans of the Great Spirit.

Valor, to be the dominant trait of the Indian character, was not to be developed until they were physically fit. But when time had produced a magnificent race of beings, their testing out process was to begin. Like all acts of the Great Spirit, it came about in a way that could not be long foretold.

It occurred after a season of unparalleled calmness and prosperity, in a joyous, bracing autumn, when the natives smelt the failing leaves, and it was too cool to doze in the half-crisp, half-sultry sunshine. It came first in the form of news from Indians whose canoes had started far towards the headwaters of Bald Eagle Creek and, like tawny Paul Reveres, brought the message of a new order of things to their peaceful, indifferent fellows in the land of the Susquehanna. And once they heard it, not an Indian rested as calmly as of yore. The bearers of tidings told of a vast upheaval of the earth, moving irresistibly eastward like the progress of some monstrous mole. Where once were smooth plains covered with groves of oaks and pine or giant ferns, or fields waving with Indian corn, were now great mountainous masses of broken rocks rifted from the centers of the earth. Springs and watercourses were loosed from their rocky fastnesses and gushed forth in torrents through the crevices in this newly formed face of nature. A force that from within could raise such huge mountains, some of them a thousand feet in height, must be titanic in its strength and immensity, almost a creator of worlds itself.

Death and destruction followed this birth of a mountain range. The peaceful natives would fall asleep one night in their cool tents along some stream on the rich plains, never dreaming of aught but plenty and contentment. During the night, the earth beneath them would rise, sometimes quickly, other times unsteadily, as if some vast monster was turning in his slumbers. Tents, lodges, campfires, Indians old and young, would be hurled to their deaths or sink to burial alive in the new-formed crannies and abysses. The sun would rise from behind a rocky peak instead of gliding gracefully into vision above the horizon. The sound of happy voices was no more, only the dull, ominous rumble of the great masses of rock, earth, and uprooted timber settling into place. And this horror was moving steadily eastward, forming a new mountain sometimes every night. As it seemed endless in its course, the Indians dwelling further east moved rapidly from the radius of the new development, but some were caught unawares when side ridges, mostly to the south, were suddenly heaved from the plains. The far-eastern Indians heard the news with dismay; it was either combat the oncoming force or fly before it. But what good was flight if mountains shot up in every nook of safety? But how to combat it was the question. All the physical force of every Indian on the vast American continent rolled together could not stay a force vast enough to heave up mountains from the plains. It was futile to concoct schemes to combat it; human energy was *nil*. It had not occurred that a supernatural power could be invoked. The Indians of those ancient simple days were much like our white people in this modern complex age; they did not know how to pray or who to pray to. They accepted everything as a matter of course; they had a physical name for every ghost.

They called the rain when it pattered on the birch-bark roof of the lodge-house, just rain, it was not the footsteps of a wraith. They called the wind when it howled dismally through the pine woods or swept shrieking, up the open bed of the river, just wind, and not a disembodied, unhappy spirit calling for surcease. They called the shadows when they fell suddenly in front of a traveler's path or hid the surroundings of a peaceful camp, just shadows, and not the dimly seen presence of a ghost or troop of ghosts. They called the sighing splash of distant waterfalls, just waterfalls, and not the song of the banshee or "'token." The crackling of boughs, or the sudden fall of a tree at night in the forest, was just nature and not unseen hands working out their purposes.

It was a very prosaic world of *facts*, much like the world we live in now. We have as many ghosts about us today as we had a hundred years ago, but like the Indians of old, we have given them physical names. But they are ghosts all the same; someday, they will come to their own. But this complete understanding of this world as a purely physical manifestation had its limitations. When human agency failed, there was nothing that drew out the reserve force. In a world where there are ghosts, the big deeds of valor and unselfish bravery are accomplished. A prayerful world is a hopeful, undaunted world. And yet these simple aborigines differed in one great fundamental principle from our modern materialists. The Indians were creedless but cheerful; they did not have the pessimistic gloom of modern faithlessness. We bemoan a faith once held but thrown away; they were comfortable because they cared for nothing before or behind. But in this crisis, when the onrush of a nascent range of mountains daily grew more imminent, physical opposition being footless, they must need appeal from it somehow. Among their number, they acknowledged one man wiser than the rest, yet he was only a very young man. Of course, his name is lost in the shrouds of time, but a name matters very little where there is accomplishment; it is only useful with society people who do nothing and need a name to prop them a brief period on the ragged edge of the inevitable oblivion. Without striving, this young man had been, by common consent, acknowledged to be the superior of all others. Distinctions of birth were unknown in those days, but his wisdom made him king, and he became the progenitor of descendants, growing less wise with each generation until, at the time of the white men's invasion, they were the dullest of their tribes.

This wise man, when they appealed to him for some recourse other than flight and to stop the destruction of their happy lands, said he must go out to the barest part of the plains, to meditate for seven or eight days. He went, taking scanty provisions to ensure high thinking, but was back after one night's solitude. He told them, when they assembled before him, that their desire to remain where they were was an inspiration, nothing less, but furthermore, if they were brave and believed, they could forever stop the onslaught of their destroyer, who was mighty but not divine.

His speech was intelligible, except for the words "brave," "belief," "divine." They dealt with a range of experiences beyond their orbit. The wise man seeing this explained them the best he could, and to the credit of the Indians, let it be said they understood.

With this much gained, he proceeded to tell them of the secret of their birth, something they had not known nor cared about before. After once they heard it, they were different beings; it was as if a divine spark from the realm where it abounds had penetrated them; they never felt the same again. The Great First Cause, who made them ("but who made the Great First Cause" was their unanimous demand, and this remained unanswered) desired to instill a new virtue, *courage*, into the supine, calm dwellers on the plains. He had permitted a Machtando or giant monster of the underworld, whose home had been many leagues toward the center of the earth, to disport himself mole-like beneath the outer lining of the globe.

Nature is wasteful of its seed, except when it has some purpose to conserve, and the lives blotted out in the monster's track were uncounted and would have availed not. But the vast body of dwellers, to the eastward, who had learned of the great changes, were to be given a chance to save themselves and make themselves, in the full sense, Men.

But here, the concourse again interrupted the wise man. "Who made the Great First Cause?" they clamored.

"That will be answered someday to each of you," said the speaker calmly, "you will laugh that you were ever dumb enough to ask such a question; it will be so simple."

At any rate, the Indians were to win their birthright, only to lose it to a race ages later, with a purer faith than theirs. Four moons from the time of the assemblage, the monster mountain builder was due to emerge, headfirst, from his chain of hills. The place chosen by him was to be on the fertile, thickly populated plains across the swelling river from what the Indians afterward called Monsey or Muncy Town. If the natives defeated and destroyed the monster, they would increase, multiply and prosper; if they failed, all would meet the fate of their compatriots to the west, not one but a horde of similar monsters would rise out of the earth and annihilate them. The Indians could conquer if they would be brave, and braver was synonymous with belief. Believing in oneself is equivalent to a creed, for God, or the Great First Cause, we all know is within us; to a greater or lesser extent, God is the power within us to do things. During the time intervening until the great monster shoved forth his Gorgon's head, the Indians were to prepare his doom. First of all, they were to shape a huge granite rock, which lay (perhaps put there by divine foresight, on the riverbank) into a spear point. This they were to smear thickly with poisons which could be dug from the earth; the wise man would show them where. Then they were to fasten the spear point to a handle made from many tree trunks laid side by side, fastened by hickory poles, and securely spliced at the ends.

All this was to be raised from the ground on trucks or wheels made from smooth beech logs and at the sides propelled by every Indian able to navigate. The logs were to be indented for each Indian's body, and his full force would help send it forward. The wise man showed them the place where the monster would emerge and where to station their poisoned ram. When they heard the ripping of roots, the cracking of boulders, and the bursting of soil, denoting the appearance of the menace, they would get ready to set the instrument of defense into motion. When the huge head, open-fanged, emerged, they were, by concerted effort, to drive the sharpened, poisoned end down its venomous throat.

The wise man had tried to make himself clear; there was little more to say. Before dismissing the concourse, however, he bade them recite after him a short prayer to the Great First Cause because that was the only part of his discourse they had not understood. Self-preservation came naturally enough, but the idealistic part, the power not seen, yet themselves solely, was too abstract, too far from immediate benefits to shape itself succinctly in their plant-like intellects. But they followed him word for word, and reverently, in the prayer. Before the mood for action would change, the young soothsayer led his people to the great flat rock and set them to drilling one end to a point. Buoyed up by their new ideals, they worked faster and more skillfully than even their leader deemed possible. Despite their vast numbers, not one worker conflicted with another; it was inspired teamwork. While they were pounding away, the wise man selected the trees which were to form the trucks or handle of the giant war spear.

These being chosen and marked, he set the enthusiastic workers constructing it as soon as the spearhead was done to his satisfaction. They say that after four days and nights of cheerful labor, the great weapon was ready to be hurled against the foe. Meanwhile, the old men and the women and children were moved far to the eastward and settled comfortably amid hills and valleys until the conflict should be over. So confident was the wise man of the ultimate triumph that he forbid families at parting to say goodbye; he determined to make faith of victory certain. He drilled the force who were to operate the ram until they handled the mighty weapon dexterously. Then there was nothing to do but to wait developments. The foe might not appear for four moons, but there was a danger of its appearance sooner. They did not have to wait until they became tired or disorganized. It was not long until they heard the awful ramble of mountains in the making. The ground shook where they were encamped as if mammoths were disporting themselves under their very feet. One clear hazeless morning, they beheld the great circular outlines of a mountain, looming against the horizon, seven or eight miles to the westward, where the night before none had been.

The "mountain builder" was almost upon them; at this rate, their conflict with him would occur that night or the next morning. In order to let them see plainly by night, the wise man ordered the plains and forests fired. When the sun sank, miles of blazing grass and tree ferns illuminated the scene with a lurid, uncanny glow. All had been silent since the morning; the monster had evidently retired below to rest before another effort.

At midnight they heard a tremendous crunching of rocks and roots, the signal that the mountain building had begun afresh. Some of the Indians almost went mad from the deafening roar, so sustained, so loud, so nerve-racking. It reached a pitch where it overpowered everything, and the tensely strained ear drums became used to it. But many of the natives were totally deafened for life. By the orange-red glare of the burning vegetation, they noted the level of the plain rising higher and higher. The work of upheaval had begun right before them; it was their chance now to stop the hideous monster and earn a patrimony of valor to send on to generations yet unborn. Amid the terrific noises, the backbone of a mountain rose into view, a mountain a mile in width and close to a thousand feet in height.

As it was settling into a permanent contour, they noticed a rending in the structure of its easterly slope; the monster, evidently apprised of his human enemies, was preparing to issue forth to give them battle. Soon the vast horned head of the Machtando, or demon, did emerge, shooting forth gaseous vapors so foul that it sickened many of the defenders. But those who could overcome their indisposition manned the ram bravely and sent it in motion after the fiendish monster. Both head and ram moved with about the same acceleration and force. But the Indians were gifted on that occasion with superhuman courage and drove the sharpened spear point into the open maw of the oncoming foe. For an instant, all seemed swallowed in the mass of sulfurous smoke, but the sharpened apex went true, coming out the back of the monster's neck. Transfixed, it could move neither forward nor backward, but its subterranean body lashed itself wildly, sending fresh convulsions through the newly formed mountain. Sooner or later, the creature might have freed himself, but for the poison so liberally smeared over the spearhead. Before he could devise a way to shake off his enemies, he was in the throes of a horrible death agony. Struggling with might and main, he was forcing the blade out of his jaws when the chilling forces of death overcame him. But he did not become still until after the entire form had turned itself completely over, causing that noticeable breadth at the termination of what we now style Muncy Mountain.

When he had gasped for the last time, like some foundry blowing off, and lay like the heights above, perfectly still, the wise man clambered out on the truck of the weapon and asked the prayers of the valiant band. "It is not for the death of the worst foe that could attack us we wish to give thanks; it is for the birth of our souls, of our new valor, of our hope for immortality."

The Indians, for the most part utterly exhausted, fell on the earth, uttering grateful expressions. They had won a notable and lasting victory. "Let none of you forget the spear," said the wise man when he bade them disperse.

And so it came to pass that Indians always carried spears when on the chase or in battle. Antiquarians have wondered at the apparent uselessness of these weapons, but they were the armament of the Indians' souls, the symbol of the grandest feat of their existence. When they carried them, it augured something great. And the mountain range which came into being was called the Machtando, or Devil Mountains, until rechristened centuries later in honor of the great Chief Bald Eagle.

II

THE SIREN

(Story of Loyalsock Mountain)

THERE SEEMED to be an unwarranted number of rafting accidents at Loyalsock Riffles, some of them fraught with loss of life. It was certainly not the worst place on the river by any means, at least to pilots who could successfully navigate Conewago Falls, with its drop of seventy feet in the mile, year after year, to say nothing of the chutes in Muncy and Shamokin dams yet would go to destruction in the shallows of Loyalsock. There was one explanation that found many followers, and that was as so many rafts had tied up at Lock Haven or Williamsport on their way, that the raftsmen had imbibed too freely and were not in the proper trim when they hit their first obstacle. But this could not hold good when numerous rafts, manned by church members fresh from the throes of protracted meetings, went down with the same alacrity as those piloted by crews "outside the fold"; it behooved investigators to learn the probable reasons from the raftsmen themselves. But the rafting fraternity was clannish and close-mouthed, as reticent about their mishaps as their triumphs, with their own revenges and rewards, and it was only when practically the "last raft" had gone that the old pilots became communicative. Then were heard many interesting reminiscences of the river.

There was one old gentleman who had rafted for over half a century and who knew the Susquehanna from the mouth of Moshannon to the dead waters of Marietta as a nun knows her beads, which was able to explain why so many rafts split up at Loyalsock. He did not profess to believe the story in its entirety, but without it, the constant wrecks would be shrouded in the profoundest mystery. Once when the grand old gentleman was in a particularly communicative mood, he was seated on his favorite easy chair on his comfortable piazza in the shadow of the Round Top; he told the story of the rafts that went to pieces over the Riffles of Loyalsock. It seemed there never was so much as a dog raft or a dugout wrecked there in the early days of rafting; the river had been run safely from Karthaus to Harrisburg for ten years before the trouble began. Then all of a sudden, there was a change; it took a hardy pilot to get through in safety until he learned the secret of the danger. Once aware of this, he took particular care not to duplicate his loss, which sometimes had mounted up even into human lives. As was generally the case with untoward happenings in those days, and in these for that matter, if we only took the trouble to inquire, man's avarice and sin and supernatural retribution were the "cause and effect" of these rafting tragedies.

To go back to the first elements of the story, let it be stated again that the Indians did not leave the Bald Eagle Mountain country suddenly, nor any other part of the State. After they had been whipped into being peaceable citizens, they were familiar figures in the marketplaces of the towns, around the old public houses and ferries, and their tents and shanties loomed along many a riverbank. Gradually only did they become less; they went quietly and unobtrusively until no one was shocked when they were seen no more.

There was a single family of Mingo Indians. Tradition had it they came from the southern part of the state and lived a short distance below the present location of the summer resort known as Sylvan Dell. They were not the only interesting denizens of that spot; Tim Murphy, the famous sharpshooter of the Revolution, spent his last days there. But to be exact, Tim's cabin stood an eighth of a mile further upstream, where there was quite a respectable-sized flat for his garden. The Indians' shanty was perched at the apex where the flat and the mountainside came together. It looked, from a distance, like an oriole's nest, literally hanging over the river. The Indian head of the family went by the name of Powderhorn, not a very pretty, but yet a serviceable cognomen. About the time they adopted trousers and stovepipe hats, the natives began anglicizing their names. In their last phase in Pennsylvania history, we read of Johnnyhocks, Little Johnny Brokenstraw, Bob Sunday, Billy Frozen Stone, Hotbread, and Powderhorn.

But the story of Powderhorn concerns us most at present. He was the last of his generation; his father and mother had been butchered by settlers on the Yellow Breeches Creek, and his brothers and sisters grew to maturity only to die of some pestilence that decimated their kind on the banks of the Juniata. Powderhorn had suffered from the horrible disease but survived it minus hair and teeth plus a palsied leg. It was hard for him to hunt, so he cultivated a taste for basket-making. He married on the Juniata, drifted north with his bride, and built for her the hanging nest in that neck of woods below the Sylvan Dell. He became an attendant at the first markets in Williamsport, where he found ready sale for his wares and, in addition, did chores for the farmers and housewives. To see an Indian today at a Williamsport market would draw a crowd, but that is because the last aborigine has gone. In those days, there were supposed to be Indians; they caused no more consternation than when a bull moose from the North Woods is strung up in front of a butcher's stall.

In due course of time, Powderhorn accumulated a family; it consisted of eight girls and a boy. The boy was a sickly specimen, early ticketed for the Happy Hunting Ground without stop, but the girls seemed full of health, were lithe, graceful, and good-looking. There was one, the flower of the flock, in whom was centered all the good points of generations behind. Powderhorn and his squaw Maggie Sue, she was named after two rich Scotch-Irish women near whose home her parents once tented; both wanted an attractive name for this most winsome of their daughters. They called her after a flowering plant, the roots of which they had both hunted and loved as modern children love candy, Sweet Cicely. The young girl developed to be sweeter than her name, and her parents, in their homely way, were sometimes sorry they had not chosen a name more imposing. Perhaps, as they grew older, they forgot the taste of their early sweetmeat. Socially the lonely Indian family was quite by themselves, as much as a parrot in a flock of sparrows. The good looks of the Indian girls, especially Sweet Cicely, made considerable of an impression on the few young white men of the neighborhood, but as the girls had no wild inclinations, they made no efforts to be civil to them. The oldest girl, when she was twenty-six, in the Warrior's Run Sunday School one

THE NEW BRIDGE, NEAR McELHATTAN
Photo by H. W. Swope, Lock Haven, Pa.

morning, told her teacher that she had never had a sweetheart. The white girls looked at her amazed, as she was far prettier than any of them.

Once, by chance, an Indian youth appeared on the scene. He came from the reservation about fifteen miles north of Warren and did farm work for old Ezra McGrady, who lived across the river from Powderhorn's retreat. He was a fine appearing young fellow, about twenty years of age, and grown to a height a couple of inches over six feet. He called himself Wild William Winters and boasted of a relationship to the venerable Chief Cornplant. Having the choice, he selected Sweet Cicely as the object of his admiration and soon was genuinely in love with her and she with him. He was her first admirer, her first love, her first kiss; all was so new and fresh; her embraces did not cast the shadow of some other man who had been there before. She was happy in not being able to measure his intensity with someone else, to compare his kisses and hand clasps with one who had gone before. The ecstasy of the first love is life's grandest elation, but how few who have experienced it are aware of its value.

There was a pathway that led from the home of Powderhorn along the riverbank; it ran about ten feet above the water and was shaded by venerable red birches, buttonwoods, elms, and hemlocks. Wildflowers and many-colored birds, sweet scents, and sweet songs made it a paradise for strayers. The path terminated at a narrow, rocky ledge often used as a seat by the lovers. On the warmer evenings, Sweet Cicely sat there and waited until Wild William, his work at McGrady's done, would cross the river in his canoe and court her on the ledge. When it was time to go home, he would accompany her up the path to the cabin and then return to his canoe, skimming across the moonlit waters like a savage warrior of old. Often as she waited, Sweet Cicely would sing. She had a sweet voice and picked up many of the ancient Indian refrains, and, coming from the south, she sang the earliest version of that bewitching piece, "Wild roved an Indian girl, bright Alfarata." It was an entrancing sight to see her sitting there, with her pretty feet dangling over the ledge, singing her love-warmed songs, while her lover sped to her side in his canoe. It was a bit of primeval life restored if it could only have lasted.

During the spring floods, rafts would drift by the lovers' rookery; when they were together, they waved to the raftsmen, just as modern folk salute a passing express train. All was good-natured, simple, and harm-less. Occasionally at dusk, when Sweet Cicely was waiting for her lover, rafts would pass, but they were belated craft, looking for comfortable eddies to tie up for the night. The young girl never waved to the raftsmen when alone, and few noticed her when the sun was gone. They swept by like wild geese hunting their night marsh. But sometimes, as they passed, she would catch herself in the midst of some song, though in minor key, and would check herself instantly, fearing that the watermen might think she was singing to attract them. She sang because she was happy, and one ought to be allowed happiness even when strangers are present.

One night when the river was falling fast, she had permitted herself to burst into song; it seemed a late hour and late from rivermen's stan-dards for any rafts to pass; the time slipped quicker when she sang until Wild William came. They had been house-cleaning at McGrady's, and the young man being a man of all work, was detained in consequence. Sweet Cicely expected this, but he seemed uncommonly long in coming. As she looked up and downstream with her eager lover-like glances, she noticed a raft approaching. The pilot, a black figure against the silvery tone of the dusk, stood motionless at his steering oar. He was alone; a pile of buffalo robes on the center of the raft showed where he slept. Where the rest of his crew were was a mystery; maybe they had mutinied at some tavern. Sweet Cicely conjectured. She was so interested in this apparition of the lone raftsman that she forgot to stop singing. The night wind springing up bore the strains of "Still Sweeps The River On" to the ears of the silent man. His alert glance showed that a slender young girl was watching him, and her singing was probably meant for him. Quick as a flash, he threw his weight against the oar and headed the raft toward shore. It was a perilous place to tie up, but he was willing to risk it. When the front logs snubbed the rocky bank, he leaped on land and tied the raft to some of the sturdiest red birches. Then he clambered up the rocky cliff to where Sweet Cicely was seated, with her feet dangling over the ledge. He moved so rapidly she was still singing when he stood beside her. She was not frightened; it was not dark; any minute, she might see Wild William's canoe launched in the current. What did the stranger want? His conduct was inexplicable. He did not lose time showing her as he sat down, put his arm, as strong as an iron girder, around her slender waist, and began addressing her in names of endearment.

The girl tried to free herself, calling out, "let go, let go, let go, *you*," but the stranger only held her more tightly. "Let go or I'll scream for help" was her next note of warning.

At this, he put both arms about her and tried to push her over on her back. That was the limit of endurance; she screamed lustily; all the vigor of her Indian lungs was asserted. The man, angered to the point where self-control was gone, released his hold from her waist with one hand and grasped her throat to silence her. He had a stronger grip than he realized, so used to bending his heavy oaken oar against resolute currents; the girl, miraculously to him, became still. He looked down on her as a panther would on a sickly fawn; the purple-pink of her complexion was now a blue-grey, the color of twilight before it dies. Some instinct of self-preservation, such as every animal possesses, caused him to turn his eyes across the river. A canoe, with two men in it, was being launched. He looked again at the limp form before him; he had evidently killed the girl; he must make his escape. But how was he to do it? On one side was the river, with the canoe of the avengers now in mid-stream; on the other rose the stiff forbidding height of the Bald Eagle Mountain. It was a perilous climb at dark, but he must go that way, as the heavy timber would protect him from any bullets they sent after him.

Abandoning money, robes, and provisions, he started up the mountain, speeding with the giant strides of fear and self-protection. The canoe, which contained Wild William and another young Indian named Bully Elkhorn, who had come to hostler at McGrady's farm, reached the shore below the ledge, and the young men clambered to where Sweet Cicely lay. She was not dead yet; every possible effort was made to revive her, but as the last streak of light vanished from the sky, she died; and they stood before death in the darkness, with the sound of the river rippling below them.

Wild William could feel the marks of the brute's thumb on her slender neck. He must have broken her windpipe. He was too stoical to cry; he belonged to a vanishing race, and death was the principal event to them; what else was there but death?

"That's pretty tough," said Bully Elkhorn, sympathetically, as he had sized up the situation "come to meet your sweetheart only to find her murdered."

"That raftsman did it, but we couldn't have stopped him, as we had no guns, and he was gone before our canoe touched shore." Taking the fragile corpse in their arms, the young men, straight and tragic looking and never speaking a word, stalked up the path, the scene of so many happy strolls in the past, to the cabin of poor old Powderhorn.

It appeared so bleak and forlorn looking out through the night; it was just a shade darker than the gloom, as the hearts of the household would be in a few minutes. The little shaggy watchdog, a sort of mongrel descendant of the true Indian dogs, barked moodily as they drew near. He saw that something was amiss. Wild William knocked on the door, and it was almost instantly opened by Powderhorn.

"What's wrong" he stammered, "I had a feeling something was going to happen; I couldn't get to sleep." He need not have inquired; his second glance showed Sweet Cicely lying limp in Bully Elkhorn's arms.

Wild William explained the story as briefly as possible, and then the body was borne inside. The next morning old Powderhorn tramped to Williamsport and tried to give the account of his daughter's death at the Courthouse. But the officials plainly regarded the Indians as outside the law; he could not get a listening ear. He was so insistent that something be done that the sheriff, to be rid of him, intimated that unless he dropped the subject and left town, he would send down and arrest Wild William and charge him with the crime, and lock up Bully Elkhorn and the old man as witnesses. Convinced of the futility of obtaining justice, he returned home and, that night, helped bury the remains of his beloved daughter in a patch of rich earth. They planted sunflower seeds on the grave.

Powderhorn was never the same after Sweet Cicely had gone. He would not go to Williamsport again, as he imagined everyone else was as unjust as the courthouse officials. He limped more than usual and complained of headaches and backaches. He often said he would like to get away. In this wish, he was supported by the rest of his family. The happy days were no more.

After harvest, Wild William and Bully Elkhorn, who had tried to trail the murderer during their leisure moments and became discouraged, decided to go back to the reservation on the Alleghany. When they confided this to Powderhorn, he said he would go along and take his family. So early in September, "they gathered up their tents like the Arabs and silently stole away." Years afterward, rumor had it that Wild William's wound had healed sufficiently to marry another of Powderhorn's daughters, while Bully Elkhorn had married the oldest girl, whose first love affair came to her at thirty.

But the shadowy essence of the ill-used Indians remained along Loyalsock Mountain, at least the spiritual part of one of them. In the springtime, when belated rafts swept down the river in search of cozy eddies, the clear, pure notes of a young girl's voice were heard from high on a ledge above the stream. Hearing them for the first time, they were so liquid, so exquisite, so far-reaching, many a pilot let go of his oar, and the uneven current would bump the raft on the sharp rocks or send it wobbling into shore. There would be a rending of thongs, a bending of bolts, a raveling of ropes, shouts, curses, thumps, and bangs; the raft, mistress of the tide but a few moments before, would be floating in all directions like so much flotsam and jetsam. Sometimes pilots or helpers would fall between logs and have their necks broken or be drowned in the maelstrom. And above the crash of breaking timbers and seething waters would come the clear, flutelike echoes of a young girl's voice. Even those who had gone through these perils and escaped with life and limb would be sorely tempted to look and listen the next time they heard it.

Who she was and what she was, this siren of the West Branch must be explained. She could not be human; she sang as if divine. No one dared stop to investigate; it was fatal even to listen. But old Ezra McGrady, from his point of vantage across the river, began to do some thinking about the matter. He had already formed an opinion of what caused so many wrecks when one night, a stranger stopped for supper and asked him, incidentally, if he knew what had become of the Indian family who used to live on the opposite shore. The man had been drinking, so his tongue ran freely; there was something about him that stamped him as a raftsman. By deft questioning, McGrady learned his name and his experiences on the river before he sent him on his way.

"Some just fate sent him here," muttered the old man as he turned about after lighting the stranger to the pike with his lantern. "Indian or not, that girl will be avenged."

The next time a party of raftsmen stopped at his house, it had become quite a resort for them on their long walks to their homes; he whispered to them the story of the strange singer with the fatal voice and who her murderer had been.

"Mum's the word, by the saints above," they all said with right hands raised. "We'll send that girl's spirit into peace, *even if she was an Indian.*"

Who could forget that rugged circle as they stood in the hallway in the candlelight? One night, the following spring, just as the last streaks of light passed from the sky, another fatal rafting accident occurred at the Loyalsock Riffles. A well-known pilot from the new county of Clinton, respected and prosperous, was knocked off his raft by the bow of another raft that had been trailing close behind. He was horribly mangled by logs and rocks, so much so that it was decided to inter his remains on the flat near the deserted Indian cabin. As they threw the sods over him, this human chuck-steak, the crowd around seemed to hear high up on the mountain, the sweet notes of a girl singing, "Fleeting years have borne away the voice of Alfarata." The men nudged one another, bared their heads, and listened. It was the last time that anyone ever heard the siren.

III

THE RED FOX

(Story of Williamsport Mountain)

IT WAS regarded as remarkable by such men of science as Professor Spencer F. Baird and others of his stamp that no fossil remains of red foxes were derived from the Carlisle and other bone caves, whereas the remains of grey foxes were abundant. At Port Kennedy, one upper molar was found in a cavern belonging to the Pleistocene period, said to be from a red fox. Apart from this, there is no evidence to suppose that the red fox existed in Pennsylvania before the advent of the British colonists. It is known for certain that they were imported from England into New York and New Jersey as early as the beginning of the eighteenth century. In 1750, an enterprising sea captain landed at New York City a cargo consisting of English and Irish hunters, English hounds, and fifty brace of red foxes. It created great excitement at the time, and the young bloods from New York, Pennsylvania, and Virginia bought out the entire shipment at good prices. It was a few years after this that red foxes began to be noticed as wild animals in the above-mentioned colonies. Other shipments followed at irregular periods, and it must be assumed that a fair percentage of the animals escaped and bred, as there was so much woodland and rough country.

It is recorded that the first red fox killed in Perry County, Pennsylvania met its death in 1787, showing that the species was gradually moving into the central part of the state. The gentlemen of English descent who lived in the manor houses along the West Branch took up foxhunting as a pastime. Several shipments of red foxes arrived from England about 1795, consigned to wealthy sportsmen at and below Williamsport. Among the most enthusiastic sportsmen of his day was old Edgar Cooper, or "Lord"

Cooper, as his friends called him. He lived in a large unfinished mansion in the Gap back of South Williamsport, at the foot of the "upper" or westerly mountain, then a very wild region. Although he had been born in Pennsylvania, he liked to pretend he was English and took pains to ignore the fact that the United States had been formed and the colonies were no longer dependent upon England. He was proud and aristocratic to a degree, yet the name Cooper would indicate that two or three generations back, or maybe less, his ancestors were part and parcel of the *hoi polloi*. He tried to look like an English country squire of the kind he had read about in books or had heard descriptions of from travelers, as the genuine article was far from extinct at that time.

One would think that with all his love for the English, he would have made frequent trips to that country, but in truth, he had never been across the Atlantic; some said he had never been as far east as New York. When distinguished Englishmen were traveling through the valley, he always managed to entertain them at "Boxwood," as he called his estate, and would talk intimately about "dear old England." As he looked the Johnny Bull and talked with an exaggerated British accent, his guests often asked him when he was last in the old country. From long experience, he deftly turned the conversation, or if cornered, fibbed bravely and said he had been educated there. In reality, he went to a district school for one term in Little Britain Township, Lancaster County. His father, an Englishman by birth, had made his money as a clothing contractor to the patriot army during the Revolution; the son owed everything to the new republic, yet he professed utmost contempt for "the common herd at the head of things."

Hunting grey or hybrid foxes was a sport followed by Germans and Scotch-Irishmen; it was below his dignity he must hunt the animal that had made the chase famous in the land of his ancestors. So, he imported, at considerable expense, six brace of red foxes from England. The arrival of these handsome animals created great excitement in the neighborhood. Tended by servants, they had as much care as children. Every Sunday, "Lord" Cooper and his bevy of more or less English friends would visit the pens and stand long and reverently before these brick-colored specimens of animal life in the realm of King George. "Boxwood," the name of the estate, came from the fact that Cooper imported a dozen boxwoods from England, which were set out on the terrace in front of the mansion. Unfortunately, all but one died; but it was too late; the name had been selected, and "Boxwood" it remained. He had better luck with the rarer varieties of native trees, of which he had quite a knowledge and possessed excellent taste. He set out groups of sweet gums" ginkgoes, Kentucky coffee trees, honey-locusts, virgilias, and buckeyes, balsam firs, red spruces, arbor vitaes, and junipers, which grew handsomely. He interspersed these with clumps of rhododendrons, hawthorns, redbuds, and spice bushes, all of which helped to hide the unfinished aspect of the house. He was a very improvident man. If he lived within his income, he could have had ample means to finish the house, but whenever his remittances came to hand, he spent it lavishly, and the work languished. He finished the stables first, letting the house progress in gradual stages. The stables were built of native stone but roofed with red English tiles and surrounded by thrifty Lombardy poplars imported from "the snug little isle."

"Lord" Cooper had married a Quakeress in Philadelphia; their family, which was small for those days, consisted of a son and a daughter. Meredyth Cooper, the son, was the antithesis of his father and was said to take after his mother's side of the house. He was genial, democratic, and broad-minded. He had refused to be sent to England to be educated but had received excellent training from tutors and in the best of private schools in Philadelphia. He was a handsome big fellow, and while devoted to outdoor sports and foxhunting in particular, he pursued them in a manly, dignified manner, after the fashion of the best type of the American gentleman.

The most prized object in the stables was a handsome English thoroughbred stallion which was said to have won the great Derby Stakes. Some years later, another alleged winner of the Epsom Classic appeared at Jersey Shore; they must not be confused, as both left a numerous progeny. The spirited Derby winner had been imported to this country in charge of a diminutive ruffian from Newmarket called Luke Pratchett. Luke boasted that he was a prizefighter and made himself very quarrelsome with the natives. One Sunday afternoon, he became impudent to two tall, lanky Scotch-Irish youths named McClanachan who came to look at the stallion, and they treated him to a terrific beating in consequence. The same afternoon a strutty duck wing gamecock, also from Newmarket heath, was trounced to the last feather by a commonplace Greeley rooster belonging to some Pennsylvania-German farmers who were immigrating to Sugar Valley. After that, Johnny Bull had his claws drawn around "Lord" Cooper's stables.

Early in the autumn, the first hunt with one of the English foxes took place. An Englishman from Sunbury, another from Harrisburg, and two from York were on hand as special guests to give local color to the chase. "Lord" Cooper, with a red coat, mounted on the English stallion, with his son and Luke Pratchett as huntsman, were the other members of the party. Unfortunately, the imported thoroughbred balked shortly after leaving the stables, and the hue and cry went out Mosquito Valley minus his lordship. It was an exciting chase while it lasted. The fox had not been given sufficient start but was game and speedy. He circled twice around the valley, over such a rough country that only young Cooper and Luke were on his trail when he made his final dash for liberty. The other four Englishmen outrun eased their mounts and trotted them back to the manor house. The fox made every effort to escape, but when he felt his strength failing and the hounds drawing nearer and nearer, sprang through an open window into the cottage of a German settler named Tobias Lehman. The old man ran out and began swearing at the huntsmen and threatened to shoot the dogs. He might have done so had not his daughter, Catharine, a very pretty blonde girl of twenty, appeared on the scene and coaxed her father into the house. During this parley, the fox escaped out the back door of the cabin and became one of the progenitors of the red foxes of Pennsylvania. Catharine was a buxom-looking girl, the typical artist's conception of a milkmaid; her coloring was good, her hair was yellow gold, and her grey eyes were large, but she had the peasant's habit of looking down and could not meet a person's gaze. There was a smallness and instability to the lips that did not measure up to her rather large, well-molded nose. Despite hard work in fields and dairy, her hands and feet were small; the latter were encased in beaded black slippers; evidently, she had expected the *denouement*.

To young Meredyth Cooper, who had been shielded from girls as from poison ivy, his father never having considered anyone good enough for him, the sight of this voluptuous mass of blonde loveliness made a profound impression. He continued the talk about the unseemly conduct of the English fox for longer than was necessary, and when he remounted and rode homeward, he felt as if he had known Catharine, as he called her to himself, all his life. Having had no predecessors in his heart, she spread over the entire area of his experience. "Lord" Cooper and his English guests had a grand jollification that night, even though they had no mask nor brush to display. They imbibed freely of English punch and rum, and towards midnight, one of the guests picked up a hatchet and said he was going out to the barn to cut off one of the fox's tails and have a brush anyhow. The others were too upset to restrain him, and he might have done it, but that he fell against a stucco figure of Britannia while crossing the lawn and lay petrified until morning. The next afternoon, Meredyth, who was glad for a chance to get away from the roistering company, rode out in the direction of the Lehman clearing. It occupied a hillside at the far southwesterly corner of the valley. "Lord" Cooper had tried to buy the piece, which comprised fifty acres, but the aged Palatine, who hated any kind of aristocrat, stoutly refused to set a price.

Catharine was collecting some large green pumpkins in a pile in the cornfield when the young gentleman approached. He stopped his horse by the stump fence, and the girl came to him eagerly, and they were soon in animated conversation. It was the beginning of a romance that burned furiously while it lasted. It was idyllic in its beginnings, a sort of earlier phase of the Maud Muller legend, but not to be without its thorny places. Six months before, Luke Pratchett, the English stud groom, had met Catharine at a country dance and had tried to be attentive but failed. There was something repulsive about under-sized men to this big stren-uous girl; many women feel the same. It is nature trying to raise the average stature of the race. No woman living will marry a homely man if she can get a good-looking one. Luke was short and ugly, and Catharine had scores of handsome stalwart admirers. Though she could not help but fancy the attractive appearance of Meredyth Cooper, who was six feet tall, athletically made, with graceful aquiline features and a sandy complexion, Catharine's principal interest was aroused by his exalted station. "Lord" Cooper's distant manner, he was the only professing aristocrat in the neighborhood, his mansion, his horses, his entertainments, all stamped him, and his son as well, as not being in the "roll of common men." To have this scion of grandeur attentive to her was far beyond the girl's wildest dreams.

She forgot that marriages seldom take place between persons in different social grades; caste encamped in the backwoods even at the close of the eighteenth century. She was a superstitious girl and went to the little mountaineers' burial ground one morning at dawn and plucked a sprig of yarrow from the grave of her girlfriend, Maggie Yost, who had died of pulmonary trouble the year before, and slept with it under her pillow that night. She dreamed of her aristocratic admirer, which was a sure sign she would marry him. This made her more anxious than ever to cultivate his attention. Luke Pratchett had noticed, ever since the afternoon the English fox had darted into the Lehman cabin, that Meredyth took solitary rides, being gone for hours at a stretch. Formerly he liked company, and Luke, whose jealousy was aroused, suspected that the young man was continuing his chance acquaintance with the fair Catharine.

One afternoon after the "young lord" had started out the road on his hunter, the groom mounted another animal and headed for a path that ran along the wooded mountainside, paralleling the highway. His suspicions were confirmed as he saw the girl come out of a clump of timber and meet young Cooper about a quarter of a mile down the road from her home. He was too angry to wait to see how they acted toward one another. Jabbing the spurs deeply into his horse, he galloped the entire distance back to the mansion, a distance of about three miles. Luckily for him, he found "Lord" Cooper in the stable when he arrived. He started to tell how he had been exercising the horse and what a fine horse he was, artfully bringing in that he had passed "Master Meredyth on the road but a half hour ago." He said it in such a way that the old man's curiosity was aroused, and he must know where and what the young fellow was doing. "Same's he's always a-do-ing, sir, courting old Tobias Lehman's daughter up by the gum-stump bridge." The old aristocrat almost had a fit; that was the worst thing he had ever heard in his life. The idea of his carefully shielded son, who was being reared for an heiress or a princess of the blood, nothing less, courting a member of the despised German race, was horrifying in the extreme. Pratchett urged him not to divulge his name as the informant, to which the old man promptly agreed, only to forget his promise as he started out the barn door.

It was a chilly night in November, and the old man was sitting before the fire while his cook, an importation from the English colony of Jamaica, was roasting a woodcock, entrails and all, on a spit. The rich aroma of the luscious bird dilated the old "lord's" nostrils, and his gouty hands were folded across his stomach as he waited for the gastronomic debauch to commence. Suddenly the door opened, sweeping in with it a gust of that incisive, crisp, steel-toned air, smelling just a bit of the moss and fallen leaves that are so characteristic of November nights in the Bald Eagle Mountains. Like a symbol of this vitalizing breeze, in strode the sturdy form of Meredyth Cooper. The old man forgot his precious woodcock and leaped from his pink plush easy chair, which had been imported from England, as if shot up from a spiral. He charged the young man with disgracing an honored name by consorting with his inferiors, with carrying on a vulgar intrigue with a scheming woman, with planning to marry without asking his father's consent, all courses of action so opposed to one another as to make the whole outbreak unpardonable. The young man listened respectfully a minute, then stooping down, he unbuckled his spurs, laying them beside his riding crop on a table, and quietly marched upstairs. In the excitement, the Jamaican, overcome with anxiety to hear every word of the argument, let the woodcock drop into the coals, and it was burnt to a cinder.

The old man, after his son had left, called for brandy and consumed a whole decanter full before his servants helped him off to his bedroom, which with rare foresight, was located on the first floor. But that ended the idyllic period of the young man's romance with Catharine Lehman. He continued going to see her but was harassed before he went and after he returned until he thought of moving into the stable for peace. His mother and sister, who had been in Philadelphia, returned and were told the whole story. They made no comment, which angered the old man considerably. It was easy to see that "Lord" Cooper's health was shattered by his son's love affair; that is, he drank heavily, and it told on his system. He had several fainting spells and would lay up for days recovering from his over-indulgences, all of which had their effect on his wife and daughter. Nothing was said, but the young man resolved to tell the girl how he was situated and give her up for the sake of the general family welfare. He loved her as he would never love again, but he believed in duty first.

The first snow had fallen when he drove out with the chinkling of sleigh bells in his low-built, old-fashioned cutter. The drive lay through a forest of virgin pines and hemlocks; old man Lehman's was the only clearing between the mansion and the pass through the mountain. The moon, striving hard to shine down between the dusky evergreen boughs that arched the way, lit up the road here and there in patches of pale blue light. The horse was jogging along nicely when suddenly, he stopped short, snorting and pawing like a wild thing. Meredyth had barely enough time to see a large red fox disappear into the laurels not twenty feet ahead. "That must be the animal that introduced me to "Catharine," he murmured, half amused, to himself. Old Lehman and his wife had climbed the ladder to bed when the young man arrived, and he had no listeners when he began his sad story of blighted hopes. He could see the girl's face plainly in the firelight; when he told her he could never marry her, he noticed, to his surprise, that her countenance never changed. She expressed the deepest regrets, but they were disappointed worldly hopes speaking; the wounded soul speaks through the face, through the eyes. Meredyth was at a loss to understand the composed manner with which she accepted her altered destiny but ascribed it to her courageous nature, inured to hardships.

Before they parted, a few tears were shed by him; her eyes showed no emotion. They pledged eternal fealty to one another; even if they could not marry, they would always love. "It is a terrible blow to her," thought the young man as he let the lines lie loosely on the horse's back and take its own gait home.

The next day he told his father what he had done, but the old man did not even thank him. He turned his back and poured out a big drink of brandy. Instead of making conditions more congenial in the household, relations between father and son were more strained than before.

In order to cheer himself up, the young man went on a trip to Phila-delphia, where he visited old schoolmates and relatives. His mother wrote him regularly, but his father never. None of them mentioned the name of Catharine Lehman, and he dared not ask after her for fear of arousing paternal ire. Often in the cold loneliness of inn bedrooms, he was sorely tempted to take out quill and paper and write to her, again confessing his hopeless love and commiserating her on the loneliness she must be enduring in that log cabin on the lonely mountainside.

But he fought these inclinations to the finish and, in April, returned home, more cheerful but with lines at the corners of his mouth, the sig-nature of his battle for soul mastery. All seemed the same at the mansion, except that Luke Pratchett acted more assertive and arrogant than when he had gone away. He actually ordered "Lord" Cooper about, a thing that, Englishman though he was, he never dared before.

The morning after his arrival, he sauntered out to the stables to look at the horses; several foals, sired by the Derby winner, had lately appeared, and he was curious to see what they were like. As he stood with Pratchett before the stall of the horse he had driven out to see Catharine Lehman the last night he was with her, the impulse to ask after her rose so strongly within him he had to bite his tongue to desist. Pratchett seemed to divine his struggle and gloated. He watched the young man for several minutes and then blurted out cold-bloodedly: "Say, Master Meredyth, did you hear of Catharine Lehman's marriage to Andy McClanachan in February?"

Meredyth tried to appear unconcerned, shifting from one foot to another, and answered "yes, yes, I did."

"I never saw a happier couple in my life, sir; she's just devotion itself."

The young man's face was ghastly pale, and Pratchett was exultant. Six months before, when the McClanachan boys had whipped him, he would not have expatiated on the triumph of one of them as a husband. Now it was different; his worst enemy would have been eligible to the hero class in order to crush his young master, of whom he was insanely jealous. It seemed to Meredyth as if the horses had lost their charm; in fact, the stable seemed to swim like the cabin of a ship in a tempest in the Gulf of Lyons. He hurried out into the balmy sunshine and, in returning

A BALD EAGLE MOUNTAIN LANDSCAPE
Photo by Charles W. Kimble, trenton, N. J.

to the house, inadvertently passed the pen where the eleven English foxes still flourished. Old Cooper had not hunted since the memorable day.

With a muttered curse, he kicked the latch loose and, pounding on the top of the box with his stick, sent the batch of animals bounding into freedom. Like seeds in a gale, they flew in every direction, but their deliverer did not watch them; he was seeking the quiet of his room. On the grand staircase, he met his father, who noted his unquiet demeanor. He suspected the cause, adding insult to injury by remarking, "well, son, that Lehman girl didn't care for you after all; she's married a fine man, and they say they are getting along splendidly."

The next thing the old man heard was the door of his son's room slamming loudly. The young man did not come down to dinner that day; he sent word he was indisposed.

In the evening, he announced that he was going to Philadelphia on the next stage and, from there, would sail for England. The first part of the speech shocked the old man, but the second part gained his consent.

"By all means, go, my boy," he said. He realized he had humiliated his son and would give him a trip to England to harmonize matters.

The next day the young fellow was ferried across the river to Williamsport, where he boarded the east-bound stage. He went to Philadelphia; he went to England. But he also went to France, where he remained, becoming one of the earliest American expatriates. Having some money in his own right by inheritance, he could not be induced to return. "Lord" Cooper never felt equal to go after him, and a trip undertaken by the sorrowing mother and sister availed nothing. He had loved once, deeply, and for all time, but in return, he held a mass of shucks. They say that in his old days, he shook like a leaf when he heard the bugle of the foxhunters in the Forest of Rambouillet.

IV

THE VIEW TREE

(Story of Duboistown Mountain)

O F ALL animals, Peter Pentz most disliked to kill a wolf. He would never do so when alone, no matter how they harassed him. Sometimes when he was with women and children traveling through the depths of the forests and the hungry packs threatened to sweep across the caravan devouring everything, he would join in the general fusillade for protection. Whenever he found settlers setting out poisons or traps, he would use his influence to get them to desist. But he showed no mercy to other animals.

He said that a wolf had once saved his life, and only an Indian would be mean enough to be ungrateful. He ascribed to wolves in general supernatural intelligence. He often pointed out that witches and spooks generally took the form of wolves when it was to their advantage to become animals for a time. That was nothing against the wolves; it was a compliment to their sagacity and keenness. Wolves in Central Pennsylvania might have dwindled to next to nothing a decade or two before they did, but for the restraining influence of Peter Pentz. "There *is* good in a wolf" was his familiar slogan.

Often when he was spending the night at the pioneers' cabins, lurid tales about wolf hunts would be retailed, but the stalwart frontiersman always disparaged these experiences. But he enjoyed hearing the children of William Crispin, a settler who lived at the foot of lower McElhattan Mountain, tell how a wolf had followed them to school every morning for a week. "William, you did wrong to shoot that wolf," he said, "it only wanted to act as a bodyguard to your little folks to keep off the bears and panthers." When all the disadvantages of wolves had been discussed,

Peter would tell his side of the question, invariably winding up with the story of how the wolf had saved his life.

Once when a pompous young lawyer said that the story proved nothing except the theory of coincidences, it is related that the old hunter became positively angry and refused to say another word all evening. He literally shamed the attorney into feeling he didn't want to spend the night at that particular cabin after all. But the host dissuaded him from going, and the next morning Peter was as genial and affable as was his wont.

"I really do believe," said one old settler to him, "if your life had been saved by a deer, the woods would be full of them today. What a pity you think you owe something to such a cursed varmint as a wolf."

But Peter could not be shaken in his belief concerning wolves, even when he was told that the wolf which saved his life might not have been a wolf after all but merely one of these witches in wolf's form. They used to say a witch loved him, and that was why he escaped the Indians so often.

No man, without immortal assistance, could have run the risks he did and lived to tell the tale. But Peter insisted that his life had been saved by a *real* wolf, and nothing could shake him. It had happened along the north slope of the mountain, which rises above the present village of Duboistown, in the days when the Indians, desperate from persistent defeats, were resorting to the cruelest deeds to impress their waning presence on the land indelibly.

Peter, with his boon companion, Almiral de Gruchy, were tramping one snowy Sunday morning along the trail which crossed from Nippenose Valley into Mosquito Valley when they noticed something stirring unsteadily in a rhododendron thicket alongside the pathway. Both men raised their rifles and were about to fire when Peter's keen eyes noticed that the object was evidently a wounded wolf and an enormous one at that.

"Don't shoot," he commanded, "let's see what's the matter with the critter."

This was a strange order, but de Gruchy believed in his companion implicitly and would have dropped his firearm even if told to do so in the face of an Indian brandishing a tomahawk. But Peter Pentz was never able to analyze the impulse which made him spare that wolf. Formerly he had killed these animals by the scores. He had been a leader of "drives" which had rounded up and slaughtered vast numbers of wolves, foxes, bears, and other so-called predatory beasts. On this occasion, he was sparing a wounded wolf, which might even prove a burden to itself. He stooped down where the creature was crouched, noticing that one of its fore paws had sustained a compound fracture, and dangled loosely from the broken joint. Evidently, it had been caught in a trap but had drawn the foot free, but not without mangling it horribly.

The injured wolf looked up at him with its dark, liquid eyes; the millennium had arrived, and it could hardly believe its senses. Peter cut some white oak twigs and shaved off the rough bark. These he placed as splints on the wounded foot, tying them securely with a piece of the inner lining of his buffalo coat.

Meanwhile, the animal kept eyeing him intently but never once offered to snap or even grind its teeth. Almiral de Gruchy stood nearby, with rifle ready, so as to fire if danger threatened, but this precaution was unnecessary. When the surgical task was finished, Peter set the wolf on its feet, and it was able to walk without much difficulty. Noticing that it was lean from lack of food—it would have starved to death, but for the timely arrival of the Samaritan—he took a piece of dried venison out of his coat pocket and threw it to the beast. This it ate ravenously, rolling its eyes with evident pleasure.

Leaving the animal in this happy frame of mind, the two hunters went their way. "I never would have thought that of you, Peter," said de Gruchy after they had proceeded a hundred yards.

"Nor I, Almiral," he replied, "some instinct made me help that particular wolf, though if I met a dozen more this morning, I'd kill everyone."

"Why don't you go back and fix that one? I don't think it's gone very far," said de Gruchy.

"No," answered Peter, "I sent it on its way rejoicing; I cannot go back."

They met other wolf tracks crossing and re-crossing the trail before they reached de Gruchy's cabin at the head of Mosquito Valley but saw none of the animals. During the remainder of the winter, both men were fortunate enough to kill a number of wolves, and Peter never once displayed evidences of the compassion which moved him on that snowy Sunday morning. With the advent of spring, Indian troubles took the place of hunting, and the bold pioneers were too busy guarding their scalps to bother about the comings and goings of the animals.

One bright August noon, de Gruchy was sitting by his cabin door, watching his cow, which was pasturing on the opposite side of the streamlet. He heard stealthy footsteps approaching and raised his rifle for protection. All at once, he heard a loud guffaw and beheld the big round face and the shock of wiry, sandy-colored hair of Peter Pentz, peering out of the underbrush. He hadn't seen his old companion for several months and jumped up, shouting, "Oh, Peter, I almost took you for an Indian!"

The big frontiersman came nearer, laughing until his thick lips stretched from ear to ear. Then the two friends shook hands and sat side by side on the door-sill, smoking and exchanging reminiscences. Peter had brought his favorite dog, Sade, with him; she was a sagacious creature and joined de Gruchy's hound Mingo in tonguing about the adjacent hillsides.

"They must be trailing a bear," said Peter, "it's a little too loud for a rabbit or a fox."

Both men instinctively took a grip on their rifles in case any wild animal should precipitate itself towards them from the brush. But they had placed too low an estimate on the character of their dog's bait. A bullet, whizzing through the air, went through one of de Gruchy's eyes, and he was a dead man in an instant. A second and a third shot taught Peter to "make himself scarce," as he was no match for a foe in ambush. He trotted down the path towards the more open part of the valley, whistling and calling for Sade to follow him. The only answer he got was another fusillade, one bullet knocking off the bucktail plume in his cap. He felt he was in for a long race, so he stopped long enough to fill his canteen at a boiling spring. He traveled quite a distance and, not hearing any more shots, began to look about for a place of safety. It would be best, he thought, to lay up for the night in a tall tree. It was a hostile country, but by morning light, he could climb down and cross the river, there to ally himself with some armed band of men. While looking about for a suitable retreat, he came into a windfall, or large opening, on the northern slope of the Duboistown Mountain.

Near the center of this natural clearing stood a single tree, a chestnut of immense height, spared as if by a miracle. Different in form from most trees of its species, it was a typical forest king. The long, smooth, serpentine trunk, at the butt not more than two feet in diameter, rose into the air upwards of ninety feet. On the top was a round, heavily foliaged head, compact as a cabbage and perhaps thirty feet in height.

Peter Pentz, big and heavy as he was, retained much of the agility of his boyhood days when he was called "the pine squirrel." Slinging his rifle over his shoulder, he began "shinning" up the tree. Occasionally he found the remnant of a branch broken off years before to take a hold on, but most of the distance was overcome by skill and sheer pluck. As he neared the leafy "top," he caught a view of the river, with the red rays of the setting sun mirrored upon it. Far to the north, at the foothills of the Alleghanies, he made out several settlers' clearings, with thin tails of grey smoke rising from the mud chimneys of the cabins. All was peace and rest, and supper-time, off there.

Further away, on the distant summits, were finer tails of smoke, probably from Indian campfires. He could discern from this "view tree" where to go on the morrow and where to keep clear of. It was with a sense of genuine elation that he grasped the first branch of the top to know that he was safe in his sylvan eyrie. He pulled himself up into the thicket, but as he did so, he was almost dislodged and thrown by a pair of Cooper's hawks striking him in the face with their stiff, sharp wings. One of his eyes was badly scraped and pained him frightfully. But he was able to draw his knife and stabbed both birds until they squeaked and gibbered in pain and flew away with checkered, unsteady winging. Then he seized the nest, which was built in a cradle of dead branches in the very kernel of the top, and hurled it, fledglings and all, to the jagged rocks a hundred feet below. He unstrapped his gun and his canteen and took out his packet of provisions, depositing them in the "cradle" where the nest had been. He twisted himself into a comfortable position to wait until morning or until his foemen had passed. The branches hung thick with prickly green burrs of unusual size; even now, some of them would be big enough to eat.

He had barely settled himself when the Indian band on a dog trot hove in sight. There were eight in the party, and four of them carried guns. He held his breath and muttered a wish that they would pass by. To his great joy, they moved by the giant tree in single file, neither looking to the right nor the left nor into the heights above! He felt he was tolerably safe. Just as he was about to heave a sigh of satisfaction, a ninth Indian, a cripple, appeared in the opening. This Indian, on account of his affliction, traveled slowly and kept glancing about him with furtive, inquisitive eyes. As luck would have it, they rested upon the shattered hawks' nest, with the crushed and dying fledglings lying about. His quick wits told him some agent, other than the wind, must have dislodged this stoutly built nest. By the looks, it had fallen recently; even if a wind might possibly have done it, it could not right now; it was dead calm. He looked into the dizzy top of the mammoth tree; he could see nothing, the verdure was so thick, and dusk was at hand. But he was not satisfied and uttered a war-whoop, which brought the eight warriors who had gone ahead, trooping to his side. He pointed to the nest, the fledglings, and certain scraped places on the bark of the tree trunk, which meant the fugitive was "up there." The Indians strained their eyes but likewise saw nothing. One of them fired three shots, but they whizzed by the hidden frontiersman's head, doing no damage. But the Indians were convinced he was in the tree top, so they sat down to wait until morning when they could see more clearly. At dark, they lit a campfire around which they sat, passing the time chanting a low, mournful war dirge. Some of them fell asleep, and the sight of them dropping over into involuntary dreamland made it difficult for Peter to keep himself awake. Sleepiness, like its earlier stage, "gapping," is contagious.

Just as the crimson dawn was flaming over the eastern mountains, the two hawks hove in sight, floating along unsteadily, as if in pain. They had nursed their wounds overnight on some remote crag; they were now coming back to try and recover their home. The Indians saw them as quickly as did Peter and wasted two good rounds of ammunition on them to bring them down. The hidden pioneer wished he could thank the Indians for this service.

As soon as the light was well established, the Indians began their scrutiny of the tree-top afresh. They fancied they saw him, and he kept wondering if one of their number would attempt to climb the trunk and give him battle in the dizzy height! But they seemed content to shoot in his direction from time to time; it seemed a marvelous circumstance they did not hit him. Perhaps they were not trying very hard but were waiting to starve him out and take him alive. It would be great sport to burn such a noted Indian killer at the stake.

Peter figured he had provisions enough to last three days; after that, he could live a while longer eating unripe chestnuts. He had enough water for several days, which was the most important necessity. The chief danger was falling asleep; if he did, he would surely tumble from his perch. How long he could fight sleep was a question he could not answer. Even the night before, it had almost gotten the better of him on several occasions. But he would not surrender to his foes; if he dozed and fell, it wasn't his fault.

All went smoothly until sunset when he felt sleep stealing on him with almost irresistible fury. Then he observed a fresh peril. The Indians, after a council together, built a hot fire around the butt of the tree. He was to be burnt out in true Indian fashion and would be killed with the fall. That was the Indian's method of felling trees before axes were introduced by the white men. His bold soul trembled.

In the distance to the south, he heard a yelping and barking. Could Sade and Mingo have caught the trail and been coming to his rescue, leading a party of pioneers? But no, it wasn't dogs barking; it was the sound of wolves, of very hungry wolves. Now there *would* be some fun. Evidently, the Indians were apprehensive as they fired a half dozen more shots, ostensibly at the top of the tree, but plainly to frighten the oncoming pack. But the wolves were dauntless. Nearer and nearer, they advanced. Soon, in the dusk, at the edge of the windfall, a long row of eyes, like the lights of a city at night, gleamed and glared at the Indian watchers. They fired several shots, which seemed to infuriate the animals, which, yelling like fiends, rushed forward *en masse*, driving the Indians before them like chaff from a winnower. The fire about the tree had not made very great headway when the wolves appeared and smoldered down to a lot of smoking embers during the excitement.

This was *some* relief to the refugee, but he hated the prospect of dropping, in his sleep, in the midst of a pack, which, now that they were all out in the open in the windfall, must contain five hundred snarling snapping animals. Then to his surprise, he noticed a black wolf, larger and more masculine; evidently, the leader of the pack, every pack has its acknowledged leader, approach the hot coals around the tree and try to beat them out with its paws. On looking closer, he noticed the animal was lame; could it be the wolf he had befriended on the Bastress ridge the winter before? Just then, the brute looked upwards; it seemed to catch a glimpse of him, for it wagged its bushy tail and began thrashing out the hot coals more vigorously than ever. The other wolves circled about, yelping and sniffing the air, sometimes rolling over one another with antic playfulness. While thus gamboling, the Indians caught them off their guard. Stealthily creeping back, they fired a deadly broadside into the pack. There was a chorus of hideous howls of pain, and a dozen brutes lay dead upon the rocks. The rest, stirred into a frenzy, turned on the over-confident Indians, surrounding them, and cutting off their means of escape. Leaping at their throats and tripping them, they laid their enemies low, like a plow in a fallow. Where a minute before had stood nine warriors, some with smoking rifles, nothing now was visible but the dark, ever-moving surface, a wriggling, howling mass of hairy beasts. They had literally buried their foes beneath them. Every few minutes, the "king" wolf, with his lame leg, would come near the chestnut tree and leap up against the trunk like a friendly dog, hanging out his tongue and wagging his tail. It took Peter some time to convince himself that the wolves meant no harm, but still, he hesitated about descending. After the pack had chewed the dead Indians into unrecognizable pulp, the lame wolf gave vent to a series of howls as musical as a bugle call, and all the pack came together in a solid phalanx and trotted off into the forest. The lame wolf remained behind, curling himself up at the foot of the tree like a collie.

Peter began to feel sleepy again; come what may, he must descend. It would be dangerous to encumber himself with the heavy rifle, so he left it in the abandoned hawks' nest. It was much harder to work down the smooth trunk than up; his heart was in his mouth, and the slightest wavering or slip meant a fall of nearly a hundred feet and ignominious death. But the same kind Fate which saw him up the tree guarded his descent, and he landed on *terra firma*, thankful, happy, free. The lame wolf got up, stretching himself like a friendly dog, and hopped over to him, jumping upon him, licking his great sinewy hands. Peter stroked and patted him many times and gave him his last piece of provision. Then man and beast went their respective ways.

V

THE BROWN BEAR

(Story of Nippeno Mountain)

THERE WERE at least four kinds of bears in Pennsylvania at the close of the eighteenth century. Today, but two varieties are found, and these, the hog bear and the dog bear, are commonly confused as one species. The hog bear is short-nosed, broad-faced, of chubby build, and makes excellent eating, his flesh being tasty like pork, while the dog bear, which is the scarcer variety, has a long pointed snout, small ears, long thin legs, and his flesh tastes like that of a canine, that is if there are persons competent to say so. The varieties which are probably extirpated were the white-faced bear and the brown bear. The white-faced bear was commonly met with in the northeastern part of the state; a good description of one is to be found in Blackman's *History of Susquehanna County*.

The brown bear was found pretty much all over the northern and central sections of the commonwealth and grew to a greater size than any of the other three kinds. He was probably related to the brown bears of Europe, as he resembled them more than our silver tips or grizzlies of the west or even the Alaskan brown bears. Some black bears have a few brown or reddish hairs, but they are not true brown bears.

The last brown bear was probably killed in Bradford County, in 1882, by Thomas Leahy, a noted hunter of that region. Another was killed earlier in the same year in Lycoming County.[1] They were accounted by far the most savage of all the bears, as the black varieties and even the white-faced bears possessed marked social instincts. Stories of how the brown bear attacked hunters or carried off calves or sheep, or even children, were plentiful along the Bald Eagle Mountains three-quarters of

---

1. See Appendix A.

a century ago. As time went on, they became generally disbelieved or confused with anecdotes of the black bears.

On the flats and table lands back of Nippeno Mountain, which slopes down to the river where Nippeno Park is now located, the brown bears made their last stand. It seemed to be their natural breeding and feeding ground, for no matter how far they wandered; they always spent part of every year at this retreat. For this reason, they were exterminated more quickly than their black relatives, which knew enough to scatter themselves and stay scattered in nearly every county in the State. At one time, there were thirty-five well-constructed bear traps or pens on the plateau of Nippeno Mountain, and some of these must have caught several victims in a season.

At an early date, probably in the first decade of the nineteenth century, there was a settler's cabin situated near the present site of the boarding house at the park. The land about it was all cleared but later abandoned as too wet by one Reuben Armpriester, who was also a hunter of some notoriety. That he was a hunter was a sign he wasn't very successful at farming, as the prosperous agriculturist has little time to stray in the woods. He had become so proficient in trapping bears that the traders from Harrisburg came to his home every spring and bid against one another for the brown bear hides. These were much affected as coats by the drivers of the passenger stages and freight wagons that ran across the mountains to Pittsburgh; each driver must have a brown bear coat or a bear robe, and this fashion lasted until there were no more brown bears, and buffalo coats and robes from the west took their places.

Philadelphia zoologists never recognized the existence of the brown bears as a distinct species, but they never took the trouble to see them, dismissing them in their brochures as a "color phase" of the black bears. Still, the men of science being satisfied, the rest of the public, including future generations, must be, so the habits and peculiarities of these interesting animals have been lost to us.

Reuben Armpriester boasted he had killed a brown bear that, "hog-dressed," weighed six hundred pounds. This is more than likely as Rhoads, in his *Mammals of Pennsylvania and New Jersey*, mentions a black bear killed by the famous Clinton County pioneer, Seth I. Nelson, which, "hog-dressed," weighed four hundred and eight pounds. As years went on, Armpriester became imbued with a single thought, and that was to capture brown bears. During his most successful season, he caught eight, but it is hard to see how it paid him to knock off from work for months when the price of hides was, in reality, very low. He raised a large family of children, who were kept in order by his industrious wife. She often complained bitterly that too much time was wasted by her lord and master with his bear hunts to maintain the household properly. The youngest child was a little boy of three named Simon, and the next the youngest was a five-year-old girl named Phoebe. This little girl was bright and precocious for her age, and if her parents had encouraged her, she might have developed into an unusual young person. But with the mother, it was all work and complaints; with the father, it was the eternal story of bear hunting. Phoebe and her little brother were given much liberty of movement and, on warm afternoons, wandered up the sloping sides of the big mountain to gather berries or acorns or chestnuts as the season afforded. They always came home at supper time, and the mother was too busy to think of snakes, so they had their way.

One bright afternoon in October, the two youngsters, after stopping at King Wi-daagh's Spring for a good drink of the crystalline water, started up the well-worn little path for their daily ramble in the woods. There were still many old pines and oaks along the mountain, some of them were not cut down until 1895 or thereabouts, and many of the tall trunks were covered with woodbine, now scarlet in its autumnal glory. Reuben was away on a bear hunt; it was his first that season. He was keen to be at his favorite pastime, as his wife was to be busy with her domestic duties or complaints. About six o'clock, little Simon returned alone. The mother, at seeing this, flew into a great state of excitement and demanded the whereabouts of his sister. As best he could, the little fellow stammered out that a great brown bear, bigger than any that his father had brought home the last winter, had come up to where they were playing and had sat down beside them. All afternoon they had played with him, and when it came time to return for supper, Phoebe said she was going home with the bear. And off they went together, so he said. The mother was infuriated.

"You little fool," she screeched, "don't you know that bear has eaten your sister; that's the way they went off *together*."

The little boy insisted that Phoebe hadn't been eaten, but was in the best spirits imaginable when they parted. His story could not be shaken. The nearest neighbors lived across the river, and the older boys went in their dug-outs and fetched them over. They decided that Reuben must be notified at once; if the little girl still lived, it would be a miracle; at any rate, he could kill the bear that had devoured his child. He would know the haunts of the big bears better than anyone else, and this bold brute would soon "bite the dust."

At dawn, a party of six men and boys crossed over the mountain in search of Reuben. They carefully observed the spot where Simon and Phoebe had played the afternoon before—it was strange, they thought, that they could find no blood nor particles of clothing. It was sundown before they came upon the unsuspecting father. They had to make a tour of all his traps, some of which were situated three miles apart, and three miles across rough mountains is no easy task, before catching up with him. He was dumbstruck but incredulous when he heard the story of his child's disappearance.

"That little boy's been romancing; either he doesn't know where his sister is, or that bear ate her; there's no other way," he concluded.

When told of the size of the bear, he said he could not believe it was one of the largest brutes. "There are only one or two of the real old fellows left; there's one, I know, but it can't be him that weighs, I'm sure, close to seven hundred pounds. I tracked him all last winter for Daniel Eck yonder in the Bastress region, he was the biggest and boldest one I ever trailed, but he always eluded me. After eating three of Farmer Eck's heifers and thirteen sheep, he had the nerve to come into the barnyard on his hind feet when Mammy Eck was milking, drove her away, and drank out of the milk pail. I *can't* believe it's him; he never came over to the river mountain; he knew where he was safe."

That night, in the solitude of the hunter's shack, a course of action was decided upon. Armpriester was to bring his two bear dogs home and see if they could take up the scent. The weather was fine, and chance might favor them. If they lost the scent, he would visit all the known bear dens in the mountains. Formerly all of these held their bruin families, but hunters like Armpriester had sorely reduced their numbers. Some of the biggest caves or dens had not been occupied in several years—it was "home to let" on every ridge.

A quick march home was made the next morning. The dogs were promptly brought to the place that had been indicated by Baby Simon, but after sniffing about for half an hour scampered off toward their kennels. That was a sign they were baffled. Armpriester was grief-stricken, rough man of the woods that he was; he broke down and wept. "It will be a long hunt; even if poor little Phoebe is alive now, she won't be by the time we find where that bear has hidden her. He will play with her like a cat does with a mouse and then eat her. Oh, my poor little girl!" He was for starting on the hunt at once, but his friends restrained him until he was given some dinner.

About three o'clock in the afternoon, accompanied by his two dogs and his two oldest boys, Lewis and Michael, he started for the brown bear country. Six or seven pits and dens were visited before dark that day, but all were tenantless save one, and out of that, they chased a small black dog-bear. Armpriester was so angry at the whole race of *Ursus* that he shot this bear and threw it over the mountain into a ravine. They camped that night on a lofty height overlooking Rattling Gap, where their sleep was disturbed by the nocturnal dissensions of panthers, wolves, and catamounts. At daybreak, they broke camp and resumed the quest.

By nightfall, they had inspected a dozen other dens, some in abandoned quarries, others in the steep and almost unscalable sides of the mountains. In one of these, a catamount family was found, and the living struggling mass, mother and all, hurled over the precipice. "You'll not keep me awake," said the frenzied hunter as he saw the fuzzy brutes strike "rock bottom."

The third day's search was also fruitless. The party had described a circle in the mountains and had closed into the center so that not a cranny escaped unexplored. "There's only one place more," said Armpriester, "and that's too near home for any brown bear. I never heard tell of one being seen there in all the fifteen years I've hunted the brown devils."

"Let's go there anyhow; it won't do any harm," said the optimistic sons.

"All right, we'll be passing there tomorrow," said the father sadly.

It was close to noon when they came upon the cave. It was in the side of a pile of loose rocks near the summit on the south slope of Nippeno Mountain. The opening was small, but a mass of great flat sandstones made a chamber, say twenty by ten. It was a peculiar formation, and no one but a skilled hunter like Reuben Armpriester could have discovered it. Once, he had caught a paltry family of grey foxes in it. He brained them all; it made him so angry to bother with "'small game." In some localities in this degenerate day, if you ask if there is any large game, the natives reply, "well, yes, we've foxes." Reuben lit his torch and went in, dragging his rifle after him. He wore a dejected look when he came out—"not a thing, but the skeletons of some cursed foxes I killed there six years ago."

Would they have to go home empty-handed? The three men and the dogs presented an unhappy-looking quintet as they sat with hanging heads on the flat stones outside the cavern. The faithful dogs seemed to have imbibed their master's dejection. During the most oppressive moment, one of the dogs began to sniff the air and bark.

"A bear, a bear," shouted Reuben triumphantly. The men seized their rifles and followed the lead of the dogs. In the midst of an old huckleberry patch, they stopped short and could scarcely believe their eyes. Was it a daylight phantasm or reality? Coming towards them, astride of the biggest bear they had ever seen, was little Phoebe, smiling and rosy! The bear looked as contented as the child, beaming happiness with his great brown eyes.

"Oh, pop, pop," she called out, "see my good playmate. Master Brown Bear, he's the best friend I've got."

Reuben Armpriester did not take in the humor or the picturesqueness of the situation. All he was thinking about was the ultimate safety of his child. He felt exactly as if he had found her playing with a rattlesnake. Quick as a flash, he had his rifle at his shoulder and was sighting it on the center of the brown bear's broad flat skull.

"Don't shoot, pop, don't shoot, don't kill my bear," the little girl screamed, but it was too late. There was a sickening report, and the huge brown monster fell forward on his breast, tumbling little Phoebe off his back into the brittle berry bushes. There she lay, unhurt but weeping piteously. The bear did not die the first shot but tried to raise himself and look at the little girl with his appealing brown eyes. A second bullet sent him to sleep, and he lay vast and ponderous, a titan of the animal kingdom. Phoebe finally got up and came over to where the bear lay and stroked his dead coat.

"Oh, why did you do it, pop? He meant no harm; he talked to me just like you do, only nicer."

"Oh, nonsense, child," said Armpriester, alarmed at her remarks, "you'd better come home; this thing's going to your head."

"But he did talk to me, pop," she continued saying.

"The child's getting a fever, I'm afraid," the hunter whispered to his boys, thoroughly alarming them.

Michael carried the little girl home and put her to bed. All were overjoyed to see her again but predicted a long illness would follow her adventure in the wilderness.

Next morning she woke bright and early, without a symptom of disorder, although she complained that "pop acted awful mean to kill that bear."

"He'd have eaten you," said the mother to console her.

"No, he wouldn't; he told me he wouldn't when I went away with him."

That night the giant bear's carcass was hauled into the Armpriester home. It "hog-dressed" just six hundred pounds, and the hide, an exceptionally fine one, was sold to the driver of a "select" stage for fifty dollars, a record price. It was a long time before Phoebe would give up chiding her father for killing the bear; she kept on insisting that it could talk just like a person and had given her presents of berries and roots, the like of which she had never tasted before. Armpriester and his wife were too happy to have her back to ever quarrel with her over this strange talk, but it worried them considerably. When they would listen, she would tell of the lovely grotto he took her to, walled with red rock and as bright as day inside.

"I'd say that was a spook bear," said Mrs. Armpriester aside, one day, "if it wasn't you killed him without a silver bullet, and I saw the fifty dollars you got for the hide."

"It's beyond me," answered Reuben shaking his frowsy head.

Phoebe stuck to her story even when she grew up, but she never found anyone who believed it, she maintained. "Every generation's worse; why my grandchildren won't even believe there was such a thing as a brown bear in Pennsylvania. It isn't in their natural histories; their teachers laugh at the idea; they think I'm romancing. But it's truth, the unvarnished truth, that I ran away with a brown bear and lived in his cave for a week."

VI

OLD PHILIPPE
(Story of Big Run Mountain)

FEW OF the present generation, or the generation past, were aware that, not far from the creek, at the foot of Big Run Mountain, stood a spacious log tavern, which was burned down during the first decade of the last century. It was run, for a year, about 1796, by old Philippe Anthonyson, an Alsatian who later became famous as the proprietor of the "Blockhauss" in Tioga County.

Anthonyson was certainly a character. He had drifted to Paris prior to the French Revolution and espoused the cause of the *people* during those bloody days. He had taken a fiendish delight in butchering aristocrats until his wing of the radical party fell from power, and he had to escape to the seacoast disguised as a carter and embark for America. In Philadelphia, he learned the prosperous trade of *Neulander*, making three trips to his native Alsace to extoll the riches and opportunities of Pennsylvania to his fellow countrymen. For every person whom he caused to emigrate, and the total was in the three figures, he received a commission from the owners of a line of vessels. The sufferings of the victims who found class distinctions and hard work awaiting them in the "promised land" brought on him such execrations that he decided to retire to the interior. He accordingly bought out the new tavern stand on Big Run, Lycoming County. It had a lucrative trade among travelers and hunters crossing the Bald Eagle Mountains as well as rivermen, and he was well-liked by his patrons.

But trouble came to him, and he had to move on again, this time to the Blockhouse Country, where he remained until his death twenty years later. Despite the unpleasant cause of his departure, it was an excellent move, as he made the Blockhouse famous throughout Pennsylvania and southern New York. "Old Philippe," as he was called, and the "Blockhauss" were one and the same; travelers went out of their roads for miles to spend a night under his roof. He was just the kind of person to keep such a resort. Rough, positive, and brutal, he allowed no nonsense or swindling, but to those who treated him decently, he was kindly and often a friend in need.

The Blockhouse was built about 1795 as a refuge from the possible hostilities of Indians by the handful of settlers who lived within a radius of ten miles of the headwaters of the stream then called Metimmue, or Wolf Run, but afterward known as Blockhouse Run.

The following year, John Williamson, a New York land agent, in the employ of an English nobleman who owned a vast tract of land in New York State, opened a rough wagon road through the wilderness in order to facilitate emigrants in reaching these lands from Philadelphia. The road passed the Blockhouse, and Williamson bought it, added to its size, and opened it as a stopping-place for the emigrants and adventurers. The trail, which took the name of the Blockhouse road, became such a great thoroughfare that Williamson cast about for an experienced innkeeper to run his tavern. He heard of Old Philippe's troubles in the West Branch Valley and sent for him. A bargain was struck, which turned out to be mutually profitable. The old man literally coined money, which he spent trying to amuse and educate his children. Many were jealous of his success; all kinds of stories were told to his discredit, but they were traceable to the unjust charges brought against him while still keeping Big Run Tavern.

The chief glamor of the Blockhouse was the excellent table. Many a tired German traveler, who could pay the price, tasted there his first elk steak, fried trout, or wild-pigeon pot pie. The smoke-house was always filled with elk meat, as the old fellow maintained an elk lick nearby. He had several Indians, whom he paid in cheap whiskey, to do the killing, and they helped the rapid extermination of *Cervus Canadensis* in Tioga County. The gables of the Blockhouse, and the sheds, were adorned with innumerable elks' antlers. Sometimes emigrants camped for days about this resort. They obtained feed for their stock from the old man, also certain supplies and liquors for themselves. It was a genial break in the monotonous journey through the dark forests and rough roads. They were delighted to find a place kept by one whom they imagined a German like themselves, for old Philippe, being an Alsatian, could speak German fluently.

But to return to the story of his unceremonious departure from the commodious tavern in the shadow of Big Run Mountain. The old fellow arrived there in the first month of 1796 and was given a rousing welcome by the mountaineers. He had come to supply a long-felt want. His earliest policy was to run the tavern in the manner of a club by making desirable patrons feel at home. Many of them, according to the custom of the day, in order to escape the dreary monotony of pulling stumps and gazing out at pine trees, would visit the tavern for a week at a time, drinking, smoking, eating, telling hunting and Indian stories about the fire, and sleeping long hours at a stretch.

In March, one of these worthy "club members" had a nightmare and, in an abortive effort to cut his bedfellow's throat, cut off the tendon of one of his feet, crippling him for life. This started a story that much brawling took place, and wives "carried on" when they heard their husbands intended to go there. But old Philippe tried to run an orderly place in a disorderly locality and generation. The resort was famed for the cooking, an old Mingo woman called Indian Mary being responsible for most of it. Philippe's three daughters, the eldest, Vieva, a girl of seventeen, assisted in the kitchen and about the house. The old man was wifeless; rumor said he formerly had one, an Italian woman, but that he had deserted her in the old country. Philippe once told a friend that she had died on shipboard on his first trip to America, leaving him with the three little girls.

Vieva was a buxom, lively type of girl with black ringlets, laughing black eyes with streaks of green in them, eyes that were always in good humor, and a full-lipped, merry mouth. Though totally uneducated, she possessed natural abilities, which might have been developed had she fallen in with the right kind of men. However, she was indifferent to the male sex, except those who were exceptionally good-looking. There was a hostler, or handyman, about the premises, one Leopold, or as he was locally called, "Lu-pold" Nancarro, an Alsatian redemptioner. He was not a bad-looking fellow by any means but densely ignorant and enamored with Vieva. Despite his efforts to charm her, she outwardly displayed little interest in him. The guests at Big Run Tavern were not all backwoodsmen and itinerant traders. Occasionally men of quality, such as Quaker landowners from Philadelphia, Scotch-Irish candidates, French naturalists, or German missionaries, stopped overnight. Old Philippe, having lived abroad, knew how to receive these gentry; republican though he was, he possessed the inherent peasant servility. When they left, he abused them roundly; he hated "blooded stock," he said.

One balmy spring evening, when the peepers and the tree toads were heralding the coming Maytime, while the transparent-winged bats were chasing insects and the air was sweet with the odor of violets and wild apple blossoms, a horseman stopped in front of the tavern. This was nothing unusual, as most persons going a distance traveled that way, but this rider and his mount were so richly caparisoned that they attracted special notice. The rider, who was a young man, by his looks, belonged to the landed aristocracy, except for his lack of the customary servant. Old Philippe and Lu-pold ran out to assist him in dismounting from his mettlesome thoroughbred stallion. When he dismounted, it was observed that he was very tall and handsome, with clear-cut, aquiline features, blue eyes, and auburn hair. He gave his name and address as "Wilmer Norris, Belmont, Philadelphia." Clearly, he did belong to the old stock. He acted the gentleman, except that his manners were more affable and democratic than most men of his cloth. He made friends easily, talked over his affairs freely, and seemed especially anxious to become acquainted with Vieva. Apparently, the dashing young girl was impressed by his good looks, but if he had been a trifle less approachable, she might have liked him better. She helped wait on him at the supper table, during which meal he asked her many questions, paying her considerable indirect compliments.

Later in the evening, he contrived to bring up his chair close to the settle by the big open fireplace, where she sat sewing. He talked in undertones, but old Philippe, and Lu-pold, who were also in the room, could not fail but catch from the drift that he was very much smitten. There was no mistake about Vieva's beauty. There were few prettier girls in Philadelphia or Europe; there was a *distingue* air about her, which attracted instant attention. This high-bred air had given rise to the report that she was not old Philippe's daughter but the child of a French nobleman and a seamstress whom he had adopted for a stipend. Her features were more delicately chiseled than the old man's, but there was a similarity in coloring, and other characteristics, which gave the lie to this pretty fancy.

Although Vieva encouraged her aristocratic admirer, she also kept him at a distance. This is a fine distinction that women understand but that many men are unable to fathom.

Wilmer Norris, despite his ballroom bringing up, could not detect the veil of reserve which the girl drew about her but pressed his attentions until the old innkeeper growled at her that it was time for everybody to go to bed. The young stranger, in deference to his position, was given use of the living room as bed-chamber. He was assigned to a roomy couch, covered with buffalo robes and brown-bear hides, by the inglenook. Old Philippe, Lu-pold, and Vieva, after seeing that all his wants were gratified, filed up the rickety stairway, holding tallow dips aloft in their pewter candlesticks. The young man said nothing about departing on the morrow, so it was inferred he would remain a day or two. He had given out that he was on his way to inspect some of his father's timberlands further up the West Branch Valley; he made no mystery of his movements. The next day was rainy; he would hardly have started anyway.

He spent as much time as possible with Vieva, who was not averse to having her two younger sisters present during the courting. They lingered around the fireside that night until she yawned and expressed a desire for bed. Wilmer Norris, try as he would, seemed unable to be with her alone. On the following morning, which dawned clear, he announced that he would leave the next day. Had Vieva given him an ounce of encouragement, he might have remained a month. On his last evening, he was more anxious than ever to spend a few minutes with the beautiful girl when others were not present. She tried, though perhaps not as tactfully as a more experienced girl, to have a third party present every moment. Wilmer was too much in love to notice that while his friendly advances were welcome, his love was not.

THE GOLDEN HOUR AT THE CAMP
Photo by H. W. T. Clarke, Conrad, Pa.

When ten o'clock was struck by the chimes of the tall walnut clock from Berks County, Vieva, rubbed her eyes, yawned for the twentieth time, and said she was dead tired, she must retire. The younger girls, who were dozing with their heads on her lap, rose up suddenly, saying that bed was a grand idea. Lu-pold had left the room half an hour earlier, but old Philippe still sat in one corner smoking his long clay pipe. The young aristocrat begged her to stay up just a few minutes longer because it would be his last night, but she was obdurate. She lit her tallow dip and, followed by the younger girls and the old man, ascended the stairs.

It was impossible for the foolish lover to sleep that night. He did not even undress but sat by the fire, drinking deeply from a brandy jug that he had brought in his saddle bag. He scorned the product of the mountain stills that old Philippe doled out. He had never felt so unhappy in his life. Aristocratic belles had smiled on him, but now he was to be thwarted by a little backwoods damsel. It seemed impossible to his imperious pride. He must win her; he would marry her, and take her to Philadelphia, come what may. She was just a little shy or hesitant because of their different positions in life; that was all, he reasoned. The brandy and his disappointment made his head whirl; he decided to go outside for a stroll. There was a fine spring a few hundred yards above the tavern; he would go there to quench his thirst with mountain water. He took a gourd from a hook on the wall, unchained the heavy oaken door, and sallied forth. A wolfish watchdog barked and ramped about viciously; it seemed as if he must rouse the entire household through his innocent stroll. The stars were out; from its reflection in the sky, the new moon had come and gone. An early cricket was trying to chirp louder than the peepers, to raise his voice above the musical crooning of the topmost twigs of the giant buck-topped white pine surrounding old Philippe's clearings.

He was walking towards the spring when he heard footsteps and sticks crackling among the maple underbrush beneath the pines. Then he heard a woman's voice, low and musical in tone; it was Vieva's, none other. "Is that you? Is that you, Lu-pold?"

Wilmer Norris stopped short, his heart thumping against his ribs, the red blood surging to his cheeks, his soul aflame with wounded pride.

There is nothing so galling to a gentleman as to have the woman he admires prefer a low-bred fellow. He thought of himself, clean-cut, intelligent, sensitive, and then of the frowzled-headed, unshaven, undersized redemptioner whom she was meeting clandestinely in the forest. It was the most humiliating event of his life. It was his punishment for loving outside his class. People are different; class distinctions do exist; he who will defy them is a blockhead of the first order.

He hoped he could slide back to the tavern without being observed, but footsteps coming up behind him told him, as plainly as words, that Lu-pold would soon overtake him. Rather than face his ignoble rival, he moved forward along the path. In another dozen paces, he came face to face with Vieva. A ray of moonlight shone on her cheeks through an opening in the pine boughs. He noted that she was whiter than the ghastly light when she saw who was approaching, that her mean deception was discovered. Wilmer made no effort to speak, and she remained silent until he was passed. Then he heard her calling softly, "Lu-pold, Lu-pold, what *has* become of you?"

The young man fully realized the awful truth; Vieva loved the redemptioner; he could have been nothing in her eyes. He plowed along the forest pathway, sometimes stumbling and almost falling over stones and roots, not caring if he did. He went on his way for several miles until he came to a windfall, where a dozen uprooted pines formed a semi-circle of a tangled mass of fibers, rocks, and earth, like a corral. He sought out a secluded spot in this tangle, where he sat down. In another minute, his face was wet with hot tears. He was paying the penalty of unwise love, reaping the harvest of tares that comes to him who dares proclaim there is no caste. He fumbled in his belt, which was under his whipcord coat, drawing out a heavy pistol. He held it up to the moonlight to see if it was properly primed. Then he put the cool muzzle against the roof of his mouth and pulled the trigger. There was a muffled, undefinable report, a lot of smoke and fumes, and Wilmer Norris released his crushed and broken spirit to the infinite.

When old Philippe, the next morning, came downstairs, his distinguished guest was nowhere to be found. It was thought at first that he had gone for an early morning walk. When he did not return at nine o'clock, a search was instituted, but no trace was found. Vieva and Lu-pold had seen him and heard the dull pistol shot in the wilderness, but they feared to tell lest they incriminate themselves.

The story of the young man's disappearance spread like wildfire; of course, old Philippe was charged with having murdered him for his money. It was in vain that he pointed to the fact that his money pouch, containing nearly five hundred dollars in gold, was found hanging over the back of the settle.

The Philadelphia relatives missed the youth in due course of time, and representatives of the agonized parents visited the scene. They went away completely mystified. In the early fall, some hunters chased a wolverine into the jungle of roots in the windfall. There they came upon the shrunken, twisted body of a young man, sitting upright, with a bullet hole in the top of the skull. A screech owl had a half-completed nest in his matted auburn hair. On the moss nearby laid a big pistol. They picked up the weapon and brought it back to show to old Philippe. That was the worst thing they could have done, as it started the story that no firearm was found near him.

Norris's parents were notified, and they directed that the remains be shipped to Philadelphia for interment in the churchyard of Gloria Dei. They threatened to have the old innkeeper arrested as his murderer, but as no motive could be shown, the matter was dropped after a time. But the tragedy killed the old man's business, and he was glad when the invitation came to run the hotel in the remote Blockhouse Country. He went there with a tarnished reputation, which could not be shaken off in a lifetime of square-dealing. His slightest faults were exaggerated, and his efforts to prevent impositions were seen as evidence of overbearing and brutal tendencies. But he made the name of the Blockhouse Country famous; he furnished cheer to thousands of sad-hearted pilgrims.

His children, despite his efforts to educate them, scorned everything done for them, marrying more or less worthless fellows. As for Vieva, she became the wife of Leopold Nancarro within a couple of months after young Norris's disappearance. It was not a happy union, as the neighbors shunned them, and after the old man had gone to keep the Blockhouse, whispered about that the couple had killed the youthful Philadelphian in order to get a dowry. All was storm for old Philippe and his family; it was like retribution falling on them for his pernicious activity in the bloody days of the guillotine.

VII

KING WI-DAAGH'S SPELL

(Story of Antes Fort Mountain)

I T WAS the unvarying custom, and perhaps the chief peculiarity of King Wi-daagh, the last ruler of the Susquehannock Indians, that any of his subjects who happened to lay eyes on him must return and see him again one year from the date. This, he imagined, instilled a proper respect for his exalted station, especially when the person who had looked at him would have to travel two hundred miles through forests drifted with snow to repeat the performance. If he but knew it, his subjects came to "hate the sight of him" for this very reason. But he had other faults. As a financier, he was a failure, even for an Indian. His bargain with the Proprietary Government in September 1700, a century after his great ancestor Pinsisseway's military triumphs, when he deeded the fertile Otzinachson Valley to the Penn family for a few trinkets and a bale of English goods, will stand out as the most one-sided land deal in history.

King Wi-daagh was very susceptible to flattery, a few grandiose compliments delivered to him by persons of the proper rank, and he would give away anything. These were probably used by Penn's emissaries, and if they had carried the farce much further, he might have given them his birthright and handed back the trinkets and the bundle of goods. Though he ever regretted the sale, he kept it mostly to himself, which is to his credit. But to the day of his death, he was pompous and overbearing to his kind, exaggerating trifles and glossing over the really important events in life. As long as his followers came back the following year after having seen him, he was satisfied. To put people to trouble seemed to be his chief delight. He was letting some splendid energy go to waste.

Wi-daagh's favorite walk was from his "palace," which consisted of a many-roomed cavern near the source of Antes Creek, along the stream, and thence westward to a small spring, where in his youth he had met clandestinely an Indian maid of inferior birth. Along the creek was the favorite pathway for Indians traveling north or south, and he invariably met troops of victims on every stroll. Much as they originally revered this august symbol of royalty, they hated the idea of having to come back a year from the date of their chance meetings with him. To each Indian who met him, he handed a piece of shell, curiously carved, and when a year later, the bearer returned, it was broken in half by the King's chamberlain as a sort of receipt to prove that the Indian had fulfilled his obligation. As a result of this oppressive custom, the meadows in the vicinity of Wi-daagh's abode, afterward the scene of his unequal bargain with the Quakers, were always thronged with Indians. Oftentimes he would keep them waiting for days before collecting their bits of wampum, which he did personally. He claimed he had a great memory for faces and would sometimes accuse an Indian of being a substitute sent by the person who had actually seen him the year before. He would talk loud and threaten, but unless his mood changed before sunset, as it usually did, it meant death to the alleged substitute. The Indians, to avoid these unpleasant complications, would have avoided the trail along the creek their monarch frequented had it not been that foreseeing this very thing, he forbid his subjects to pass north or south any other way. Some did go many miles out of their course to keep clear of him, but spies reported them, and in some cases, they fell into the hands of hostile tribes, whose penalties were more severe than Wi-daagh's. The only comfortable way to avoid their king was to stay at home, and Indians who had to travel east and west were envied, but some of these who were unlucky enough to have crossed the Susquehanna, and met the king at the spring, were forced to return like the hapless travelers on the trailway of Antes Creek.

As he grew older, he was mortified by the knowledge that most of his subjects acknowledged the Penn family and not himself as the real rulers of the realm. He protested that he merely thought he was selling the Englishmen right of way through the Susquehanna Valley; he did not expect them to attempt to be his overlords. That was his feeble defense to go down the ages against the paltry sum given him for his property. He was humiliated when one year, his chamberlain reported to him that four hundred Indians whom he had met on his walks had failed to return to pay their respects at the expiration of the year. The official gave the king a certain number of shells each day he went walking and, in that way, kept track of the size of the returning parties. A party of fifty innocent Juniata Indians who were found camping along the mountains at the south side of Nippenose Valley were seized and accused of being some of the renegades. Despite their protests that they had never been in that part of the country, all were sentenced to be burned at the stake. Had it not been that a delegation from the Proprietary Government happened along opportunely, this cruel sentence would have been carried out. One of the Quakers seeing the captives lying about in the hot sun in the meadow, bound hand and foot, learned their story from an interpreter and intimated to King Wi-daagh to abrogate the punishment.

That night, while the Quakers slept, an ear was cut from each of the fifty prisoners, their goods confiscated, and they were turned loose. Even this sentence seemed shocking to the Quakers, but it was too late for further protests. But the backbone of Wi-daagh's rule was crushed; he lived the balance of his life a broken-hearted man.

Even before his death, his sons and sons-in-law quarreled over the remnants of his domain like buzzards struggling over a dying horse. Perhaps if he had not estranged his subjects by his silly idea of making those who saw him return in a year, he might have rallied them around him and forcibly broken his contract with the Penns. Only a handful of Indians, and mostly from his immediate household, attended his funeral exercises. No doubt, the bulk of his subjects feared they might be exacted to come back the next year and call on his corpse. Attired in full warrior's regalia and with face painted, he was buried where the fish house now stands on the Lochaber estate. How the later owners of this magnificent property came to erect this little pagoda above the remains of the fallen chieftain is unknowable and belongs properly to the subject of divination. If only the weight of the fish house could have weighed down the ghost, then the best interests of divine justice would have been conserved.

King Wi-daagh's ghost was as unhappy as the living tenement had been. He had not been in his grave a week before he acquired the habit of taking midnight strolls through the Gap to the small spring at the foot of the upper mountain. Few Indians traveled at night, as lights were uncertain and expensive, so there was little to relieve his churlish loneliness. But he was occasionally seen by Indians from distant points, who were unlucky enough to build their campfires along the path. When he loomed up before them from the back of the blaze, he would hold out his hand as if trying to give something to the campers. Obviously, a spirit could not do this unless it be the *double* of a living person, and he would sink back into the gloom and vanish. For some odd reason, those who saw him always found themselves back in Antes Gap a year later, no matter if they had left there after their first visit, vowing never to return. They always met the regal ghost on their second visit, and he would flit about them like a hazy rainbow before he dwindled out of sight. After the second visit, the travelers did not find it necessary to return.

When the Indians were driven out of their beloved valleys of Central Pennsylvania, they took special care not to warn their supplanters of King Wi-daagh's ghost and his propensity to make those who saw him pay a return visit. They would have a laugh at their haughty conquerors if a ghost with far less substance than a jellyfish compelled them to do homage in this manner. It would be the triumph of the Indian spirit over Anglo-Saxon matter. Many a self-important Scotch-Irishman, through a chance meeting with the spook, was compelled to tramp back from the Chillasquaque, the Mahantango, the Codoras, or the Swatara. Why they came, they could not understand. As the anniversary approached, they "felt queer in the head," as they phrased it, and an unaccountable impulse started them in the direction of Antes Gap. They always felt easier after their second meeting with the ghost, but the trips usually wound up with a long siege of insobriety and plenty of curses heaped on the offending apparition.

In a later day, after a hotel had been built at the northerly entrance to the gap, travelers and farmers would come into the cozy barroom nights with hair standing on end and eyes bloodshot and dilated, order a drink of whiskey, look about to judge the crowd, and say, "I saw an Indian, all gotten up in war paint in the gap; I was scared out of a year's growth when he tried to hand me something."

At first, the landlord attributed these Indian stories to the alcoholic properties of Nippenose Valley cider or Rauchtown applejack, but as each frightened guest told a similar story, he concluded there must be "something back of it."

He also noticed that about a year after the first fright, the same men would turn up in the bar room, considerably cooled down, but saying that they had just come from a second experience with the Indian, and this time they were sure it was a ghost. It helped the trade in the bar, and as time went on, the genial landlord "saw through it all," and rumor had it he too had met King Wi-daagh. But the wives of the solid citizens who met him never became convinced. When they heard the story, they laid it to too much good cheer at Jersey Shore or the cozy hostelry in the gap. The ghost never appeared when two persons were together or to folk in carriages or wagons. He reserved himself for lone pedestrians. Wi-daagh in life had a similar predilection. If he came upon one of his subjects alone, the wretched savage, awed by the presence of supreme Highness, often prostrated himself on his face. When a crowd was present, more reserve was displayed.

It happened that out in the summit country east of Loganton, there lived a bright young fellow named Lot Clingerman. He had received a good common school education and had once cherished an ambition to teach. Hard work on his father's farm and some incidental prop timber and paper-wood operations had blocked his hopes of going to "Normal," and he secretly nursed a bitter disappointment. He liked to talk with persons who had been away from Sugar Valley and had come home professing a contempt for their own Dutch blood. "You've got to get away from the Dutch if you want to amount to anything," was their very silly refrain.

Lot began to feel that if he "got away from the Dutch," he would become a great man. It was his Dutch associations and not his lack of education that had prevented his success thus far. He professed a dislike for everything savoring of Dutch. He criticized his aged father to his face because he spoke with a Dutch accent, yet Lot talked as brokenly as his parent if he had only known it.

"The Dutch ain't progressive" was a jewel of wisdom he interjected into every conversation. "When I get away from these Dutch, you'll see some hustling," was another of his aphorisms.

In short, all the failures and imperfections of his family were blamed on the Dutch blood; to hear him talk, one would have thought he came from a different race. The unfrocked priest is not the worst apostate; the Pennsylvania German, who is ashamed of his race, is the meanest renegade of all.

Lot had met a pretty girl at Pine camp-meeting who lived along Antes Fort mountain. She professed to be of Yankee origin, and this made her doubly desirable in his eyes. He must have had some pluck, for he proposed marriage to her on the strength of a job he imagined he'd get. The girl liked his looks, for he was a line big specimen of manhood, but said she wouldn't take him until he had the job. In his heart, Lot said, "those Yankees, ain't they the slick articles."

He got into correspondence with an old friend who worked in a mine office at Butte, Montana, a fellow who had left Carroll four years previously. He promised Lot to place him, eventually finding him a situation in the same office. The young mountaineer was beside himself with joy. He borrowed money from his father to make the trip and started away in high glee. It was harvest time, and all the horses were busy; he was too close to hire a rig, so he walked over the summits, through the Gottschall Hollow to Rauchtown, and from there across the broad valley to Antes Gap. He intended to take the train at Antes Fort but would stop first and say *au revoir* to his sweetheart.

It was a sultry midsummer night, almost full moon, when he reached the smooth macadam road leading through the gap. The katydids and crickets were chorusing loudly. His big suitcase, which looked heavier than it really was, swung from a strap across his shoulders. To show he was "citified," he wore a brown derby with a ridiculously narrow brim, such as no city man ever owned, and kept it jammed on his head though he perspired freely. He crossed the small suspension footbridge, which spans the creek near a group of summer cottages, and started out the forest path which led in the direction of his sweetheart's rather remote residence. As he neared the little spring, he saw a tall figure emerge from behind a white oak of stupendous proportions, it is called "the Indian oak" by the way, and walk towards him with a brisk step. "Say, he walks like a New York banker," thought the young "know-it-all."

When the figure drew near, there was a flimsiness and instability which made him feel that New York bankers must be made of very frail stuff. He was further surprised when the stranger held out his hand as if to give him something, and he noticed the hands quiver and melt into vapory smoke at the fingertips. He would have grasped the hand had not the specter vanished into thin air. He supposed he was overtired from the long walk; he had heard of folks having hallucinations under such conditions and decided to say nothing of his adventure to his sweetheart. It was to be their parting night; he had only seen her thrice before, and then it was at "camp" in a crowd, and he wanted to make a favorable impression. The evening passed off better than he had expected; he knew he was a "winner," to use his own language, but this was the handiest work he had attempted. The girl agreed that after he was settled at Butte, if he would send for her, she would come out and marry him if he paid her railroad fare.

Lot Clingerman did not see the Indian King's ghost again that night, but he reached Antes Fort station in time to catch the westbound morning train, which connected at Lock Haven for Tyrone and Pittsburgh. He got along very well in Butte, and he had been there nearly a year before he realized it. He saw many girls out there whom he liked better than the one he had left on Antes Fort Mountain. He was growing less and less anxious to send for her. What he wrote her is not disclosed, but one of his letters to his father ran something like this:

Dear pop:
Say, I do like it out here more every day. Say, I am getting along just grand. Say, they put it all over the Dutch out here. These people know how to hustle. Say, I will be out here one year today a week, but I guess it will be another year or two before I can spare the time to come east. Give my best love to mom and all the rest.

Yours,

Lot

He went out of his boarding house to drop the letter in the box. It was about ten in the evening. On his way back, an uncontrollable desire seized him to go east. He had just posted a letter saying he wouldn't do so for a year or two, and now he was filled with the desire to start at once. He wasn't homesick, not he; there wasn't an ounce of sentiment in his body. He was as stolid as quartz. He could not check himself from continuing his walk to the railroad station, where he found that a through train for St. Paul and Chicago would pass through town at 1:15 that morning. He found himself walking briskly to his boarding house, where he packed his belongings and scribbled a note to the general manager of his office, saying that he had been called east on urgent business but would return as soon as possible. He paid his board bill and asked the landlady's son, who was a chum of his, to deliver the note for him in the morning. He got to the station before midnight, but the wait seemed of no moment; he was so determined to go.

All the way to the east, he was in a state of dazed exultation. He did not know why he was bound east, but he was glad to be going there. It was almost dark when he got off the eastbound train, "number sixty-eight," at Antes Fort. He realized that he was carrying the same suitcase; it was considerably heavier than when he went away, but on his head was a new and more up-to-date derby. Carrying the heavy case, he started out the road leading to Antes Gap. He passed the brightly lighted hotel; it was a temptation to watch the jolly crowd through the bar room windows. But he was east on "urgent business" and could not tarry. He came to the suspension bridge and crossed it, starting out the forest path, just as he had one year ago that night. He could not reason with himself why he was doing this; all he knew was he *must*. He saw the "Indian oak" rising like a sable cloak against the reflected lights of Lock Haven. From behind it emerged a tall slim figure, with a quick, nervous step, just as he had seen it a year ago. The apparition came near and held out his open hand as if he wanted something. Lot Clingerman came to his senses. "What in hell am I doing here?" he said aloud.

His uncouth words shocked the effete shadow, and he vanished. The thought flashed through the young man's head, "shall I keep on and see that girl?"

But another voice answered no and began naming over a dozen girls in Butte whom he liked better.

"Shall I go out the Gap and see the folks for a day?"

Again a voice said no, "they'd think it queer to see you after sending you that letter that you would not be east for a year or two."

He felt more sound and sane than he had in a year, and he wondered why. There was nothing else to do but to wander back to Antes Fort and wait for the westbound mail due about seven-fifteen the next morning. On the way, he stopped at the little hotel at the beginning of the gap. Like all the rest, he ordered a drink of whiskey, eyed the crowd critically, and then blurted out, "boys, oh, boys, I've seen a spook; what do you know about it?"

A good many of those present knew a good deal, some more than they cared to tell. One old tottering, clean-shaven German, who would have looked better if he had a set of false teeth, got up from a chair in the corner and, flourishing his heavy sassafras cane, exclaimed, "Poys, I feels tam sorry for that spook; he vants to gif folks somesing, ven he can do dat, he'll come no more."

But in the general talk that followed, it was agreed that it would be pretty difficult for an airy form to hold or give out anything material, which shows that a bar room can contain metaphysicians. "Put if he didn't make efferbotty dot sees him come back von year from date, ve'd forgive de rest," broke in the old German.

Lot, who was draining a heavy schooner of beer, hit the glass on the bar with a thud. "So that's why," he said to himself, gritting his teeth, "I had to come back to this God-forsaken region tonight."

VIII

CAVES OF THE BALD EAGLES

(Story of Aughanbaugh Mountain)

PHILIP TOMB was very fond of telling about a wonderful cave that he discovered while on one of his hunting trips. It contained many square rooms, stone benches, tables, and altars, bearing unmistakable signs of having been cut by hand. He was very explicit in his descriptions of the interior of the cavern but equally reticent concerning its exact location. Sometimes he would say it was "up Pine Creek," which is a pretty extensive territory, and on other occasions, "on Tumbling Run." As there are four or five Tumbling Runs in the State, it would lead to further mystification.

There is an old legend that the Indians who mined silver in the Bald Eagle Mountains had a cavern where they concealed themselves when pursued by eavesdroppers, and this was probably the cave visited by Philip Tomb. He evidently thought he would discover some of the silver bars and, for that reason, wished to keep the exact location secret.

This cave of the silver-mining Indians is situated on the side of the westerly mountain at Aughanbaugh Gap, near a stream that was once known locally as Tumbling Run. The name has since been changed several times, and it is now shrunken to a tiny rivulet; even the springs in the famous Little Valley, which helped feed it, seem to have lost their pristine fullness. It never tumbles over the rocks as in the old days; the only thing that tumbles now are the rocks as they roll down the chute into the hopper of the big stone-crusher.

Poor Aughanbaugh Mountain, stripped of its timber and water courses, and the quarriers delving deep into its sides! Sooner or later, if they extend their operations at the present rate, the Indians' cave will be uncovered, and new light thrown on this strangest of antiquities. Evidently, the natives had been mining silver for centuries, and successfully, else they would not have constructed such a solid and spacious underground labyrinth. It was first built as a council chamber for the chiefs and captains and, from this, developed into a storehouse for the silver before it was apportioned out at the close of every twenty moons. When the Europeans arrived and began to harass the Indians and later got an inkling of their mining operations, it was used as a haven of refuge.

Skillful in darting through the trackless forests and dropping out of sight, they could run to cover when surprised by their jealous supplanters. Several Indian miners were captured and tortured fiendishly, but they would not reveal the secrets of the mines. The barbarous manner in which they were treated by these invaders explains why the Bald Eagle silver mines got no further than into legendary history. But the last Indian died with the secret, and Philip Tomb, and one other man, were the only representatives of the pale faces who stumbled into this subterranean fastness.

An Indian whom we shall call Huntsman's Cup was the last chief who carried on the mining operations on a large scale. In the midst of his labors, he was summoned to New York State to join in a general defense of his tribe, but somewhere near the border, he was surprised at his campfire by a band of cross-grained Germans, and with his entire party perished.

The Germans, who were on their way to make a settlement in Chemung County, New York, did not know the mining story and, after the massacre, made no effort to find the ores the Indians were transporting. Possibly the rich silver bars are lying somewhere in the woods on the headwaters of Babb's Creek.

For years afterward, Indians camped near the mouth of Pine Creek annually and were said to be carrying on silver mining. They were importuned and annoyed but kept at their work manfully. When they did stop coming, they said it was only because of the angry ghosts they encountered; at least, that is the story told by a younger Indian named Billy Douty, who was brought to the mountains at a later date to try and re-discover the mines. The writer visited the reservation along the

Alleghany River in May 1908 but learned that poor Billy had been hit by an Erie midnight flyer while returning from a roistering bout at Salamanca a couple of weeks before. That ended any chances of learning the ghost story from him.

But there was the one other white man, besides Philip Tomb, mentioned earlier in this story, who chanced into the cave. He was glad to get out and said that he knew why Philip Tomb had been so chary about renewing his acquaintance with the place. But there are reasons why he was prejudiced. He was a Civil War renegade. When hostilities between North and South had reached a fever heat, and every man available, even grandfathers, was wanted for service in the field, the draft was instituted to enforce patriotism. In Pennsylvania, some whose duties at home made them dubious about enlistment submitted cheerfully when their names were drawn, but others, with little or no excuses, rebelled against the system. Some even crippled themselves, others took to the woods or went west, and one worthy, after filling up with hard cider, got into bed and sat there with a loaded shotgun in hand, ready to "pepper" any draft officers that chanced his way. In the wilder regions, several marshals and officers were shot, and considerable ill feeling was engendered among persons with "copperhead" tendencies.

The renegade in question said he had a big family to support and wouldn't enlist. All he had was a wife and one half-grown daughter, a girl old enough to learn dressmaking. He had a next-door neighbor who went to the front in 1861, leaving a wife with eight children, besides an aged father and mother, dependent on him. But that made no matter with the renegade; his family was *big* in his eyes; he wouldn't fight in any war that had been caused by a squabble over slavery. "A man's a fool to fight for Uncle Sam; the country never was run right, let it go to smash now and begin over again," was another of his anti-enlistment broadsides.

But maybe on account of this loud talk at night around the post office or at the railroad station when the evening train came in, he became a marked man with the draft officials. It was not long before his name was drawn and a notice sent to him to report on a certain date at Williamsport. Two men about his age, neighbors, were drawn at the same time; the draft had fallen heavily in the little mountain hamlet. Bright and early, the chosen three were at the station. Two of them were surrounded by weeping mothers, wives, and children, while the third stood nearby chewing tobacco and whittling a stick of white pine. His cool demeanor wasn't noticed until after the train came in and the two men climbed on board.

"Aren't you coming along, Mike?" yelled one of the conscripts as the conductor gave the signal to start.

"Hell, no," he answered, "let 'em send for me."

There were enough copperheads in the crowd to enable him to sneak away unmolested, and the train started down the valley, carrying the two brave-hearted patriots. When they reported at the recruiting office, the absence of the third party from Mountainburg was noticed. The conscripts admitted they had seen him at the station but said he had shown no inclination to accompany them. A telegraphic message was sent, ordering him to come down on the evening train, but he did not put in an appearance. A sergeant was at the station when the train arrived, and as the recruit did not get off, he boarded the westbound train, which left five minutes later. Arriving at Mountainburg, he was told that his man had left the station fifteen minutes earlier, saying he was going home. The agent declared that he handed him the message personally. The sergeant was incensed clean through and requisitioned a horse and carryall that was tied back of the station to quicken his speed to the renegade's home.

The fellow's cabin stood at the edge of the pine forest, and all the windows were brightly lit as the officer approached. He knocked at the door, which was opened by a half-grown girl.

"Where's your pop?" demanded the sergeant.

"He's gone to Williamsport to be a soldier," said the girl looking him squarely in the eyes.

For a minute, the sergeant was puzzled; he might have missed the man in the crowd at the depot, but on the other hand, he had been told by half a dozen reliable people at Mountainburg that he had not boarded the train. Then he realized he was being hoaxed. He angrily demanded that the girl tell the real whereabouts of her father, but she remained firm. Then he commenced a search of the shanty, but he only found the renegade's wife sitting calmly on the back steps smoking her pipe, listening to the katydids. Threatening wife and daughter with arrest, he left for the station, a baffled man.

Afterward he was told that while he was arguing with the girl at the front door, a dark figure carrying a rifle under his coat emerged from the chicken house at the back of the yard and disappeared into the inky depths of the pinewood. The sergeant returned to Williamsport on the midnight train, and a reward was at once offered for the conscript. It would seem like money easily earned, but some of the natives sympathized with the wretch and warned him whenever the trail grew hot. Besides, he knew the mountain paths; his pursuers did not; perhaps the sympathetic natives mystified them at times. But every day, it became harder and harder to get provisions to him; his family was under surveillance and couldn't go, and it was often difficult for others to spare the time to carry his dinner bucket over seven or eight miles of mountain byways.

Down on Aughanbaugh Mountain, the evergreen timber grew thicker and blacker than on any other mountain in the chain of the Bald Eagles. Even today, what few of the "black-tops" that survived the lumbermen richly deserve their picturesque appellation as they rear their somber heads from among the other trees. It was here that the renegade made his headquarters; few would trail him into this deserted region.

He was frightfully lonesome, and some of the nights were very cold as he bivouacked in the junkie, too hungry to find much comfort at having cheated Uncle Sam. His conscience began troubling him, and that added considerably to his woes. It was hard to put in the time; the days and nights seemed interminable; sleep appeared to have deserted him, and hunger alone kept pace in the solitude. His friends left pails of provisions as regularly as they could, but he often had to go without two of his three meals. This empty feeling may have helped the birth of his conscience; it often does. He saw lots of game but was afraid to shoot, fearing the shots would betray him. He was even afraid to kindle a fire. He imagined he was getting all manner of diseases; every cracking twig was a captor approaching, every shudder of the leaves an accusing voice. His mental state was hideous, stumbling about in the hemlock glades, trying to figure out what to do next.

Late one afternoon, worn out from his aimless travels, he sat down on a rock, watching some yellow birch leaves floating on the glassy surface of a small pool. He buried his face in his hands, cursing himself and his luck with an endless stream of blasphemies. In the midst of his lamentations, he felt a cold breath on the back of his neck, like a breeze from some underground vault. He looked around; the air seemed to issue from a crevice between two upright rocks, weather-beaten and lichen covered. He cut a stout pole and was able to pry one of the rocks aside. It disclosed an opening into the side of the mountain, sufficiently large for a man to crawl through. At the sight of this, the outlaw forgot most of his troubles; even his conscience became temporarily diverted. Then he got down on his hands and knees and crawled into the opening. At most, he expected to find the den of some wild animal, probably a large black bear. He had not moved more than a hundred feet when he found himself in a vast room, the ceiling of which was at least twenty feet high. It was square in form and neatly walled up, the work of skilled masons.

Beyond was a doorway that apparently led into another similar chamber. But he was too much surprised by this one room to want to venture further just yet. At the far end, in one corner, was a pedestal cut out of granite or ganister that looked like a sacrificial altar. In the center of the room was a square table cut from a solid block of gray rock. Grouped around it were a dozen or more stone seats. Along one wall was a stone couch or reclining chair. The atmosphere of the place was soothing and cozy and not too cool, so the visitor seated himself on the reclining bench to make out whether or not he was dreaming. If he wasn't, then he was face to face with one of the greatest of curiosities. It must be of Indian origin, he reasoned, but what Indians were such skillful masons and stone cutters? They must have been a race far superior to the people he used to hear his grandfather tell about. These had considerable trouble chipping an arrowhead evenly. He took off his heavy hunting coat and put it back of him as a pillow. His torch began to burn down to the end, but somehow he was oblivious. He heard air currents, almost musical in their vibrations in the inner recesses of the cave. He would go and explore every foot, but he didn't; he just sat and speculated. One of the air currents took an unexpected course and blew out the torch altogether.

He fell sound asleep the same instant the light was extinguished. He must have slept several hours; that is how he figured it out. In the midst of a sweet dream about being home and free from disgrace, he was roughly awakened by a hard firm hand shaking him by the shoulder. He opened his eyes and looked up. The gloomy cave was illuminated by a silvery light, like the fox fire of many candle power.

Close by him loomed the figure of an Indian chief, fully seven feet tall, silver-grey in color, like fox fire. Around him were grouped other Indians, some more vague of outline than others with clenched fists and menacing expressions. The whole scene was enough to have made him die of fright; it was worse than a hundred Southern battlefields.

He did not die of fright or even faint; his ancestors had been brave men, and what was strongest in his make-up sustained him now. He gazed boldly at this army of sepulchral inquisitors. The tall Indian chief began to speak to him in a strange tongue, but soon the words seemed to find equivalents in his brain. He may have jumped at the purport of the speech from the tone of the voice and the movement of the lips. At any rate, he knew the meanings. George Moore says, "The Gods speak not in any mortal language; one becomes aware of their immortal Presence." But at first, he was too dazed to act on the demands. Seeing this, the huge Indian seized him again by the shoulder and tried to shove him off the bench. The heavy hand pressure lacked something; we are not impelled forward by a fog. All the while, the Indian was talking angrily. "Get out of this place," he seemed to say, "you are a vile coward, a renegade, a runaway, a poltroon. This cavern never sheltered one of your kind before; you are making it an unfit place even for the matchless spirits of brave warriors who lived long ago. Begone, wretched craven, do not pollute this pure atmosphere with your foul presence, be gone!"

With these last words, he strove harder than ever to dislodge the half-dazed, half-stubborn intruder. All efforts might have failed had not the other Indian shades swept forward, and their combined effort, like a night wind, tumbled him from the couch. He fell to the stone floor, cutting an ugly gash on his forehead. Stumbling to his feet, he lunged towards the opening as best he could. He plunged out into the darkness, and as he did so, he heard the tall gate-rock which he had dislodged fall back into position.

He fell into the pool, extracting himself with difficulty. He sat for some time by the pond, gradually coming to his senses as he saw shafts of light sifting through vague openings in the tall trees. But these soon closed up, giving way to drizzling rain. As the drops touched his face, he got up, burning with a new resolve. Wiping the clotted blood from his brow, he started down the hillside, over the jagged rocks, and along a trail that followed Tumbling Run to the river.

When he came in sight of the railroad track, he stopped and stripped off his red shirt. He threw it over one shoulder and leaned against an original white pine tree, which, until it was felled a few years ago by the contractors who built the double track, was known as "the deserter's tree," and waited. In the distance, he heard the treble whistle of the morning train coming through the mist. He got out on the ties and began waving the red shirt frantically. The engine was almost upon him when the crew noticed the demonstration and threw on the brakes. The renegade climbed into the coach and dropped heavily into one of the rickety seats. The conductor appeared for the ticket but was told that Uncle Sam would pay the freight. This angered the conductor, who started to pull the bell rope. The impudent passenger grabbed his arm, whispering, "Say brother, don't do it; I reckon you'll get reward enough by carrying a damned deserter into Billsport."

IX

PATHFINDER'S CHILD

(Story of the Round Top)

TO LEVI Cornprobst, everything Indian was detestable, except the beauty of some of their women. And these he regarded more as chattel than as rational, feeling human beings. He may have had a sense of honor in regard to his relations with white girls, he said he had at any rate, but he would deceive an Indian girl without a qualm. His constant motto was, "The sooner the Indians are gone, the better for the country." Wrecking the lives of Indian girls was helping along the demolition of the race and affording him pleasure as well. It was a labor of "love," put plainly. Being good-looking and stalwart, his campaign against Indian women was assured of success. A homely man could have butchered warriors and old squaws to his heart's content, but the copper-colored girls would have turned their backs on him and disappeared into the forests. Levi's good looks were a fatal magnet that drew the maidens to their destruction. There always was a peculiar fascination about handsome white men on the part of Indian girls. Nine times out of ten, they preferred a sturdy Scotch-Irishman or German to any sinewy member of their own race. Few of these respected them individually or as a race; consequently, their attachments were foreordained to end in physical ruin and suicide. No Indian girl could stand the taunts of her jealous sisters or former lovers when betrayed by a white man. She would invariably wander off to some cave, like a woodnymph, and stab herself in the breast with a poisoned arrow or else tie a heavy rock about her neck and leap off a ledge into the bowl below a waterfall. She would emerge a frail and willowy spirit, to flit about on moonless nights awhile and sob, and then become a part of the elements from which her soul originated.

"The Indians are here to be killed, and their women folks to be loved," was Levi's code of justification. His parents said that he had been born in the Palatinate, but this he always denied indignantly. He knew where he was born, he said; it was right in the shadow of Fort Dietrich Snyder in Schuylkill County. Wasn't his godmother Dolly Hope, who later became the bride of the fearless Snyder himself? German or not as he may have been, Levi Cornprobst was often taken for young James Brady, who met with such a melancholy death at the hands of the natives.

It is related that a week after the burial of the "Young Captain of the Susquehanna," a party of backwoodsmen met Levi walking near the Bull Run graveyard and took to their heels, thinking it was the gallant hero risen from the dead. But the resemblance, if it existed, was superficial, as Cornprobst was altogether lacking in those noble qualities of mind and heart so noticeable in this young martyr of the West Branch. Levi was very proud of his cumbersome German rifle and, on the walnut stock, had cut five nicks, which meant five Indians had fallen to his unerring aim. Six was his lucky number, he contended; he must get one more before peace was declared.

"Damn those Quakers," he would say, "they're trying to smooth things over while we are working to rid the country of the Indians; why can't they let us alone?"

Despite the five nicks on his rifle stock, the Indian girls still "made up him," ties of blood did not matter much when a handsome, six-foot frontiersman was within call.

"After a man's known a hundred Indian girls, then it's time to find a white wife," he would say.

It was down in Dry Valley that he first ran across Polygalah. She was the most winsome Indian girl who ever crossed his path. "I'll bet she had a white man for a father" was the highest compliment he paid her. But that is doubtful, as apart from a light or pinkish complexion, she was a Monsey maid in every particular. Her father, Greatshot, was a noted hunter and sometimes warrior, and at the period when Levi met his daughter, he was encamped trying to heal a bad gun wound in one of his feet. As he could not travel and fight, he professed the greatest friendliness for all the white men in the neighborhood, and there was

THE RIVER AND THE ROUND TOP
Photo by H. W. Swope, Lock Haven, Pa.

not one who helped him in his trouble. But the wound would not heal, "Some white devil's put a spell on me" was the way he summed up his ailment when none of the secretly hated race were present.

Levi somehow managed to get together a lot of salves and medicines in his cabin, and these he doled out in small quantities, provided Polygalah came after them. He could have given all the stuff to the wounded warrior at once, or taken it to him daily, as he lived but half a mile away, but he wanted to lure the maiden, that was certain.

From Polygalah's point of view, she would have been deeply disappointed if there was no medicine to go after; she felt enough modesty to make her want an excuse for often going to the young pathfinder's shack. She was a medium-sized girl, neatly formed, with features clearly defined. Her hair was of a softer texture than the "manes" of most Indian girls. She was not "flat-faced," a noted Indian peculiarity. Levi noticed this; if she had been flat-faced, a single night in her company would have sufficed.

"When I meet a pie-face," he once said, "I shut my eyes and think of the most beautiful girl I have ever seen."

With Polygalah, it was different; he looked at her with open-eyed admiration. He could not see enough of her clean-cut mouth and nose, her dancing hazel eyes.

The Indian girl was wildly infatuated with him, never had she beheld such a handsome man. She would have gladly laid down her life for him at that time. Levi was then close to twenty-one years of age, over six feet in height, powerfully made, with aquiline features and a shock of stiff, dark red hair. He bunched it together at the back of his neck and tied it with a piece of black ribbon. Polygalah always liked to stroke his hair when she called; if possible, she would put a fresh twist to the ribbon under the pretext that it was coming undone.

Levi was like a catamount watching for his prey; when he got her where he wanted, he pounced on her, and after that, everything was easy. During the hegira of the romance, Polygalah forgot there was such a thing as marriage or duty. She was prostrate, smitten, helpless. She stayed so long on her visits to the pathfinder's shack that old Greatshot fussed and fumed, which did his wound no good. But in his dependent state, he feared to forbid his daughter's visits, else trouble might result. Levi was too big and too ugly a customer to trifle with.

"When I get well, I'll ambush and kill him," was the way the old deer slayer mapped out the future of the youth he should have been angling for as son-in-law.

These were the happiest days of the fair Indian girl's career. The very fact that her lover made no promises, in fact, never once discussed the future, left her in a delightful state of uncertainty. She was always fearing that some morning she would find him gone. Literally, she wanted the man because she could not have him.

There had been a young warrior tenting with her father during the early days of his mishap, named Little Johnny Brokenstraw, but Polygalah's rudeness to him had driven him to parts unknown. The young Indian, when he left, vowed vengeance on every white man.

Polygalah never cared for Indian youths when white men were about, and Little Johnny Brokenstraw labored under the double disadvantage of being a homely Indian. That was absolutely inexcusable. But he had loved Polygalah with all his heart and could have been good to her and knew it. Hence his sulks for weeks in the depths of the tall timber after his departure.

Meanwhile, Polygalah's sojourns at Levi's hut were longer and more impassioned. Some of the frontiersmen started the story that she had deserted her parents and gone to keep house for the pathfinder. But she was occasionally found about the parental tepee, downcast and sullen. At Levi's shack, she was all affection and smiles. At length came a time when the glum countenance she wore at home was extended to her hours at the abode of her lover. Things had gone amiss; she had been compelled to confess to him that she was to have a child. This angered the young man, and it is said he struck her down when he first heard the news. Whether he did so or not cannot be proved, but this much is certain; he tried to discourage her visits from that time on. But she continued coming on one excuse or another, despite his abusive treatment whenever she put in an appearance.

One morning she arrived to find the inevitable had happened. Levi had stripped the shack of everything of value during the night and disappeared. Polygalah sat down on the doorstep and wept; she had lost her lover, now she would be taunted almost to death. She thought of the poisoned arrow, of the leap over the waterfall, but she also remembered her stricken father, whose gangrenous foot was growing worse daily. Indians being Spartans, she decided to go back and confess everything. Indian children were often born out of wedlock, and she was to have one by a really handsome white man.

Old Greatshot took the news unflinchingly, as did his squaw. Under his breath, the old huntsman muttered, "Great Spirit, give me strength to get well and ambush and kill that dog."

To her surprise, Polygalah received very few taunts. The neighboring Indians pitied her on account of her father's condition. They would not add to her burdens.

A week before her child was born, Little Johnny Brokenstraw, who had heard everything, appeared on the scene and offered marriage. He had built himself a grand lodge-house on the north slope of the Round Top, a beautiful mountain in the Bald Eagle range, in a region that abounded with game and where white men were few and generally inoffensive. But Polygalah indignantly refused him. She would rather be the castoff plaything of a handsome white man than the wife of a homely, undersized Indian. Little Johnny Brokenstraw, repulsed a second time, "gathered up his tent and silently stole away."

The child, a fine boy, was born, and two days later, Greatshot breathed his last. The baby was called Little Levi Greatshot, accidentally putting a part of Little Johnny Brokenstraw's name into the composite cognomen.

Dry Valley was a poor place for three unprotected squaws to live, there was a younger daughter, Orchis, also a pretty girl, so they yielded to the entreaties of some of Greatshot's former comrades, and moved west with them, happening to camp in one of the mountain ridges directly south of the Round Top.

But Little Johnny Brokenstraw did not come to see her. He was devoting all his time to seining shad and trapping wild pigeons. He liked to see how many he could destroy in a day for the ruthless love of killing. He must have imagined each one a miniature Levi Cornprobst. But fresh and more serious hostilities broke out between the settlers and

Indians, and Little Johnny gave up killing shad and wild pigeons for the
more edifying slaughter of white men. He had a special antipathy against
Germans. Somehow or other, in days of truce, he had acquired a heavy
German rifle and, with the renewed hostilities, was able to cut five nicks
in the walnut stock. In addition, he had five scalps, four red and one
black, as proof positive of his prowess. On some fine days, he wore these
as a cape around his massive shoulders, the black scalp in the center.

"I'd like to make it an even six," he oft confided to his brothers-in-crime.

They knew what he meant by this; he had his eye open for Levi
Cornprobst. But it was for the young German to make the first move
in this game of life. He had tracked Little Johnny Brokenstraw with the
same avidity as the Indian had trailed him, but for a different motive. He
blamed the Indian for putting false notions in Polygalah's head; without
him, she would have given less trouble when she found she was to be a
mother. But all this was utterly unfounded.

One bright morning in the Indian summer, Little Johnny Brokenstraw was sitting in the grass in an open space where there had been
a windfall, warming himself in the fitful sunlight. The woods about
him were a riot of bright yellows, pinks, crimsons, and purples. Nature
seemed to tell her glory in the hickories, tulips, lindens, gums, and
maples. The breezes swayed the scarlet garlands of the woodbine like
Greek dancers. The dark pines and hemlocks were like somber Quakers
who took no part in Nature's Mardi Gras. The tall tree trunks were
alive with squirrels, red, grey, and black, seemingly in harmony on this
occasion, gathering their winter store. The creek nearby had been reju-
venated by the fall rains and spread foam broadcast as it swept over the
stones and driftwood. A belated dove was reiterating to an obstinate
loved one the plaint a-coo, coo, coo. Rejected, after the long courtship,
it hurled itself across the open space with the velocity of a catapult. A
few flickers, perched perpendicularly, were calling peremptorily to one
another, "quit, quit, quit, quit, quit!" There was a pale blue haze over
everything, like sunlight in half-mourning, especially over the conelike
outlines of the distant Round Top.

Little Johnny Brokenstraw, though dreamy like his surroundings,
was awake to danger. When he heard a soft tread in the woods, very

different from a startled deer, he looked ahead, all attention. The German rifle lay ten feet away; that was his one act of carelessness. He rued it when he saw the tall form of Levi Cornprobst emerge from the timber on the opposite side of the creek. It was probable that he saw Levi first, but it was by a close margin if any. The pathfinder raised his rifle, and the Indian had only time to take to flight, unarmed, to escape the bullet sent after him. That was the beginning of a chase that lasted all that sunshiny autumn morning. Little Johnny Brokenstraw was noted for his fleetness, but on this occasion, he had met his match. Even though the white man stopped several times to reload his rifle, the Indian could not elude him. The shots missed every time, but the quarry was becoming exhausted. He stopped for breath every time Levi did, but he noted that his pursuer gained more from these rests than he. He knew that the rifle was loaded; once he gave up, he was a "good Indian," and everyone knew what that meant. On one occasion, when he fell over a big log, for an instant, he lacked the initiative to get up. He had some reserve force, so he sprang to his feet, redoubling his efforts. But his lungs pained like molten lead; he was burning up inside. His tongue hung out; he thought his distended eyeballs would drop from the sockets. His feet ached, and every muscle was sore. He wondered what condition his foe could be in, running as fast and far and carrying a heavy German rifle as well. He had crossed several ridges and bounded through Love Run Gap and then to further tire his pursuer, cut across the eastern slope of the Round Top.

As he was running down the mountainside, in the direction of the river, with a vain idea of swimming to safety, he suddenly came upon an Indian encampment. It hadn't been there the day before; evidently, they were homeless, driven hither and thither by the warfare. His bloodshot eyes noted only squaws, a dozen or more of them. Then he tripped over a basket and fell to his knees, waving his long arms and trying to articulate a cry of defeat and fear. An old squaw was seated by a pile of stones that had been heaped up to make a hearth for the campfire; near her, resting on a stump, was a loaded musket.

Levi Cornprobst, rifle in hand, a half minute later, appeared on the edge of the camp, his face fiery red from overexertion and anger. Trembling as he was, he raised his firearm to aim at the kneeling figure of

Little Johnny Brokenstraw. At this moment, the figure of a young squaw, fairer of complexion, daintier and more slender than the rest, bearing in her arms a lusty, chubby baby boy, it was none other than Polygalah, threw the child and herself between Little Johnny Brokenstraw and the bloodthirsty pathfinder. Holding the child aloft, she silently dared him to shoot. He let his hand slide along the barrel until he held the rifle at the tip; could he kill Little Johnny Brokenstraw without endangering this child? He was not given much time for reflection as the old squaw, who was sitting near the loaded gun, slipped her hand to the trigger, and fired. Shot through the abdomen, Levi fell forward, groaning and twisting with agony. Little Johnny Brokenstraw rose to his feet, shouting, "I've got my sixth scalp at last." But there is no record that Polygalah ever married Little Johnny Brokenstraw.

X

CONRAD'S BROOM

(Story of Lower McElhattan Mountain)

IT IS difficult to view the north slope of the lower Bald Eagle Mountain at McElhattan without catching a glimpse of the Crispin Fields. A great circular clearing is carved out on the mountainside one-third of the distance from the summit; it is a conspicuous landmark for miles. At a distance, it gives the impression of being well-kept and smooth, but if you visit the ground, it will be found to be fast growing up with young *Pinus rigida*, sumacs, and blackberry vines. To all intents, it is a part of the surrounding woods, for the fences have rotted or fallen down. A short distance below the western corner of the fields is the famous "lower gum-stump spring," a source of sweet, pure water, which increases into a stream of no mean proportions, a much larger stream than that which flows from the "main gum-stump spring" about a quarter of a mile further west.

It was near the "lower gum-stump spring" that William Crispin, a settler from New Jersey, said to be of English descent, erected his log cabin, and commenced clearing the surrounding land. His former home was in the northern part of his native state, where mountains abounded, hence his selection of a hillside plantation in Central Pennsylvania, when river-bottom lands could have been purchased cheaply. On his way up the state, it was a tedious journey in those days, when farming implements and household goods had to be transported in ox-carts or horse-drawn wagons over rocky or muddy roads, he met, wooed, and wed an attractive German girl whose home was near Weisersburg, afterward called Selinsgrove. A good-sized family was born to them, all handsome and healthy, of whom the oldest son was named Conrad, after the immortal

Colonel Conrad Weiser, about whom Crispin's wife had heard so much in her youth.

The section now known as McElhattan was a wilderness even in the early years of the nineteenth century; it has retained much of its delicious old-time flavor still, but then it was a primitive Arcadia. Once Conrad told his father that every morning a large black dog followed his three little sisters and himself to school. When it came too close and showed its teeth, they drove it away by throwing pine knots at it. One morning after a snowfall, the father accompanied the children to school; he wanted to see the dog himself. He was able to see it and shoot it; the familiar dog turned out to be a big black wolf. It was just when the hardy pioneer had gotten a nice farm tilled; he had to grub out and burn hundreds of trees to do so, to say nothing of piling up countless rocks, that he caught a heavy cold which developed into pneumonia, and he died at the early age of forty-five.

Conrad, who was fifteen years old at the time, became the head of the household and the continuer of the farming enterprise. He was a stout boy for his years, willing, alert, and cheerful. He took up the tasks with vim, aiming to leave nothing unfinished that his father had commenced. He was his mother's idol, like most boys who make good in any sphere. By the time he was twenty, he had the farm and livestock in good order, so much so that the sentimental German mother continually said, "Oh, if your father could only have lived to see all this!" Chief among the stock was a large flock of sheep, and it was told with special pride that there had not been a single one taken by a wolf or panther since good William Crispin's death. This spoke volumes about the watchfulness of Conrad and his younger brothers. In the yard, about the comfortable cabin, were a goodly number of chickens of the old-time breeds, Creeleys, buntiea, sprucies, toppies, as well as brown ducks and white geese with black heads. The little girls vied with their brothers to keep the foxes and weasels from destroying these and guarded them well.

During the long winters, Conrad practiced other accomplishments. He was an expert basket-maker with oak or willow withes and grew some broom com back of the house, from which he made some excellent besoms. He also was proficient in carving out hickory axe handles.

At the time of the young man's twentieth birthday, about ten families were living on the fertile plain within the semi-circle of mountains, now included in the boundaries of Wayne Township. Most of the families were of Scotch-Irish origin, but there were several "mixed-households" where the husbands were Scotch-Irish and the wives German.

On the sloping river bank, near the "big bend," and close to Spook Hill with its crumbling palisade of Fort Horn, lived a German couple named St. Galmier. While their name sounded more French than German, they spoke the tongue of the Fatherland, in fact, could speak but a very few words of English. They were most probably of Huguenot extraction, coming from ancestors who had fled to Germany from France during the massacre on St. Bartholomew's Day. They were past middle age and childless when the Crispins appeared and began clearing their farm near the lower gum-stump spring. Old Christ St. Galmier, it was said, was a butcher by trade, but he had long since abandoned everything except tilling a small garden patch and eternally fishing for shad and salmon. A few stalks of tobacco grew in his meager front yard; from this, he made his own smoking materials. He was an unsociable follow, sullen and uncommunicative, and his wife, who was his counterpart, was further cut off from friendly intercourse by almost total deafness.

A couple of years after the birth of the Crispins' first-born, Conrad, old "Mammy" St. Galmier became the mother of a girl. At least, she said she did and proudly exhibited a very beautiful infant. Local gossips were limited to one or two individuals in such a small community, but these could not hint at the baby's parentage if it had been a foundling. As Conrad Crispin grew sturdy and strong, the little St. Galmier girl, who was named Elizabeth, developed slight, blonde, and winsome. No such beautiful child had ever been seen in the West Branch Valley, Vashti McElhattan of an earlier generation, who ran off with an Indian, not excepted.

Vashti was also a blonde, of much the same type; there have been no blonde girls in Wayne Township since, not one. At school and in the out-door religious festivals, the mutual fondness of Conrad Crispin and Elizabeth St. Galmier was noticed and commented upon. The St. Galmiers were pleased, but the thought of it struck terror to good Mother Crispin. She had always feared the elder St. Galmiers, with their dark, mysterious past, and their supposed daughter so ethereally beautiful belonged to the world of black art in her eyes.

Down at Weisersburg, there was an old woman, a witch, who had the Black Book, the *Sixth and Seventh Books of Moses*, and she fancied she saw an affinity between the fair young girl and this awful old "hex" of the long ago. What the resemblance was, she never would tell, but she kept warning Conrad to beware, beware. This opposition only fanned his interest, and as he was such a good boy in every other respect, his mother did not like to make it too hard for him. But when mother and son, as they sat side by side on the doorstep, watching the sunset behind Mt. Pipsisseway, indulged in heart-to-heart talks, the demoniac origin of Elizabeth was never neglected.

"That girl was not born to that old woman," the good mother would say, "she is a she-devil that took the form of a beautiful girl, deceiving the old couple and coming into this world to do mischief. You could not keep her if you married her any more than if you tried to keep the snow on the roof from melting when Spring approaches."

"How do you know all this, mother?" the young man would plead.

"Never mind, son, I know more than you think; someday, I will prove it to you."

Then, the sun having sunk behind the majestic peak, they would get up to go about their duties. But these words always threw a pall of gloom over Conrad's otherwise happy and hopeful nature.

Whisperings of Mother Crispin's opposition, and the causes of it, spread about the settlements, keeping many friends away from Elizabeth. It had one advantage to Conrad; no other lads noticed the exquisite girl; he did not have the annoyance of rivals. He would have won out, though there were a dozen, as the girl cared for him alone. It seemed as if her destiny directed her to him.

Twenty years old in the backwoods was accounted as a good age; much was done by boys and girls of that age and younger. To celebrate the occasion, Mother Crispin asked Conrad, as his birthday drew near, to name a wish, and she would grant it if in her power.

"I'm going to marry Elizabeth someday, mother," he replied, "I want you to really know her; can't I have her here for supper on my birthday?"

The mother would almost as soon have entertained one of the black wolves from the forest, but she loved her son, and he should have his way. Besides, "the day of reckoning was drawing near." A wolf in sheep's clothing could only play the farce a certain length of time before blowing up like a bubble. Conrad invited Elizabeth in the presence of her parents. They beamed at this compliment to their strangely neglected, beautiful child.

"You will have a grand time," they said, "Conrad's mother is such a great cook."

Elizabeth had passed her sixteenth birthday two months before, was tall and graceful like a dryad, with hair of a peculiar golden tint and blue eyes kept ever at "half-mast" to hide the mystery of her soul. She had marked peculiarities for one so young. Even if there wasn't a story extant of her ghostly origin, she was different from girls of her age, so much so that during her brief schooldays, her fellow pupils dubbed her "Cracky." The Irish schoolmaster, a drunken lout with a Dublin University degree, predicted she'd "go to the devil or marry the President." She would not learn, though she was naturally clever. There is much potential energy in such young persons, though the devil often does inherit most of it.

Conrad's birthday dawned bright and clear, an ideal day in late Summer. As the afternoon advanced, the Round Top and the lower McElhattan Mountain assumed the tone of dark heliotrope, while the air smelled like that exquisite flower. There was a pale gold mantle above the crest of Mt. Pipsisseway.

Mother Crispin outdid herself with the supper; it was all in readiness for the arrival of the ethereal guest. Conrad seated himself on the doorstep, within call of his mother, looking across the clearings in the direction from which Elizabeth would come. As he sat there, the good woman came out, bearing one of the brooms he had made the winter before but had never been used.

"Let me sweep off the steps," she said, so the young man arose while she swept industriously. He was leaning against the house when far in the distance, he espied his sweetheart. Mother Crispin saw her at the same moment.

"Conrad," she cried, "I told you that Elizabeth St. Galmier is a devil, a witch; now, to prove it, put this broom under the steps, and you'll see she will not be able to walk over it."

"Oh, mother," said Conrad ruefully, "how can you say such a thing? It would be awful to do that; you might as well scatter mustard seeds or put a sieve on the steps; if she were a ghost, she'd have to count the seeds or the holes in the sieve before she could proceed."

"I am right, Conrad," said the mother forcibly, "I know that girl's secret; hurry, put this broom under the steps."

Conrad was hesitating. "You do it, mother, if you wish; I can't."

"It would not do any good if I put it there; a witch's lover must do it if the truth is to be shown."

Elizabeth was still too far out to see them, and there was a fringe of paw-paw trees along the fence which hid the cottage. There was time to make the test, to prove for all time the fair vision's innocence or guilt. Quickly seizing the broom from his mother's hand, he thrust it under the steps and ran down the path toward his loved one. Both looked happy and beaming as they drew near the cabin. Mother Crispin was at the door to greet them. As they came in front of the steps, Elizabeth suddenly paused. For a bare instant, the bright young smile vanished off her lips; her eyes never smiled as far back as anyone remembered. She stooped down and drew the new broom from out of its hiding place.

"Oh, Mother Crispin," said she, the old gaiety of her voice fully returned, "how did this fine new broom get under the steps?"

She rested it against the house, went up the steps, inside the cabin, and the little supper party proceeded. But before grace was said, Elizabeth presented her lover with a pair of mittens and a pair of beaded deerskin moccasins of her own knitting. Never had she seemed gayer or more witty. Conrad felt sick at heart, but he had to laugh at her jests; he could not be glum in the presence of such a radiant object. Mother Crispin was also in good humor; hers was the elation of victory, while the other children were joyous because they were young and the supper tasted good. Altogether it was a most successful party; they sat at the table a good hour and a half, partly joking and bantering. There were many sincere good wishes for Conrad's future happiness and Elizabeth's.

About ten o'clock, a late hour for mountaineers, the young girl started homeward, accompanied by her lover. There was a young moon with its horns pointed to the east.

"Don't they look like the devil's horns," said Elizabeth as they emerged from the wood.

Conrad thought that very strange talk but said nothing. All was congenial and gay, and they kissed a long lingering goodnight as they parted at the St. Galmier cabin. When she opened the door, her pet cat, a huge brindled creature with six toes on each foot, trotted out and rubbed himself against her skirts. The young moon, reflected horns downward, was dancing on the calm river when the young lover started back to the mountain.

"Elizabeth, oh, Elizabeth, was there ever anyone like you in the world," he kept repeating as he treaded his lonely way.

A great horned owl perched in a white pine tree with supernaturally long branches insisted on answering "no, no, no, no, no!" whether from the elation of the entire affair, or the broomstick episode, Conrad could not sleep that night. Through the closed window, he could still hear the owl reiterate, "no, no, no, no, no-o-o." He dozed off a little while just before daybreak.

At six o'clock, there was a knocking at the door. Conrad opened it and found old Christ St. Galmier waiting outside. There had been a white frost, and the old man's face looked as ashen as the dew-enameled grass.

"Elizabeth's very sick; she wants to see you at once," said the old man in German.

Without waiting to find his cap, the young lad followed him to the cabin by the river-side. He found the girl in bed, breathing heavily and only partly conscious. He could not be sure if she recognized him or not. All day and all night, he remained with her, the old couple meanwhile plying her with herb remedies.

By the following morning, she seemed to improve and opened her droopy eyelids, smiling sweetly with her smooth, arched lips. But she never uttered a syllable. Conrad felt he should go home for a few hours, so taking advantage of her favorable condition, he started away.

When he was returning, after dinner, he met old St. Galmier halfway.

"Elizabeth's dead," the old man muttered, "she passed away suddenly fifteen minutes ago, just after she had begun talking to us so nicely."

"What were her last words?" said Conrad.

"Oh, something about she wished you'd always believe in her."

The rest of the way, the two men walked in silence.

Conrad was ushered into the presence of the dead, but great was his surprise. Though life had only vanished a brief half hour, every trace of her former beauty was missing. It seemed like the corpse of an old wizened, wrinkled woman and not a sixteen-year-old girl. The bright gold hair had faded to an ash or silver color. Even the teeth had fallen out. Conrad was shocked but made no comment.

In the ensuing hours, he helped old St. Galmier construct a coffin out of pine boards, which the aged man had recently bought at young Billy McElhattan's watermill to build a bed. Several neighbors called during the afternoon and left, shaking their heads, after viewing the remains.

At nightfall, the young man felt he ought to sit up with the dead, but duty to his mother called him homeward. One of his good friends, Hugh McMahon, offered to do the office for him. On his way home, a screech owl chasing a mouse scurried across the path in front of him, flapping its big flat wings. He should have turned back as it meant bad luck, but didn't. That night he slept but had troubled dreams. Though it was chilly, he always kept the window of his room open. It seemed he saw a female figure astride a broomstick flying across the horned moon, a cat upon her back.

At dawn, he started for the house of sorrow. Midway he met old Christ, leaning on a staff and puffing for breath as he hobbled along. "My God, Conrad," he exclaimed, "Hugh went out for a drink of water about midnight, and someone stole our corpse; the pet cat, overcome with grief, has also disappeared."

Conrad turned white as the hoar frost and trembled like an aspen. The truth was now revealed, though he dared not offend the old man by telling it to him. He hurried to the cabin, carefully examining the premises, but could see no earthly way that the body could have been removed. McMahon, sobbing like a child, sat on a log by the river; surely, he was not to blame. The only charitable thing to do was to say that the body had been stolen by persons unknown. After consoling the grief-stricken couple as best he could, Conrad returned home.

His mother met him at the door. "My God, Conrad son," she said, when he had told her everything, "I knew it was so, and to further prove it, that new broom has vanished."

The young man made a search; it was nowhere to be found, and gone also were the moccasins and mittens given him by Elizabeth.

"It must have been she I saw last night riding athwart of the moon," he mused sadly.

XI

THE GIANTESS

(Story of McElhattan Mountain)

WHEN THE great flood of St. Patrick's Day, 1865, laid bare, in the bed of McElhattan Creek, the gigantic statue of a giantess carved out of black flint, the old settlers and the few Indians who remained at Nichols' Run predicted a series of disasters to the neighborhood. Every time the swarthy monster, with its sullen, angry, but not unlovely countenance, her form enveloped in a loose mantle was disclosed to view, wars, pestilences, famines, floods, and general misery ensued. And all this in less than three hundred years as the figure was carved from stone during the last years of the sixteenth century. When it was uncovered by the flood of 1865, the accounts which appeared in the Clinton County newspapers heralded it as a relic of remote antiquity, and it would have been generally accepted as such had it not been for the "old timers" who knew the legend of its comparatively recent origin. For once in its career, it was only a seven days wonder. The paragraphs in the papers attracted a few antiquarians to the scene, and the native mountaineers marveled and brought their families, but the closing events of the Civil War and Lincoln's assassination soon overshadowed it.

A freshet in September broke the drift pile which had diverted the stream from its original course, and the "Giantess of McElhattan," as she was called, was covered once more by the rushing current. For a few weeks, those who passed over a prostrate beech tree that served as a footbridge nearby could see the angry, vengeful features of the giantess peering up at them through the clear water, but sand and pebbles and branches of trees drifted across it and were giving it a brand new shroud. With the spring of the next year, the face was entirely covered, and only the sable outlines of the breasts were reflected through the limpid depths. In another year, these were covered, and with it went the last memory of the Giantess to rest until Destiny sends her forth again. The old men, when they first saw the figure shook their heads, muttering, "there's never going to be an end to the war." That was the direst prediction they could make. When the death of the saintly Lincoln was reported in the little mountain community, the old men raised their knotted forefingers and whispered, "see, it's coming true; there's never going to be an end to the war now." But hostilities did not break out afresh, and the last Confederate forces surrendered within the next couple of months. When the ruin of everything didn't happen, the wiseacres laid it to the fact that the stream, having resumed its old course, had put the Giantess where she could do no mischief. And how time flies!

The floods of nearly half a century have swept over this strange figure since she was last seen; the old men who knew her story are all dead, and but few of them passed it on to succeeding generations. The essence of a living thing is within, an inanimate object without. Death releases the spirit of a living thing; with one of iron, or bronze, or stone, it lives from generation to generation by word of mouth. And now will be told the story of the black-flint giantess, as nearly as it was related by the Indians to the old men and by the old men to appreciative juniors.

Like most of the great works in Central Pennsylvania that date back to Indian times, the Giantess was an emanation of Pipsisseway, the great king of the Susquehanahs. He was the bravest of warriors, the joiner together of kingdoms, the mighty peacemaker, the patron of legendary history, of arts, of agriculture; the one rounded-out personality in an otherwise unfinished and undeveloped period. Unfortunately, this humble chronicler of the greatest of Pennsylvania Indians does not know his real name. He called him Pipsisseway in several other stories because he liked the sound of it because it had a distinctive flavor. The old settlers and the few Indians he knew spoke of him as the "great king of the Susquehanah Indians," but nowhere was the real name obtainable. But he was an actual man nevertheless, and his deeds are a better immortality than a high-sounding name. We know Shakespeare's name but little of his life; we know of this Indian king's life but nothing of his name. But at any rate, the "great king" was the inception of the Giantess.

In his early youth, probably when he was eighteen years of age, he had made a hunting trip to the Ohio River to chase the fleet herds of antelopes in company with several other Indian princes of about his own age. The chase took place in the realm of a western chieftain, whose son was Pipsisseway's particular friend. The young heir to the kingdom of the Susquehanahs was too impressionable in those days to make a good hunter. He would start out boldly enough, but a beautiful view, or sunset, or waterfall would divert his attention from the fleeing objects.

It was during the frenzy of the hunt that he stopped to make the acquaintance of a beautiful young girl of noble blood, a relative of some kind to the young prince whom he was visiting. She seemed to him the most exquisite object he had ever gazed upon, and it is a known fact that we never see anyone more lovely than those who charm us at eighteen. Our standard of perfection is formed then; heaven help him who aims low, for he can never go higher in the future. This Indian beauty was famed all through the valleys that opened into the great basin of the Mississippi. None could equal her charms of person or mind; she was a star of the first magnitude. Pipsisseway was ardent in those days, and he wooed and thought he'd won this fair idol of the west.

He returned to the Susquehanah country to tell his father and brothers of his conquest. Just after he had obtained the old monarch's consent, he heard the news of her marriage to a young warrior in the west. The blow was a crushing one to the proud spirit of Pipsisseway. He could have stood it better if it had been something hidden away in his own heart, but he had informed his family of his romance, and they must watch him every day recovering from it. That is why persons suffer who are crossed in love; it is the half-pitying, curiously interested faces of those about who probe the wounds deeper. A wounded animal hides in a cave; a wounded love should be hidden in the caverns of our soul. A trip into some distant region, like the Great Lakes or the New England coast, might have enabled the humiliated prince to escape all this, but he deemed it cowardly to run away, and affairs of state, in which he assisted his father, required his presence at home. Besides, he had observed that when persons get on fire, they invariably start running, but the flames burn no less fiercely. He might escape espionage at the Great Lakes but find his sorrow burning into him just the same.

The royal lodge houses were erected where the village of McElhattan now stands; the one occupied by the King of the Susquehanahs stood on the present site of the railroad station. The unmarried sons, surrounded by their retainers, lived in their own encampments, that of Pipsisseway being where Youngdale now flourishes. It seems strange what attracts village-building to certain localities and religiously passes others by. For centuries the Susquehanah kings lived where stand the group of houses at McElhattan station. When the Indians retired, and the settlers took up the ground, the site had to be favored above all others.

For years the eldest sons of the kings lived on the site of Youngdale; it, too, became the choice of the settlers for a village and shipping point. The captain of the warriors, or rather the second in command to the king, usually maintained his war lodge at McElhattan Springs. Though there has been no permanent settlement there, it has proved a popular tenting place and resort. Man feels inherently lonesome because of the mystery of life; he likes to live where others have been before; it gives him a certain spiritual sense of security.

Half a mile further up the beautiful stream now called McElhattan Run, at the foot of the "High Banks" where there is an inexhaustible supply of fire-clay, were situated the royal pottery works. They were part of the kingly perquisite and were usually superintended by the rulers' brothers. No one could make or even buy pottery from any other source; it was, for generations, a most profitable monopoly. Some beautiful work was turned out and, had it been less perishable, would have been the most attractive souvenir of the vanished Susquehanahs. In Pipsisseway's reign, it had attained a state of perfection, and bowls, pots, kettles, and ornamental pieces from this plant were bartered for as far west as the Missouri River. Susquehanah pottery had as respected a name as Wedgewood.

A short distance beyond the pottery works, in a cave dug in the side of the big McElhattan Mountain, lived an Indian sculptor. He had been captured by Pipsisseway's father in one of his expeditions to the south and put to doing menial work around his lodge-house. With only the crudest tools, he had carved some figures of animals out of soapstone, and these had given the young Pipsisseway his first inclination towards art and sculpture, of which he later became such a conspicuous patron. He had obtained the slave's freedom and installed him in a roomy cave to carry on his work, liberally providing him with necessary implements and materials. He openly said he preferred sculpture to pottery making, which angered the potters who had given the best years of their lives to perfecting the plastic art. After executing numerous smaller pieces, the ex-slave was commissioned to carve a huge female figure out of black flint. It was to resemble, as closely as Pipsisseway's descriptions could convey, the beauteous but false Indian maid on the banks of the Ohio who had saddened his young life. When it was finished, the young prince pronounced it a complete success, except that it looked more severe and ill-natured than the original. The sculptor worked for weeks trying to soften the expression, but to no avail; he only made it more sullen, more forbidding. Pipsisseway was disappointed, as he wanted the figure to wear the benign and smiling expression that had captivated him. The old sculptor explained that if he could have seen the living model, all would have been different; under the circumstances, he had done his best.

A date for the erection of the statue was set. Pipsisseway had been utilizing a number of hostages in building a pathway from the Seven Springs to the summit of the upper or "big" mountain, and this was now completed two-thirds of the distance. The young prince was seized with the idea of having the statue set up at that point which would make it a place of resort for his subjects, being such a great artistic wonder, and at a place where the view was expansive and ennobling. Before the figure could be moved from the studio, the sculptor was waylaid one evening and foully beaten to death by artisans from the pottery works. He had escorted the prince, who had been visiting him, to his lodge house and was returning to his cave when set upon by these fellows. They were jealous of the attention he received from the prince and the fact that Pipsisseway and his suite no longer visited the clay works. The guilty parties were soon apprehended, flayed alive, and roasted to death by slow fires.

The gigantic statue, drawn on a truck by five hundred slaves and prisoners of war, was placed in position at the head of the mountain path.

It was regarded as strange that all the trees near the statue died of blight in a few days, leaving it in the center of a patch of desert. To this day, vegetation will not grow there; it is a conspicuous sight for miles, known locally as the "little bare place." The following spring, all seeds planted in the valley refused to sprout, and a terrible famine was promised.

Ironwood, the old king, consulted his soothsayers, and they said that this trouble was caused by a curse put on the statue by the dying potters and advised hauling it off the mountain at once and burying it, out of mischief, in the bed of the creek. Pipsisseway felt badly but was an obedient son, and he superintended the lowering of his favorite effigy. Even as his minions were diverting the course of the creek to prepare a proper burial place, there descended a plague of wild pigeons. These birds, by countless billions, flew so swiftly and, in some places, so low that they beheaded such men, women, and children who were not quick enough to find shelter. The tops of most of the trees for a space ten miles in width were cut off as neatly as if done by axes. For three days, the earth was inky black under this canopy of the winged multitudes. As soon as the plague subsided, the work in the stream was quickly completed, and the statue was smothered beneath rock and gravel.

After that, the affairs of the kingdom moved smoothly; good crops, good weather, and good cheer were the watchwords. In the course of time, King Ironwood passed away, and his eldest son, Pipsisseway, was crowned as his successor. Then began in earnest the golden age of Indian art and sculpture. Many colossal statues were constructed, but none seemed to have the innate perfection and dignity of the disgraced and buried Giantess. Despite her forbidding countenance and unlucky associations, she was an artistic gem; it was a shame to let her lie submerged to gratify a superstitious idea. Pipsisseway ordered her dug out of the bed of the creek and set up on the site of the home of the nameless sculptor who modeled her. The night after she was in place came a cloudburst and a terrifying flood. The Indian towns were washed away; there was a heavy loss of life; courtiers and soldiery escaped drowning by climbing the trees. When it stopped raining after the fourth day, the Susquehanna River reached from mountain to mountain. Pipsisseway and his queen, Meadow Sweet, with their infant son, were away at the time, or they might have fared badly. When the waters subsided, a wet, marasmus slime lay all over the fertile plain. Fever broke out among the natives, more dying from it than had perished in the flood. Most of the courtiers and royal serving maidens were stricken, and Death seemed to have taken his permanent abode in the kingly circle.

Pipsisseway had sent his queen and the son and heir to his mountain retreat on the high pinnacle which overlooks Quinn's Run, the mountain that the sun sets behind in such regal splendor. They remained in good health, and the king himself seemed to be able to ward off the dreadful malady. He boasted of his vigor, in fact. Unfortunately for him, he stuck too closely to the flood country, superintending the drainage work and the rebuilding of his towns. When everything was pronounced safe, he sent for his family and celebrated their homecoming with a grand review of his warriors on the plain in front of the new "castle." That night he complained of feeling badly. The medicine men were summoned and pronounced his disease the dreaded "swamp fever." Pipsisseway being less than thirty-five years of age and powerful physique should have had no trouble in recovering. He had, however, worked hard during the twelve years of his reign and perhaps was what modern physicians call "run down." In any event, he lost strength steadily, despite all that medical skill could accomplish.

Wise men and fortune-tellers were finally called into consultation. They decided unanimously that the rehabilitation of the black flint Giantess was not only the cause of the late flood but of the king's illness as well. They recommended that unless the figure were immediately submerged again, the royal sufferer would succumb. Accordingly, the mammoth sculpture was buried a second time but with more dispatch than ceremony. Pipsisseway's condition seemed to improve slightly after this, but only temporarily, his vitality was gone, and he died two months afterward. The wise men who predicted their monarch's recovery if the statue was reburied were frightfully tortured, but that could not bring back the departed spirit. But from princes to slaves, all agreed to leave the black Giantess lie at the bottom of McElhattan Run.

Over two hundred and fifty years passed away, a flood opened the sepulcher, and white faces peered down on the revengeful countenance of the flint colossus! Then as if back to dreamland from a half-awakening, she returned, and when she wakes again, what will be the change that greets her vision?

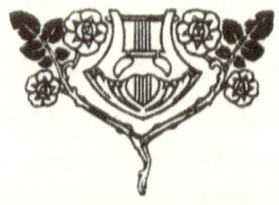

XII

MARY GOES OVER THE MOUNTAIN

(Story of Castanea Mountain)

MARY WOULD go over the mountain on that particular evening. Her best friend, or as she called her, her "companion girl," Dolly Hope, now Dolly Snyder, had become the mother of twins in her cabin on the Nittany side of the mountain, and Mary must visit her. Mary was only sixteen but a strong, well-developed girl for her age, and Dolly, who had been destined for a stirring history, was but a couple of years older. Mary, who was a daughter of old Patt Gillaspy, the Indian fighter, lived with her parents in their comfortable cabin by the creek. Above them loomed the "dark and somber ridge" of the Bald Eagle Mountain, inscrutable and silent, hiding the mystery and rage and rancor of the Indian hordes who ranged behind it.

The Gillaspys had only recently moved "up country," having abandoned a well-cleared farm in Buffalo Valley because the old fighter thought the country there was much too slow. His wife and older children protested, but Mary, who was born too late to have participated in Indian carnage at the old home, was eager to move into a land of adventure.

"Sure, she's more like myself than any of the boys," was Patt's way of expressing his approval at the position she assumed. But despite high hopes, the Indians refused to molest the Gillaspy family; there was absolutely no provocation to shoot one down, and the old man secretly wished himself back at his comfortable farmstead near Derrstown.

"Some day," said Mary, "we'll get all we are looking for."

What kind of Irishmen were these old Indian fighters anyway, with such names as Brady, Sweeny, McLaughlin, Dougherty, Callahan, McKeehan, Costikan, and Gillaspy; they were clearly not Scotch-Irishmen, but if they came of Catholic stock, what became of their Catholicism? Old Patt Gillaspy once was seen inside a Lutheran Church in Dry Valley at some special services, but that was the only time it could be "laid against him." He was a brave fighter but could do more harm than good in times of peace as he loved dearly to provoke the Indian's ire.

It took fully a year before he could pick a fight with some Indians. They were continually passing up and down the creek, the path led not fifty feet from his cabin, yet they refused to stop, refused to become embroiled, even when his savage cur Links snarled and bit at their heels.

Sometimes when the old man, with his long rifle across his shoulder, was coming from the landing where he kept his canoes and would cross the path directly in front of a file of passing natives, he whispered under his breath remarks detrimental to the Indian valor and morals. The tall aborigines merely looked angry; their beady eyes would flash, but further than that, they made no move, always to old Patt's discomfiture.

One night, however, the chance came, and there was almost bloodshed. A party of eight Indians, six men and two women, camped near the landing without asking Patt's permission. He would have refused, so it is just as well they didn't. He did not know they were there until he noticed the red glow of the campfire through the tall white pines which lined the water's edge.

The old man was in a fury. Seizing his trusty rifle, he declared he'd drive "the damned Indians away or kill them in doing it." In reality, he had some provocation. His rye field was only a short distance from the fire; a spark might ignite it at any minute.

Mrs. Gillaspy understood her husband's fiery disposition and intense antipathy to Indians and dreaded his visit to the encampment. She had visions of an episode like was performed later by a certain Frederick Stump when this worthy frontiersman owing to trouble between some Indians and his nephew's wife, killed the four offending warriors with six Indian women and girls for good measure.

As luck would have it, all the Gillaspy boys were away from home the night in question, and the older girls were afraid to go, so it devolved on Mary to accompany the old man to the landing to "keep him straight." The combined strength of the household could not prevent him from loading his rifle and slipping his scalping knife in his belt, but Mary, "his girl," as he called her, might keep him from turning the front lawn into a slaughterhouse. The Indians were seated in a circle around the blaze of rich pine, which must have thrown their massive faces and fancy costumes into bold relief, like in one of Blakelock's paintings. Near them was a small pile of early roasting ears and melons, which they had probably filched from some farm further up the creek. In a bucket scooped from a block of basswood, one of the squaws was stirring some beverage; evidently, a high old time was soon to begin. The sight of so many Indians in a happy frame of mind furthered the choler of the old man. Sighting his rifle at them, he approached near and gruffly ordered them away. Pointing to the fire, he commanded them to put it out, but as they were too surprised to act quickly, he seized the bucket of brew and threw it into the blaze. There was a splutter and lots of blue smoke, for there was something spirituous in the decoction, but the fire kept burning. Kicking it with his boots, the old man separated the embers, calling the Indians all kinds of names as he worked. He had forgotten the rifle, and the hot fire ignited it, or else he hit it against something; at any rate, it exploded, a bullet barely grazing a squaw's cheek.

But the Indians, all except one big brave, who was younger than the rest, maintained their composure and let the old pioneer have his way. When the rifle exploded, the old man dropped it on the head of this young fellow, who it was afterward learned was known by the name of Billy Frozen Stone.

The young Indian sprang to his feet, cursing in English, and hit the old man with a stinging blow across the mouth with his open hand, felling him to the ground. Patt yelled with pain and would have stabbed the man, but for his helpless position. Two of the older Indians, fearing they might stir a hornets' nest if they hurt a member of the dominant Irish race, lifted Patt to his feet and apologized profusely for the incident.

The young Indian slinked out of sight, but not before casting a few sharp glances at Mary, who witnessed the scene from a respectful distance. The others considerably cowed gathered their pots and baskets and started in single file down the creek. By the light of the dying embers, the old man gathered up the roasting ears and melons left behind and took them to his house. These were to be a slight balm for his bursted rifle.

The family breathed easier when they saw the door opened, and Mary, with the old man leaning on her shoulder but minus his rifle, come in. He looked pretty seedy after his knockdown and was covered with ashes and mud. But he clung tenaciously to the roasting ears and melons.

"We'll eat these tomorrow," he repeated over and over again.

The next day he got up feeling all right and walked to his nearest neighbors to tell them how he had been attacked and ill-treated by wandering Indians.

The report spread throughout the neighboring settlements, and threats were made to shoot the next Indians that appeared. This came to the ears of the unfortunate participants in the unpleasantness, who had located themselves in Castanea Gap about where the reservoir is now. There were extensive beaver dams in the creek, and they had resolved to catch a few of these valuable animals. They knew the complaints might result in a hot-headed band swooping down on their camp some night and butchering them all. The two eldest Indians started out to make a personal visit to the cabins of the leading settlers to apologize and explain. They only made matters worse by this, for when they admitted that they were trapping beavers in the gap, it infuriated everyone, especially the younger pioneers.

"What right have Indians to trap those beavers?" was the constant rallying cry. "It's too early in the season; their hides aren't very good; we wanted those hides ourselves."

But at first, no active measures were taken to stop them, as the settlers were too busy with their crops to kill a few Indians. Jacob McCarty, a level-headed young man, was deputized to give the natives a hint that it would be best for them to quit trapping and leave the neighborhood. If they refused, it was understood, they would have to pay the extreme penalty "after the crops were in."

McCarty was a born diplomatist and delivered the warning with courtesy and tact. The Indians said they were only too glad to cease trapping and move away but asked permission to finish drying their "summer skins," as they called the beaver hides they had taken. They had killed, all told, thirty-nine beavers. McCarty told them there would be no objection to this, and matters were left that way.

There were a few settlers in Nittany Valley, among them Dietrich Snyder, a young veteran of the warfare in the Blue Mountain country, but they all shunned the pathway through the Gap since the Indians tented there. There was another path into Nittany, very steep and rocky, which led up the face of the Bald Eagle Mountain and had its beginning not far from where the infirmary now stands. It led through a forest of white pines and white hemlocks and was as black in daylight as at night. There were six copious springs between the beginning of the path and the summit of the mountain. It would be difficult to believe that now, as since the timber has gone, the water courses have dried out, and the face of the mountain is as parched and arid as an alkali plain.

In those days, it was different; in addition to the darkness, the path was infested with animals, every spring had a full quota, and it seemed like passing through a zoological garden to follow it.

Travelers with more ammunition and time than business used to try and count how many animals they could kill along the way. Jasper Gillaspy, Mary's oldest brother, held the record for a long time with seventy-one kills, which included three bears, five wolves, two wolverines, and a fisher.

When Mary Gillaspy heard that the stork had visited her "companion girl," there was nothing else in her mind but to visit the valley; her father and brothers warned her not to attempt to go through the gap; the Indians they thought were gone, but there might be one or two lurking about. The path up the mountain was less dangerous; if she waited until tomorrow, they would accompany her, but Mary stamped her foot and said she was going now. There was no stopping her, for, at sixteen, she was already mistress of everyone in the house except her mother. In almost every household, each member has their particular tyrant; Mary's mother took special delight in trying to thwart everything she wanted to do. She stormed and fumed against Mary's proposed trip across the mountain, but the girl had now reached a size where she could hardly be restrained by main force unless her father or sisters cooperated. But while they feared the dangers of the mountain road and sought to gently discourage her by refusing to accompany her, they offered no violent opposition.

Mary went. With a red shawl around her pretty chubby face and kindly curiosity beaming out of her clear brown eyes, she started away, walking briskly as was her habit. As she was going through the back gate, Jasper called to her and, running to where she was, handed her an old navy pistol, loaded and primed. She thanked him for his interest and, as a final dig, told him she would not waste ammunition on little birds as he had done but would save it for no smaller game than Indians.

"Sure, and she may meet some of the gay lads," said old Patt.

"If she does, they will act pretty quiet," replied Jasper, "they've had a couple of pretty good lessons since they touched this locality."

It may have been Jasper's marksmanship or the fact that dusk was falling, but Mary noticed the forest was quieter than she had ever known it before. Once a big black squirrel ran across the path, and another time a wild turkey hen; she heard the twigs crack a couple of times as if deer were near, but that was all. The evening was so still that the odor of the evergreens was heavy and oppressive. She stopped at a few of the springs as the steep climb made her perspire, and she was a girl a little inclined to stoutness, but she was making good time on her journey.

The top of the mountain was very different from the sides. The summit was almost bare of living timber, while the sides were a jungle of forest monarchs. There were dead trees a-plenty on the top, none very tall, scrub oaks, pitch pines, and hemlocks, which had given up the ghost at an early age after their unequal battle with the elements. They were barkless, silvery white in color, gnarled, twisted, and torn into every conceivable shape. Some of their broken limbs were supplicating, others defiant or menacing; all the pines and hemlocks had their tops smashed off and stood like an array of headless specters. One tree had its trunk so bent that it resembled a human being in the attitude of prayer. They were always creaking and complaining to the mountain breeze. A little thin grass and white fireweed grew at their roots in this Golgotha of the woods.

As she emerged from the green timber, her keen eyes detected something ahead, which at first looked like three huge brown stumps beside the path. A second glance showed the "brown stumps" to be three Indians wrapped in their blankets, for it was cool on the summit. One of them, the youngest, displayed a keenly sharpened celt to his companions, who were much his senior. She walked boldly forward, and just as the Indians became aware of her presence, she recognized the young Indian as none other than Billy Frozen Stone. Recognition was mutual, and he jumped up, brandishing his weapon. His older companions grabbed at the trimmings of his trousers, but he was off, tearing along the path in the direction from whence Mary was coming. The canny girl took it for granted he meant no friendly greeting, and left the path, and ran for her life. The Indian followed and would have caught her, only she stopped and, from behind a dead oak, took aim and fired at him. Her aim was fairly good, for Billy Frozen Stone howled with pain and, holding his hand over his left side, wheeled about and hobbled back to the path. Mary wandered some distance along the summit, almost to where the ridge dips down to Castanea Gap, but as it was growing dark, she plucked up her courage and returned to the path. To her surprise and horror, she found the young Indian resting against a tree, with his hands vainly trying to stay the copious flow of blood that poured from his left side. When an Indian is badly hurt, he turns deep blue, and this fellow's complexion was the shade of the berries on Solomon's Seal.

Mary had never taken a course in "first aid to the injured," for such bright ideas were unknown in those days, but she was the equal to any emergency. She quickly tore a thick strand off her woolen skirt, for this mountain girl, like her modern sisters, wore no underwear, and with the aid of a stick, made a tourniquet and bound it around the young Indian's waist. Up to this point, the wounded brave had taken little notice of her, but with the loss of blood being checked, his mind began to co-ordinate, and he looked up and recognized her. To her wonderment, it was not a look of gratitude or forgiveness; it was a look of hate. Mary was grieved, she had all but killed the Indian, and now he felt badly because she was bringing him back to life. But she didn't care what he thought; she was doing her duty, and she didn't want to be known as an Indian killer; they said her father had killed an even dozen in his day.

He continued to rest against the tree, gazing at her more intently and maliciously as he got a better grip on his consciousness. Mary looked about her. The other two Indians had gone; evidently, they scented trouble no matter how the encounter came out and decided to put miles between them and the fated spot. Mary got to daydreaming about Dolly Hope's babies, whether they had blue eyes like their mother or black eyes like their father, and whether her folks would suppose she was at her friend's home by now, and so on, until she forgot her proximity to the wounded warrior. Maybe Billy Frozen Stone had hypnotic powers and was soothing her like a blacksnake does a robin. He was watching his chance.

When her thoughts were far away, he lunged forward and caught her plump white throat in his vise-like grasp. Mary was stunned for an instant but, with her sturdy arms, struggled hard to shake herself free. The struggle must be brief; she would be strangled if there was a delay. But nature, rather than her agility, came to the rescue. As they tumbled about, the Indian's tourniquet gave way, and the blood which had been dammed inside burst forth like a freshet. She felt his grip relax and, with her own hands, wrenched herself loose. It was none too soon, she was fainting, and the Indian was all but dead. If she hadn't been such a stalwart hardy girl, he might have died with his fingers clenching her throat. She sighed a sigh of relief when fanned by the night wind; she came to herself and saw the fate she had escaped.

The Indian, drained of the last drop of blood, lay dead on the rocks, hideous and shriveled in his desiccated condition. The brave girl consoled herself that she had only prolonged his life temporarily when she bound up his wound; sooner or later, it would have been fatal. She had no regrets but felt rather happy about how she managed things. Then she walked back to the spring nearest the top of the mountain and washed her face and hands.

A golden harvest moon was up to the level of the summit by this time; she smiled to herself when she looked at her blood-stained skirt, tom off to the level of her dimpled knees. She was perfectly composed as she passed the dead body for the second time and resumed her journey to Dolly Hope's cabin in Nittany. Just as she left the summit with its grey-white ghostly trees, a great black wolf skulked across the path, not twenty feet in front of her.

"You are out after your supper pretty quickly, old boy," she laughed and pointed the pistol at him just for fun, at the sight of which the beast drooped his tail between his legs and moved faster.

It was midnight when she reached the cabin of her "companion girl." She hated to disturb the sleepers, but the watchdog performed that service for her. Dietrich and Dolly noticed her torn skirt all spattered with blood.

"Kill a bear?" they queried.

Mary could not tell an untruth. She first admired the babies and then, before dawn, told them the entire story. That was the last Indian Mary ever saw in going over the mountain.

XIII

THE FATE OF ATOKA

(Story of Mill Hall Mountain)

AMONG THE earliest settlers in the Bald Eagle Mountain region was a young man named Constant Iba. He came from that portion of Lancaster, which is now included in the County of Lebanon, from the vicinity of old Heidelberg or Shaefferstown. He was descended from the hardy band of Jewish missionaries, who, having heard that the Indians were the lost tribe of Israel, penetrated the wilderness to re-convert them to the old faith.

They laid the foundations for their first synagogue about 1704, nearly a third of a century before the Germans, Huguenots, and Welsh appeared in the fertile Lebanon valleys. They may have given the name of Lebanon to the county, and the seat of justice, who knows, but at any rate, there are villages in Lebanon, Lancaster, and Berks today which possess names more Jewish than German, such as Hummelstown, Newmanstown, Rothville, Lauterbach's, Goodhart's, Steinsville, Klinesville, Strausstown, and Shubert.

Jewish surnames are everywhere, though their bearers, through the intermarriage of their ancestors, are strong adherents of the Lutheran or Reformed congregations. And their dark, strong, passionate features may have found their most notable exponents in the strain called the "Black Dutch."

But the Jewish missionaries were flat failures; the Indians instinctively wanted to trade with them rather than hear the story of Moses; they became imbued with the material possibilities of the new land, and they scattered to the four winds.

THE MEETING OF THE WATERS
Photo by H. W. Swope, Lock Haven, Pa.

Intermarriage seemed to be their new watchword; their sons and daughters made light of the Jewish tradition. Though Constant Iba was clever at barter and trade, he was more of an artistic nature.

That was inherited from his father, the Cantor of the congregation. He composed many touching chants on the long sea journey to Pennsylvania, hymns that everyone from the captain of the ship to the young rabbi overseer predicted would bring the stolidest native to the verge of conversion. The Cantor was speedily discouraged and tried farming with better success. There were not enough Jewish girls to go around, so he wandered down to the lower reaches of the Schuylkill and wooed and wed a Swedish maid. The son, Constant, looked more like his mother than his father, but he had the dreamy, artistic spirit of the latter. Like some artistic souls must, he was disappointed in love.

When Constant, more handsome and brighter than the other lads of the neighborhood, paid court to a pretty German girl, the stern father said to him one night, "I hear you are not a good Christian; I want my daughters to marry good Christians, I don't want anybody else coming to see them." As the girl remained silent throughout, Constant never went to see her again.

A month later, he struck out for the wilderness above Shamokin. Either he nursed a deep hurt or wanted to feed his artistic inclinations; at any rate, he selected about as retired a spot as could be possibly located. He erected his one-roomed log cabin a mile west of the present town of Mill Hall, in a gully near a good spring, at the foot of the mountain. There was no view, very little breeze, and the land nearby was so rocky that it has never been cleared to this day. Here the young man settled down to lead the life of a hunter and trapper. The ground about him being so poor he cleared a small garden patch along the banks of the Bald Eagle Creek, and there he went daily to work while the weather was good. He set out some grape vines, and old settlers remembered his as the first vineyard in the neighborhood. He may have inherited this taste from his ancestors in Asia Minor. He had no sheep nor goats, however, but at one time, a string of sixty-five wolf hides sunning near his cabin showed how futile it would have been to emulate the herdsmen of old.

If he cherished a grievance of any kind, it was deeply buried in his heart, for he made a most cheerful companion. Hunters liked to get him to join their parties, and his happy demeanor and uniform courtesy put added zest into the chase. Most of the hunters were very young men-they were the "old hunters" with the prolific reminiscences of the next generation; they truly enjoyed life to its fullest extent. The word "old hunter" is a misnomer; all the great hunting is done by men when they are young. Hunting was a stern necessity, but that generation of nimrods made it also a perpetual lark.

During the spring and summer months, practically all the hunters went to their homes "down country," as permanent settlements had hardly begun to any extent, and during this period, the Indians were Constant's companions. They thought so much of him, he might have converted them all to Judaism, but he cared little for the old faith, or any faith, for that matter. "There must be a Good Man who rules us. He gives us all a fair show," was the only religious comment he was ever known to utter.

Solitude developed rather than retarded the growth of his personality, and by the time he was eight and twenty, there was a beautiful light in his soft grey eyes, the token of a developed and well-finished individuality. He had good looks, courage, and honesty. He had never found the necessity to tell a lie; with such attributes, he was "master of his fate." Sometimes as he sat before his cabin door on calm summer afternoons in the "golden hour," with the forest silent save when interrupted by the "bang, bang, bang" of the pileated woodpecker breaking through the bark of a hemlock tree to extract the injurious beetles, he would think over his lot and consider it a just one.

"If I had a wife," he would reason, "I would have to leave this life; after ten years of it, I am fitted for nothing else; I could not make her comfortable in a town nor here. I am well off as I am."

Then the giant woodpecker would answer with his loud "bang, bang, bang" as if in affirmation. Then he would laugh to himself, "that bird knows me by heart; I wouldn't shoot him for that reason,"

Constant loved birds and even the animals—he could not kill a deer and even hesitated over a buffalo. The Indians would say to him when they started on their expeditions, "we will kill the elks, buffaloes, and deer; you can slay the panthers, wolves, and bears."

He once had a peculiar experience with a bear. One evening he heard a cough, strangely human, outside his cabin, and lighting his rushlight went out to investigate. He found a huge bear sitting on his haunches with a bullet wound in the region of the lungs, vainly trying to cough up the lead. Being fearless, he stroked the bruin's head, and the animal became docile. There were no "wild animals" in those days. It took a hundred years of dogs, repeating rifles, poisons, and traps to make them wild in this country. He gave the beast a large dose of snuff and red pepper; it sneezed and retched violently, and although the bullet did not appear, it lodged more comfortably, and the bear suffered no longer. The grateful animal lingered around the cabin for days until an Indian's dog appeared, and it took the cue to drop out of sight.

A couple of years after this episode, he always said that it was in November 1758, he was cooking some supper in the big open fireplace when he heard a sound like a cough outside. It wasn't quite the same as the bear's, but he laughed to himself, "that bear's back again with another bullet; as sure as anything, he can't cough as loud because he's older; he'll have to wait until I'm ready to go out and doctor him."

He heard the cough again a couple of times; he listened more intently, and he concluded it came from a human being. He opened the door and looked out but saw no one. There had been a skiff of snow the night before. The day's sunlight had not served to melt it all, and cold darkness was settling in. He heard the cough again; it was not more than fifty feet away in a cedar thicket. Hurrying to the spot, he beheld a beautiful but very pallid young girl sitting on a moss-covered hemlock log, holding her body erect with her hands, and oh, so sick, weak, and dejected looking. As she saw him, she opened her large grey eyes in surprise and tried to speak but could only cough. Dressed in a badly soiled costume of buckskin, trimmed with beads, with a fisher's skin for a collar, and the skirt badly ripped from a long tramp in the forest, she might have passed for an Indian girl, but for her dun-colored hair, light eyes, and rather fair complexion. Constant was trying to think of something to say to her, but before he could do so, her arms gave way, and she fell forward in a swoon.

The young man picked up the precious burden and carried her to his cabin, and laid her on his comfortable couch among the buffalo hides. Then he poured a drink of rum down her throat to revive her. He noticed that the soles of her moccasins were worn through in places, and her pretty feet were rough from the uneven ground. She wore a frayed pair of military leggings, probably a gift from some white man. He took a couple of warm stones from the back of the fireplace and put them at her feet, which seemed to "bring her to" more than anything else. He rubbed her white hands, and gradually consciousness returned. She seemed thankful to be in such comfortable surroundings, but no word escaped her lips as to where she had come from, and Constant, considering himself favored to have such a visitor was careful not to ask. Maybe she had dropped from the clouds; then it would have been sacrilege to inquire! She did not sleep well that night but tossed about, moaning and coughing intermittently. The young trapper knew a thing or two about the ancient remedies and brewed some Blue Mountain tea, but it did not relieve her cough very much.

The next day she was quite weak, and several times he thought she would turn into a fair spirit on his hands. But he was a careful nurse, it was a labor of love, and he kept her alive by the sheer persistence of his attentions. He violated his scruples and shot a young deer and some grouse and quail that she might have delicacies. At the end of ten days, she began to improve and, evidently liking her physician, told a few things about herself. At least she told her name, and where she came from.

She was none other than Atoka Strahan, the beautiful mixed-race girl and foster daughter of the old Mingo chief, Arrow-Wood,-whose stronghold was high up in the Sugar Valley Mountains. Constant had often heard of her; what a prize to have come to him when every pioneer and all the Indians of rank who saw her aspired to her favor. She seemed so satisfied in Constant's cabin that he began to lose all fear she would want to return homeward. Whether she would have or not was settled by Destiny, which sent, when she was well enough to move about, a blizzard of unprecedented ferocity and duration.

The cabin, situated as it was in a gully, was buried to its roof—the inmates would have smothered had it not been for the generous stone chimney. Atoka made no attempt to go now; she was stormbound until spring. Her manners were easy and gentle, and there was a charming frankness to her voice, all of which added to the irresistibility of her physical beauty. Any man who saw her half a mile off would have loved her, let alone being stormbound with her in a lonely cabin.

Constant had a hunting dog before the snow began, but he never found out if the poor animal was buried in it or escaped before it was too late. So they were the only two living things about. Luckily there were plenty of provisions in the cabin, and a path was dug to the woodpile, so they neither wanted for food nor fuel. Every time the snow melted a little and Constant feared his fair captive might grow restless, a fresh blizzard ensued, and her stay was reinforced. It seemed to him the Snow God favored his suit, that it knew from his first glimpse of her that he loved Atoka. He could not compare it with that weak attachment for the German girl on the Swatara; this was greater, grander, permanent. He was glad he wasn't a Christian, for if he was, he might have married the German girl and never have been stormbound with Atoka.

This half-breed girl could speak German, although her father had been a Scotchman and her mother a Lenni Lenape, whose second husband was Chief Arrow-Wood. She had picked up the German, she said, in her early childhood in Lancaster County, and it formed the medium of conversation between her and her new protector. She seemed so gracious, almost affectionate, in her attitude toward him that once after they had been stormbound for a month, he made bold to tell her that he loved her.

She was sitting on the bed propped up against the wall, with one hand behind her head; he never forgot how she looked. It was a long while before she answered him. "I am very sorry. Constant," she said, "no man ever treated me as you have, or could, but I cannot love you; I am pledged to another."

The young man said no more but wondered why she seemed content to linger so long with him if her heart belonged to some other man. But he accepted things as they came, and their relations continued as genial as ever.

As the days wore on, he was considerably worried about her cough; his remedies had ceased to be efficacious, and he could get no others.

Once, she had a slight hemorrhage which increased his fears. While recovering from this, but evidently believing she was going to die, she told him her love story.

At Fort Augusta, where she had gone with her mother to sell beads and feathers and blankets, outside the palisade, she had met Captain Evan Morgan, a handsome young officer of the British colonial forces. They had loved each other from the start, and later when he had been sent to a fort near the mouth of Tiadaghton, he had disguised himself as an Indian (Arrow-Wood was hostile to the British) and come across to see her at her father's fortress high up in the elbow of Bull Run Gap. He had promised to return one week from that night, but he never did—she could not hear tell of him again—especially as the English soon after evacuated the fort. She had watched and waited, but in vain, for over a year, and one day feeling particularly despondent, started for the Susquehanna to try and investigate for herself among the trappers who ranged up and down the river. She had become cold and tired; how she got as far West as Mill Hall Mountain, she knew not, nor how long she had been traveling when Constant found her. She knew she loved Captain Morgan; there must be some good reason why he did not return; she could love no one else. She wound up this confession with a flood of tears which set her to coughing frightfully. If she hadn't begun to cough, Constant might have told her something, but he hadn't the heart, even though it might have helped his case. At the mention of the name of Morgan, he was illuminated.

The young captain, disguised as an Indian, was mistaken for a spy by his own men and killed by them—it was probably the very day after he visited Atoka. He was heralded far and wide as "Morgan the Spy" many had doubted his duplicity, and Constant vowed to himself he'd set the poor fellow's memory straight if he lived until Spring. But he feared to tell the delicate girl that her lover was dead. With the gradual lessening of the severity of winter, her health did not improve as he had hoped. She had several more serious hemorrhages, which left her weaker and more pallid. Every day she told Constant how much she owed to him, and once she took him in her arms as he leaned over the bed, saying, "let me kiss you for your goodness to me." But it was not a kiss of love.

One rainy night while she slept, a strange-looking bird fell down the chimney and flopped about the stone floor, wet and broken-winged. Filled with horror, Constant opened the door and kicked it out into the darkness. Then he sank down on his easy chair of buffalo hides exclaiming to himself, "something's going to happen; the worst's to happen; a bird in the house is our family token of death."

The next morning brought sunshine for the first time in weeks, and Atoka seemed stronger and brighter, and more tender. She even insisted on helping him cook dinner and supper. After the evening meal, when she was putting the wooden dishes on the improvised dresser, there was a "bang, bang, bang" outside like the triphammer bill of the pileated woodpecker breaking through the bark of some hemlock tree.

"That's unseemly," she said, "for that bird to get busy as early as the fourteenth of March."

She had scarcely uttered these words when she was seized with a violent hemorrhage and would have fallen to the floor had not Constant caught her. Tenderly carrying her to the couch, he laid her down among the robes. She soon pulled herself together and wanted to sit up. She was ghastly, yellow pale, about the hue of her dun-colored hair, but her unearthly complexion made her more beautiful than words can describe, so he always said. He had sat beside her on the bed and held both her beautiful cold hands in his. They were rather large hands as were her feet, but shapely and dexterous; she had been noted for her basket making. She raised her head and laid it on his shoulder, saying, "I want to tell you something." He put his cheek against hers while she whispered, "I love you more than I ever loved Morgan, lots and lots more, it only came to me recently, and I hated to tell you because I feared you'd think me changeable, but it's true, it's too great a thing to keep, I'll love you forever."

He was so thrilled by what she said he had not noticed that her beautiful cold hands were the temperature of ice, and her loving stare was glazed and rigid. With the last word, her lower jaw dropped, her head fell to one side, and Atoka was no more.

Kissing again and again the dead clay-like lips he had never touched in life, Constant laid the beautiful image out full length and spent the night resting beside her, never sleeping but watching, admiring, worshipping the deserted tenement that had held her rare spirit. A few days later, he buried her by the old rotting hemlock where he had first met her.

He never moved from his cabin at the foot of Mill Hall Mountain; settlers came in by droves, the game became scarcer, and most of the old hunters he knew moved further west. But Constant Iba remained close to the grave of Atoka.

XIV

FOR THE GLORY OF INDIAN SUMMER

(Story of Mount Eagle)

MANY PERSONS have wondered what was the origin of the words "Indian Summer." Only recently, a correspondent wrote to the New York *Evening Sun*, asking for this information. But the paper, usually so explicit, did not give a very definite reply, except that it was first known in written language in 1794. The Lenni-Lenape used to say that Indian Summer was more properly the name of a girl, though it was also the name of a season. Lena-kit-chita was the name of the Indian maid, and it also corresponded with the word meaning this most delightful period of the year.

Five or six centuries ago, there was a notable encampment of Indians on the slopes of Mount Eagle in the Bald Eagle range. At that time, this region was a stronghold of the now-vanished Lenni-Lenape. This picturesque and valiant tribe had a particularly courageous chief called Chau-wa-lanne, or Forked-Tail Eagle, whose personal bravery and charm had much to do with cementing the clans into closer union. He maintained his regal lodge-house on the summit of Mount Eagle, believing that he was descended from the king of birds and must live as in an eyrie. The remainder of the settlement was upon the lower levels of the mountains and in the ravine below. It has come down to us that over fifteen hundred souls made up its quota. Five hundred of these were trained warriors, the pick of the tribal organizations. There was not one of them who stood under six feet in height; they were an "old guard" of an earlier day. Chau-wa-lanne himself was taller than any of his warriors, with that keen eye beneath busy brows and sharply curved nose so characteristic of stout-hearted men. Though very tall, he was willowy and graceful; he could outjump any member of his tribe, and he could outrun the swiftest deer. In the chase, he always outran his game; he considered it beneath his dignity to stand still and shoot.

An eagle flies above its prey until it falls exhausted and is overcome easily, and this was precisely the method of Chau-wa-lanne. Once he chased a giant panther through the forest, up trees, and down again, leaping from one rock to another, crawling over ravines on grapevines and prostrate logs, but he tired the animal and broke its jaw with his iron hand without a struggle. Struck with pity for the magnificent brute, he dragged him back to his lodge and made him a pet. The animal was readily tamed and made an admirable "watch-dog.'"

There was a giant forked white pine near the lodge-house; its spiral, buck-topped pinnacles seemed to unite with the heavenly dome. Two pairs of eagles made their nests in the cage-like tops, emblems of perpetual good luck to Chau-wa-lanne, living beneath. In every way, he seemed to be one of the chosen of Getchi-Manitto, the Great Spirit.

It does seem as if some souls are selected to do the big work in this life. All is so easy to them, every wish so quickly gratified. With others, it is a painful struggle, a long siege of disappointment, unappreciation, and uncongenial tasks. It is a case of striving only to be beaten back until one sinks into the inactivity of despair. The Great Spirit has cast such to play minor roles. But with Chau-wa-lanne, to wish was to realize; life is a success to the divinely anointed. But unlike a few of Infinity's favorites, he did not become vain and overbearing. The sharp, keen outlines of his dominant face showed that enervation, the indolence of happiness, could never be his. His was a warrior's part, a mountaineer's part, a hunter's part, the attributes of his fanciful eagle blood. His father, Wiponquoak, or White Oak, a noted chief before him, had died a lingering death from wounds received in one of his victorious battles when Chau-wa-lanne was only nineteen; responsibility coming upon him at this early age helped to develop his Spartan qualities. But like Alexander, he longed for fresh worlds to conquer; he longed to incite warfare in distant tribes. But none would provoke this human tower of strength. At twenty-four, he was like some great pinioned bird, seeking to unfold wings designed to rule the high air.

It was at this mentally mature period of his life that love was born. Always a hunter and a soldier, a man's man, his romances had been few and far between. Furthermore, he was so beautiful physically, his ways so engaging, that a nod would have brought any woman to his side, even if he had not been a king. When love settled down like a dove in an eagle's nest, it was for the beautiful maiden Lena-kit-chita, or Indian Summer, daughter of the famous captain Woakus or Grey Fox. By birth, she was not the equal of Chau-wa-lanne, few would have been for that matter, but her blood was noble, of the rank of many noted chiefs and warriors, even if she could not claim kinship with Chau-wa-lanne. Caste was firmly adhered to in those days; the Indians saw the evils of misalliances much more intelligently than we of today with all our ancestral societies and heraldic manifestations. It was generally the custom for an Indian King to marry a woman who was related to him to "keep the rank in the family," but there was no positive barrier against a union with an unrelated person, provided she was of noble blood. Lena-kit-chita, being well-born, and the most beautiful of her tribe, could not be discriminated against; the loyal subjects rejoiced at their beloved monarch's decision to take a wife who might send his seed down the ages. It was a genuine love match, at least after all these years tradition declares that it was, although there had been an earlier lover in the life of Lena-kit-chita. There was no doubt but that it was Chau-wa-lanne's first affair.

An Indian could not burst the bonds of caste through being a warrior or a hunter, no matter how superlatively brave he might be, or if he was a weapon-maker or artist, but if he possessed the gift of second sight, was a wise man, he could raise his social status next to that of the king. There was a poor widow in the camp; her husband, in his lifetime, had trapped pigeons, making coats out of the sunrise-colored breasts of the male birds; in other words, he was an Indian draper. This aged woman had one son, whose spiritual gifts had made him the most noted man in the settlement. They called him Wili-wili-han, or the soothsayer. Despite the fact that mentally he towered above every Indian of his tribe, physically, he was at a disadvantage. His stature was short; his shoulders were not broad, and his frame contracted or puny. He had a large head, a bigger head than even the giant Chau-wa-lanne, but his features were irregular; on one side of his face, the profile was good, the other side defective. In most self-made men and women, the left side, which controls the right hand, is most fully developed. That is the side we make ourselves; the other is the side we are born with. On the left side, there was divinity in Wili-wili-han's face; on the right, clownishness, like the right side of Lincoln's face.

The young soothsayer had worked hard to perfect his art, his nearness to the infinite; it showed in the serious, though not harmonious, lines of his countenance. In the camp adjoining to that of the widow and her gifted son dwelt Woakus or Grey Fox, the famous captain. Besides his squaw he had several sons and daughters, including one girl named Lena-kit-chita, or Indian Summer. How she got this strange sobriquet, none can tell, but it came to be most appropriate as events shaped themselves. She, of course, knew young Wili-wili-han and always spoke up for him when others ridiculed him.

"He will be the greatest one among you," was the tenor of her championship.

When the other boys and girls threw stones at him and would not let him play their games, Lena-kit-chita would always run to his side and comfort and amuse him. She was a stalwart lioness of a girl and once or twice soundly thrashed well-grown boys for molesting her favorite. Wili-wili-han was shy by nature; he had limited powers of expressing himself, but as best as a "silent man" can, he conveyed his gratitude to his fair protectress. She often stopped at his humble lodge and asked him to accompany her on walks in the woods. Neither would speak much on these excursions, but both were thinking deeply.

Once, and once only, did Wili-wili-han kiss the smooth, round cheek of his friend, but one kiss to a spiritual man means more than a thousand to a lecher. The gist of the young man's thoughts was that someday when he was famous, he would ask Lena-kit-chita to marry him. She must care for him; else, why would she stay away from her other and livelier companions to amuse him? Why would she fight for him? Why would she ask him to go with her on so many walks in the forest? Why would she hold up her smooth, firm cheek so he might kiss her? But again, why should she marry one so eccentric, so physically disproportionate, so ill-born, so poor? But he was underrating himself; he had a distinctive personality and was far from being what would be called homely; his mystic gifts had already found him marked favor with the king. He was now a nobleman by courtesy; every honor accorded to rank was exhibited towards him. All he would have needed was a little courage, and Leha-kit-chita was his in those days. While he was hesitating and repining, Chau-wa-lanne had espied the fair maid himself. He commanded that she be brought before him, and she was delighted at this signal honor. Arraying herself in her best, in a coat of the breasts of male wild pigeons, with a collar and cuffs of opossum fur, she attended the regal youth at his lodge house on the summit of Mount Eagle.

It had been a case of love at first sight with Chau-wa-lanne when he had seen her at a distance; Lena-kit-chita, the sixteen-year-old girl that she was, had always admired her stalwart king. Now when they met face to face, each was illuminated with a consuming love. Much as she had secretly cared for Wili-wili-han, she had always felt that he lacked something-now she knew, it was physical beauty. Before her stood the great slim muscular Chau-wa-lanne, six feet five inches in height, with the features of an eagle, the muscular development of a panther. He seemed typical of the world he ruled: above him soared the eagles, screaming their treble fury, nearby growled the pet panther. Back of him was ranged his personal bodyguard, composed of youths of his own age and almost similar height. Lena-kit-chita stood probably five feet eight; she towered above Wili-wili-han, it seemed, but in the presence of her king, she felt a more equable sense of proportion. She could hardly speak for her rapt admiration of his charms. When he talked, his attractiveness was enhanced. He had a clear, well-modulated voice; his manners would have captivated any woman; he was so considerate, so polished. It was a clear sense of *noblesse oblige*. There is no reason for a king to pursue a long courtship when he knows all about the object of his love. He had investigated Lena-kit-chita before he sent for her; her birth he was familiar with before; her character had been pronounced spotless. She was not surprised when he wound up the interview by asking her to become his

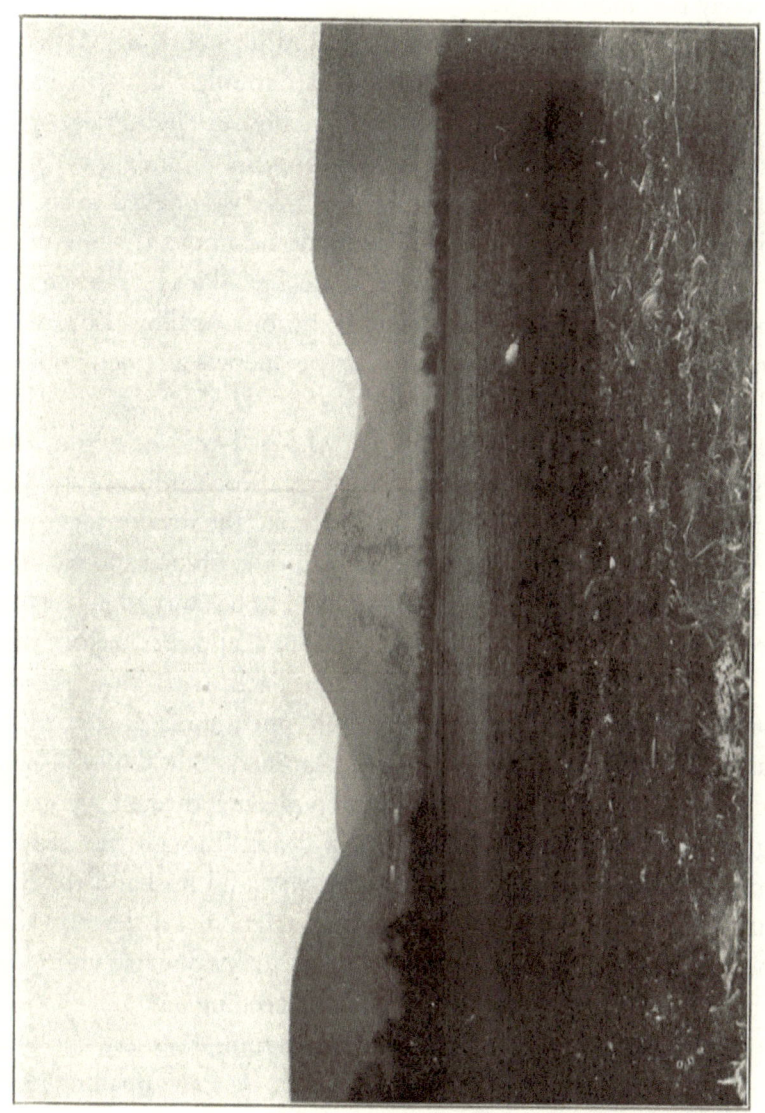

A DISTANT VIEW OF THE BALD EAGLES
Photo by H. W. Swope, Lock Haven, Pa.

bride. He would not have invited her to climb Mount Eagle for less. She accepted with such genuine cordiality that the young king felt assured that he had found a jewel, a loving mate. She was asked to set a date, naming a day two moons hence.

The wedding, which occurred in the beautiful month of May, was attended by Indians from far and wide. Chief among the participants was Wili-wili-han, who had lately assumed the post of High Priest upon the death of the venerable Indian, Pethakwonn, or Thundergust, who had performed this office for so many years. If he was grieved to see his one and only love marrying another, he made no outward show of it. He had been one of the first to congratulate Lena-kit-chita when her betrothal was announced; it seemed to give him an unalloyed pleasure. There was no pettiness, no rancor in his nature; life was an open book to this philosopher.

After the ceremony, the happy couple, who had eyes for no one but themselves, went for a short trip down the creek in a sumptuously decorated canoe built of white or "canoe" birch bark. The royal bridegroom was his own steersman while the bride reclined on cushions and robes of mountain cat and otter. They were so overjoyed to be away together that they prolonged the trip considerably; six moons had passed before they returned to their eyrie. Soon after they came back, Lena-kit-chita was seized with a heavy cold, which developed into pneumonia. It seemed for a time as if she must die and leave all her happiness. But Wili-wili-han, who had been summoned to minister to her, pulled her through the crisis, drawing her back from the yawning jaws of death. Though she escaped the grim reaper, she did not improve as her watchful husband thought she should. There was a racking cough, an emaciation, a listlessness that betokened perhaps a permanent affection of the lungs. She had chills and fever, which reduced her vitality lower each succeeding day.

To make matters worse, the summer was waning fast, and the long rains which would last until the advent of winter were an appalling prospect. When the equinoctial rains betokened that summer was no more, Lena-kit-chita moaned and cried for the fair days that had gone.

"If I couldn't improve in the sunshine, how could I do better in a constant storm," she wailed as she tossed her shapely form about on her couch of buffalo robes. But she was really not a complainer; she had no desire to make Chau-wa-lanne's lot harder than it was. She was suffering intensely, and anyone would have bemoaned a fate that offered no respite. There was a natural drainage on Mount Eagle, there were no pools to hold water, but even at that, the constant drip, drip, drip was disheartening and depressing.

One morning, when there had been a steady downpour for five days, the fair sufferer underwent a more severe chill than usual; Wili-wili-han, who had occupied a tepee near the royal quarters ever since she had been stricken, was hastily summoned. He applied all his remedies and saved her heart's action from collapsing. When she recovered sufficiently to be calm, she sent for Chau-wa-lanne.

"I am better, my beloved, but I have strong reason to believe I will never get well."

The king tried to encourage her, but she shook her curly head, "No, I can never improve while these storms continue; I wish that there was a season like my name, Indian Summer, a season following the summer when the glad sunshine of happier days would succeed the depressing equinoctial rains, a period of warmth and life before we feel the winter's blast. I have only rain and snow to look forward to now; the rains chill me, and the mound of the snows will prepare the way for the mound which will soon be heaped above my remains."

She could say no more after this; sobbing, she sank back on her pillow, exhausted. Both the King and Wili-wili-han were deeply moved by her words; they realized the truth of what she said, but they seemed powerless to alter climatic conditions. They stood in silence before the fair invalid until a drooping of her eyelids told them she had fallen into a doze. Then the two powerful men of the tribe withdrew, each trembling with a sense of his own impotence against the forces of Nature. As they stepped outside, the drip from the eaves trickled upon them and ran down their backs. Chau-wa-lanne turned and laid his sinewy hand on the wise man's shoulder.

"Soothsayer," he said impressively, "I have a favor to ask of you."

"Anything I can do will be my greatest pleasure, sire," Wili-wili-han replied.

"You have infinite power, or as nearly so as a mortal can possess it," the king resumed, "won't you intercede with the forces of nature and restore the health of my beloved queen ?"

"I have tried in every way, master," answered the wise man, "but of no avail; my medical potations have sufficed to a certain point, but no further; my fervent prayers may have kept her alive, but in a sad and almost hopeless state."

"But can't you," broke in Chau-wa-lanne, "ask the Great Spirit, the Getchi-Manitto whom we have always served, to send a new season, whose sunbeams will restore the color to Lena-kit-chita's cheeks, and make despondent nature glad again, before the pall of the ice king?"

"I do not see how mortal would dare to expect such a benefice," replied the soothsayer, "Getchi-Manitto created seasons that seemed best suited to the needs of most of us. We might all be rebuked for our presumption."

"Wili-wili-han," said the King, "Lena-kit-chita is a young woman of saintly life; she should be spared to the natives as an example of goodness; I firmly believe the Great Spirit will listen."

"Whatever you say is true, my king," said the wise man, "your faith gives me the strength to ask this blessing. I will tonight retire to an inaccessible cliff on this same mountain and ask as you request."

Chau-wa-lanne shook him warmly by the hand, and the two men parted.

The King re-entered the lodge-house, finding his queen awake. "Darling Lena-kit- chita," he whispered, "Wili-wili-han has promised to ask the Great Spirit to send a new season, an Indian Summer, beautiful like yourself, to bring you back to health, to make all Indians happy, before the onset of winter."

The sufferer smiled cheerfully: "Wili-wili-han is a great soul," she faltered, "I know he is favored by the unseen power. I have perfect faith in his accomplishment if he petitions it."

After fasting all day, at dusk, the High Priest attired himself in his official robes, hanging to his person every talisman and cabalistic token he possessed. At dark, he emerged from his tent into the drizzling rain. The leaves on the trees were bedraggled and falling; the earth soggy and oozing; he could appreciate that it was a time when invalids would go downward instead of upward. He followed a trail to the crag known as the Eagle Rock, which overhung Machtando, or as it is now called, the Bald Eagle Valley. There he paused, with arms uplifted, and muttered his mystic invocation.

When the words were said, he fell on his face and, in a loud but respectful voice, chanted, "Oh, Great Spirit, who has ever been the friend of the race of Chau-wa-lanne, and have favored this young ruler oft-times, think of the sufferings long-continued of his queen. My prayers and libations have failed; there seems but one chance to restore her back to health; this one chance is the creation of a new season, a fresh spell of sunshine and color, to succeed the dreary pall of the rains. Oh, Great Spirit, ordain it for the glory of Lena-kit-chita, of Indian Summer, best and truest of her tribe. Let her live on as an example of purity and god-liness to her race. One and all need this new season; it will bring joy and hope to the entire people of Lenni-Lenape."

It was then and there that he heard the rustle of an angel's wing. He arose and walked slowly and sadly back along the trail in the drizzling rain. Out of the darkness had come an answer of blessing to the invalid, but it also contained evil tidings as to the future of his race. Furthermore, he could not stifle the thought that Lena-kit-chita might have been his wife, his share of the glory of Indian Summer. He lay awake all that night, thinking over his message from the Infinite of his lost love and how he wished to prove his unselfishness.

Towards dawn, the patter of raindrops ceased, and he heard birds singing in the trees. Could he be in a trance? A shaft of sunlight, like midsummer, shot through the flap of the tent. He got up and looked out; a scene of rare beauty met his gaze. All the autumn foliage was gleaming in the warm sunlight, the mauve of the beeches, the buff of the hickories, the ochre of the tulip trees, the yellow gold of the maples, the maroon of the oaks, the titian red of the sumacs. The woodbine, which curved Laocoon-like over cedars and pines, was magenta colored in contrast to the dark greens of its captives. The grasses were pink and gold; the earth was dry and firm. Over all hung a delicate haze, like a mantle of the Great Spirit shutting out the rains and leaving in only the light.

Overjoyed, he ran to Lena-kit-chita's lodge, finding her standing at the door, a look of rapture on her face. "Oh, friend and queen," he cried out, "this is your weather, your days for good health and happiness; it is all for the glory of Indian Summer, of Queen Lena-kit-chita!"

The queen looked at him; her voice was choked with emotion. "How can I express my gratitude, wise High Priest; from an invalid, hopeless of ever getting well, you have made me a well woman supremely happy in this beautiful world."

"You owe no thanks to me," said Wili-wili-han, "it is to the Great Spirit that we owe everything, who has done this for you, to show that he loved the Indian race. Our people will always be remembered while this, the fairest, most mystic season of the year exists."

"Do you mean that some time our seed may grow less?" said the valiant King Chau-wa-lanne, who appeared on the scene at this minute.

"Surely there will never be any just like your queen and your Majesty," replied the wise man, evading the question. But in his heart, he knew the awful tragedy which loomed ahead of his people, like a rock hidden by mist, in a ship's course; the voice in the night which granted his petition had told him this. He bowed and walked away, feeling sick at heart, for he knew that his race would vanish, only to live as ghosts, filmy and vaporous as the mists of Indian Summer. With such a fate, no wonder Getchi-Manitto could give them a new season, an Indian Summer as a last indulgence.

XV

THE LOST CHORD

(Story of Beech Creek Mountain)

FOR SOME time, I had been anxious to meet the strange young man. I was just as curious as his unenlightened neighbors to know why he had constructed a bungalow fashioned after the style of an old-time log cabin high on the steep face of Beech Creek Mountain. Where he had come from was the chief mystery, for though he talked freely about himself, he was always reticent about his beginnings.

He had studied art in Paris and Dusseldorf, had been a war correspondent in South Africa, had been on the stage in Shakespearean dramas, and had followed mercantile pursuits in Philadelphia. These occupations had been told to me by as many different persons; it was hard to reconcile them into one personality, into the chronology of a young man of scarce thirty years. His ultimate retirement from the active world at such an early age seemed surprising; I was just beginning to live at the same age.

Of all the persons in the neighborhood, he seemed to take most kindly to old John Ruhlin. John was a mountain tramp by spells but at other times worked diligently on his sister's farm. While not a man of education, he was experienced in the world and its ways and could entertain the strange young man, as he had me, with his experiences in all the counties of mountainous Pennsylvania. He was very proud of the intimacy he had contracted with the stranger; it made him the spokesman of the one interesting figure on the mountain. In his way, he was now just as much of a recluse as the stranger; yet within the limits of a dozen counties, he had gone through as much as some men who have circled the globe.

He was an optimist who felt like Leibnitz that "this is the best possible world." He was reconciled to its injustices by forgetting all about them. Can it be that misery, after all, is a phantasm and that the good and happy parts of life alone are real? It would appear so because some say, frankly, they cannot see the side that gives others a melancholy tinge to every thought.

The old man was delighted to have the opportunity of introducing me to the stranger. "You are sure to like him; he's a broad gauge man; he'll not go back on you like some of your friends, and that one in particular who you helped most."

But I said to myself, if this strange young man is in comfortable circumstances like it is claimed, he is *true* for that reason; only the dependent is disloyal, and then only after he has extracted the last favor obtainable. But there are some persons with a sense of honor, no matter how indigent in condition, but that has been bred into them by generations of gentle ancestors. Conscience is only one of the many happy faculties awakened by refinement.

It was a dull, overcast afternoon when we started to climb to the young recluse's retreat. A pathway led from the gorge road over the face of the mountain to the "first bench." From there to the bungalow, the climb was very steep, and would have been arduous to some, were it not for the long flights of wooden steps with guard rails, which extended all the way to the door. The cottage, a long, low one-story affair, was of frame construction, covered with slabs with the bark on to give the impression of a log cabin. There were spacious piazzas on the front and sides, but the back abutted against the steep mountain. There were several armchairs made of rustic wood, but otherwise, porches and cottage seemed uninhabited.

When we reached the last step, we paused for a moment to admire the gorgeous view which opened out before us through a vista in the tall chestnut trees. The deep green of the forests seemed to stretch as far into the valley as the entrancing "meeting of the waters" of Beech Creek and Bald Eagle Creek. Beyond that were miles of farms, in their browns and greens of late summer; the town was hidden behind groves of buttonwood and linn; in the distance rose the overpowering vastness of the Alleghany plateau. While thus enraptured, the door opened, and the young occupant came out quietly; we were unaware of his presence until he stood beside old John and squeezed his hand.

"I'm glad you both enjoy the scene," he exclaimed enthusiastically, "most people complain they're out of breath when they get here; the view is secondary to that."

I turned around and got a good look at the young fellow; I always like people on first impressions. If I don't, and they later "grow on" me, I am sure to eventually feel again that first distrust or dislike, for everything in life is a circle. I am free to confess that I liked this young man's looks. He was about my height, with hair a shade darker and slimly but athletically built. He was dressed more like a businessman than an artist; his hair which was worn longer than the prevailing fashion, alone revealed his artistic temperament.

He invited us to enter the house. He wanted "to show us around," he said. Inside was a great hall or living room with a tremendous open fireplace, big enough for half a dozen men to stand in; on either side was a bedroom, one for the master, the other for the colored help. He explained that a family of faithful servants were the only persons who would live with him on the mountain. They had only one drawback; they were in constant terror of mythical wild animals. They must have studied a copy of William Cox's inimitable book *Fearsome Creatures of the Lumber Woods* before they came there, he said. In front of the fireplace lay a rug made from the hides of two enormous panthers. "Those were two of the last panthers killed in this state; the famous hunter who shot them presented them to me. He was a mere boy when he slew them; as most of the great soldiers were boys, so likewise were the great hunters."

Above the mantel hung the drab-colored head and faded horns of Jim Jacobson's elk, "the last elk killed in Pennsylvania." It was the most valuable natural history specimen in the state.

These relics were enough to cement a naturally congenial association, but my eyes kept wandering towards the bookcases along the walls, to a pretty porcelain statuette of a shepherdess that stood on a wall bracket above the piano. The young man watched me to see what interested me most; he was clearly proud of his possessions. When my eyes rested on the pretty bit of porcelain, however, he hazarded that I was surprised to find a grand piano on a mountain. "It was quite a piece of work to get it here; there is an old bark road not a hundred feet from the cottage; we brushed it out and carted it up that way, but it was a trifle rough."

John Ruhlin, who had seen all these curios before, put his head through the door leading to the servants' quarters. He found them in the kitchen, so he went in to talk with them. "Water seeks its own level," but that is said in no spirit of discredit to old John. He liked to hear the folks tell of strange sights and sounds that bothered them at night; that was more vital than some discussion of a point of ethics. But I was not to be side-tracked that easily, though I wondered why I should feel more concern about a twelve-inch statuette than Jim Jacobson's elk or the Beech Creek panthers.

"That's a very pretty little figure on the bracket by the piano," I ventured.

"Yes, it is, rather," said the young man nervously. It evidently worried him that this one artwork possessed a magnetism all its own. I walked over as near as I could, leaning across the piano to catch a better glimpse. For some reason, the object fascinated me. It was a work of art that would have attracted attention anywhere and clearly an individual piece. It was exquisitely done, even to the smallest detail. It represented a young girl with coal black hair, wearing a Nell Gwynn hat of dark blue with a black wing in it, clad in a Basque costume of electric blue, carrying a wand in one of her pretty white hands. There was such archness and vitality to the *toute ensemble*; I almost felt as if I was in the presence of a living person. The figure had large blue eyes; they reminded me, oh so sadly, of someone now in far distant Tien Tsin, as did the black lashes and brows, the straight nose with its saucy, retrousse tip, the full upper lip, pouting with seriousness, the alabaster whiteness of the complexion, the arms, and hands, to all of which porcelain was an able ally. The figure was trim and jaunty. The little white-stockinged feet in their high-heeled gilt slippers seemed ready to trip off the pedestal. I would not have been surprised if it suddenly assumed normal size and conversed with us. I could not take my eyes off the statuette. I was embarrassed; I began to feel almost as if I were staring at the man's *intended*. I looked at the young fellow again; I think he had begun to accept me as a kindred soul; he now seemed deeply moved by my interest in this cherished object.

"You really like that figure, do you?" he asked me.

"I certainly do," I made reply. "In fact, I never saw an inanimate object which appealed to me as much; I was untouched by the Venus de Milo, even by the Winged Victory."

"I am glad to hear you say so," he said, "that little bit of porcelain has a peculiar history; it is the leading factor in my life at present—I was almost on the point of saying that it was the cause of my settling on this wild mountain—but do I know you well enough to tell you that?"

I assured him that I could understand any spiritual adventures of an artistic nature and that no sensation he felt would be unrecognizable to me. I had experienced nearly every pang that can come to a person of artistic apperceptions. These words seemed to reassure him, but it was some time before he began the story.

He sat down before the piano and closed some sheets of music which had evidently been frequently played. At another time, I would have asked him to play for me, but now I wanted to learn the romance of the exquisite porcelain statuette.

"Three years ago," he said, "when I was foolish enough to have been engaged in business in Philadelphia, I was called to Pittsburgh on an important matter. I always traveled by day, if possible, and on this occasion, it suited very well, as I received a message about ten o'clock in the morning and boarded the first fast train I could get after that. I got in the car just a minute before it started and was lucky to find a seat by the window. After it started, I looked around to size up my fellow travelers; I am a democrat and ride in the day coach. I always liked to give people names, occupations, and destinations; I had become quite adept at this and in sketching out the life's histories of each. Directly in front of me sat a grizzled war veteran bound for a soldiers' home. Across the aisle from me sat two foreign women, flat-faced and uninteresting. 'Johnstown or Latrobe will get them,' I figured. In the seat in front of them, I saw a young woman; her head was turned away at this moment, looking out at the West Philadelphia station. When she turned around, I saw she was the most beautiful being I had ever beheld. Her profile was fascinating; such a pretty turned-up nose, such a pouting upper lip, and such smoothness to the skin, such a well-rounded, dimpled chin, such deep blue eyes, such lustrous black hair, and brows! She wore a big felt hat, a Nell Gwynn effect, with a black wing in it; her suit was of some soft clinging goods, electric blue in color, and there was a band of dark blue velvet around her white throat. I hastily drew out pad and pencil to draw the witching features, but between the train's motion and her frequent turns of the head to look out of the window, I failed utterly. I tore up my unfinished sketches and threw them on the floor.

"But there were times while I was gazing out at the Chester Hills or at distant Mount Gretna that I felt she was looking at me. I turned around once or twice, and she blushed and buried herself in a book, *Marie-Claire*, it happened to be. I felt if I knew that young woman, I could love her as no woman had been loved before; I knew her and loved her enough as it was to offer myself—if I but had the privilege of her acquaintance. I wondered if any man had been to Paradise by kissing those pouting, serious red lips. I wondered if any man had assumed parity with the Gods by an embrace. She seemed to be a lady; she had every indication of refinement, but that made the barrier against meeting her the more insurmountable.

"As the train swept around the bend after crossing the primeval gorge of Conewago Creek, and the first glimpse always so inspiring, of the broad, island dotted, hill-horizoned Susquehanna is revealed, I recited to myself: 'You are more beautiful than the landscape, with the bronze-green hills widening to god-speed the steel-grey river, with its circular islands, where the Kildeer and the Halcyon hover, with the somber mountains in the distance, under the low-hanging leaden sky; I will never forget this day because of you whom Fate has in her hands to let me see again, or I forever live in loneliness.' By the way my lips moved, I wonder if she suspected my litany! As the train was passing the Paxton furnaces, I saw, to my dismay, that she was putting on her coat and adjusting her books and papers as if to leave at the next station stop, Harrisburg.

"This blessed communion with beauty was to come to an end; I could scarcely believe my senses. Such a radiant and harmonious creature coming into my life should be a more permanent element. I had never felt quite as happy, quite as much in harmony, at peace, in tune, as with this young woman in electric blue, with eyes to match, to whom I had never spoken a word. I felt like a musician who has found the *lost chord*, where the living world and infinity are linked by divine rhapsody. All the music in my soul welled up in a song of happiness; life with this rare being would have made me a superman.

"But now the brakes were being thrown on, and the cumbersome steel cars were coming to a halt beneath the murky shed. The sweet, graceful little creature got up, satchel in hand, and started for the door. I did not know what to do—should I follow or remain where I was? Pursuit, that most primitive of masculine instincts, got the upper hand for an instant. Perhaps she would be getting on another train; I might ride in it to find out where she lived. I ran through the empty car and out on the station platform; I got there just in time to see her dainty figure ascending the iron stairway leading to the waiting room and street. I hated to follow her; she might lose any good opinion she had of me—and stamp me as a 'masher.'

I state that she *might* have had a good opinion of me because a woman who made me feel so spiritually exalted, literally born anew, must have received some beneficial influences from me.

"There is one-sided love of the carnal kind, but spiritual love ought to come from harmony, and harmony defined is 'two or more different musical sounds produced simultaneously.' We would have been congenial had we but met! Yet with many persons, men as well as women, I feel out of harmony, to a greater or lesser extent. If you play the piano, you will notice how sometimes an inanimate object will be in *accord* or in harmony with your instrument; it might be a table, a chair, a guitar, or even an oil stove that vibrates in sympathetic ecstasy.

"One night in an old house in Baltimore, a full chord was drawn across a mandolin while one of John Field's Nocturnes was being played on the piano. Some of those present were frightened, thinking a ghost had touched the strings; perhaps harmony *is* a term for ghost; there may have been unity between the pianist and some long-vanished player of that mandolin. That is my theory of it: there is *thought* back of every act, all your *wave theories* to the contrary.

"I was so attuned to the personality of this beautiful girl, she appealed to me as no one ever had before, and the sweet echoes are still stirring with an ever-present still, small voice, the inmost recesses of my soul. At first, I cherished the vain thought that I would see her again—I traveled by the same train in hopes that the calculus of probabilities might again send her across my path. I had often seen the same persons on trains, on outward and return journeys of the most complicated sort. There must be a similarity of purposes, a common channel of impulse, to explain such coincidences. Feeling that innate spiritual nearness to the beautiful girl in blue, I fancied that if she ever traveled at all, she might probably ride on the same train with me again. But in this, I was disappointed; my fair traveling companion was not to be met with. I made diligent inquiries in the capital city, where I had many good friends, but to no avail. I had to find solace in the lines, 'How wide the world, how small its particles.'

"I saw several young women after that, who were beautiful, talented, attractive, but they did not produce in me that spiritual exaltation, that divine harmony, which I had felt when in the presence of that fair being in electric blue.

"Was the lost chord just touched that one afternoon, now gone forever?

"It was a depressing thought to have realized that such possibilities for the ideal life can exist, only to have them ruthlessly swept away. I could accept no lower valuation on life than I had felt that afternoon on the train. If the lost chord was engulfed in the trackless sea of melody, I would mourn it, but I would also live up to the standard of perfection, as far as I could, that it had developed in my spirit. I could not and would not shake off the effect of that happy afternoon. It taught me the futility of everything else except trying to help others and the value of artistic perfection. Through this brief taste of *harmony*, I was able to do better work in literature and art, despite an overmastering sadness in my spirit. I was often reminded of George Moore's words, 'The sadness of life is the glory of art.'

"I decided to give up my business occupation and take a trip to Paris. There I had studied art as a boy; it would seem pleasant to revive old associations and memories. These had been the most vivid of my life, up to the time I had been touched by the divine that afternoon in the day coach on the Pittsburgh express. In Paris, I found that the keen memories of the past were pale and dull compared to my latest experience. I had touched a plane of living far above earthly custom; the past could not help me any more than that it emphasized the thrill of my 'lost chord.'

"One afternoon, it was lowery and overcast, and a few raindrops were falling, weather much like that when I had traveled with the fair being whose blue eyes matched her dress, I stopped before the large show window of a shop on the Avenue de l'Opera, a few doors from the American consulate. I was compelled to stop by some impulse within; it felt like a minor species of the thrill at seeing my beloved.

"In an instant, my eyes were drawn to that porcelain statuette, which you see here, the replica in miniature, of my love on the train. There were the blue eyes, large and of a peculiar shade, like electric blue, the shining black hair, the pallor of the complexion, the pouting red lips, the rounded, dimpled chin, the alabaster throat, the blue costume, in color if not in mode, like my love had worn.

"I went into the establishment and made inquiries; it was, as I believed, an individual piece. Beyond that, even the proprietor, polite though he was, could give me no information. It had passed through several hands; the artist could hardly be traced. I bought the little figure and hurried with it to my hotel. There I opened the package and feasted my eyes for hours on this perfect reproduction of features that I had tried to sketch on the train with such ill success.

"Whoever the artist, he must surely have seen this girl, or else she had appeared to him in a mental presentiment. It was steeped in her personality. We cannot produce an *ideal* without models; this girl's individuality was too marked to have been evoked by an artist's whim. There was some hidden connection between my losing the fair original and the finding of this faithful reproduction. I felt spiritually re-awakened since my purchase on the Avenue de l'Opera. It seemed as if the purpose of my trip, which had been previously kept from me, was accomplished.

"I returned to Philadelphia four weeks earlier than I had intended. I would not trust the precious statuette to my trunks or even hand luggage. I carried it with me at all times in a cardboard box wrapped in cotton.

The package was about the size and shape of one that might contain a thermos bottle, so it attracted no attention. Never did an ocean voyage seem shorter, more propitious. I was on American soil and in my rooms in Philadelphia, almost before I realized it was like a 'dream voyage.' I had often reasoned that if the possession of this inanimate statuette gave me such spiritual aggrandizement, how much more would be gained through the original who actually lived and breathed?

"It was some satisfaction to think that I lived in the same world, probably only a hundred miles from her. I could visit her in my dreams—at times. I carefully opened the box, took out the figure, and placed it on a table, or music stand, beside the piano. That evening, I was in a state of reverie and introspection and sat down at the piano and played a few bars from Vincent d'Indy's 'Chant de la Cloche.' The room was dark save for the light of a lamp and the dying embers of Lykens Valley coal in the grate. When I struck the first notes, to my surprise and infinite delight, the porcelain statuette began moving towards me, tripping lightly and in perfect time with the music. Here was an inanimate object, or one supposedly so, that was in harmony with my instrument, with me. I had always believed that each inanimate object retains a particle of the soul of its maker; that is why some articles of furniture are so hateful, and others become prime favorites. But all are more than *things*.

"When the statuette reached the edge of the table and could proceed no further, I imagined I saw an appealing look in those electric blue eyes—but it may only have been a light cast by some chunk of the soft coal splitting and sending up a fresh blaze. I ceased playing and caught the little figure in my arms, holding it against my heart. I fancied it felt warm to my touch, not frigid like porcelain, but there again, I may have been deceived by the warmth of the room. I always detested the story of Pygmalion and Galatea. My story was not quite the same; I loved the soul that inspired this bit of porcelain, just as the idolator is devoted to the unseen pod represented by an image. I put the statuette back on the table and began playing. It moved in perfect tune; no other objects in the room stirred. It would have been a miracle if they had. I was in harmony, in *rapport* with the real girl in electric blue—this speck of her personality, in this exquisite bit of porcelain, was attuned to the vibrations of my spirit. 'Are we not made for one another like notes of music,' said Shelley.

"I placed the figure in different corners of the room; it always tried to come nearer to me when I played; it only moved in unison with the notes; it was the 'poetry of motion.' I felt that somewhere, on the other side of the black gulf of space and time, the real girl in blue was waiting for me, perchance, was calling for me. At times her spirit might be crying out, but she could cry until she was speechless; there would be no response. She might not know what caused her sense of soul loneliness, her spiritual isolation, her lack of harmony with her surroundings. She might possess everything visible yet lack some unseen element to make her happy. There is no famine so racking as soul hunger. She might never think of me during her distress; doubtless, to her consciousness, I was a blank.

"Through this little statuette, *subconsciously*, she was sending her spirit's message to me—to come to her—to awake in her the lost chord; to do it in the present when she was young and could enjoy. 'Oh, if we had met when life and hopes were new' is a regret voiced by many mature lovers who come together after the fires of youth have burned low.

"Through this little statuette, my desire to see the original was quickened; it would not grow less until appeased.

"In the midst of these psychic experiences, I decided to retire for a time to the mountains to paint the sighing pines, the rocky heights, the sunsets of cerise. I happened upon this particular spot by chance. The piano and the little porcelain figure came with me; all else is purely local, even to the servants. But after I had erected this bungalow, I found I was too distracted to paint; all my concentration was centered upon the statuette, its inmost secrets. At first, I feared I was suffering from some aberration; then, a light was shown me, I was illuminated. When I played, it might be from Vincent d'Indy, Mozart, Schubert, Schumann, Wagner, or any worthy composer; the figure moved with a series of steps that had certain fixed limitations. They were like the first spirit rapping heard by the Fox sisters in 1848; an effort was being made to communicate with me. I cannot believe that the girl whose eyes matched her dress knows directly of it; the statuette is merely an *antenna* for subconscious thought waves, a central station of telepathy. Thought moves through a system of alternating currents, which must be recharged at regular intervals. My soul's *want* is that young girl—hers is *me*, even though she may not understand. Nature's chief concern is keeping alive the race; to do this best, those most congenial must be thrown together and by design.

"The unseen powers are helping the girl in blue and me, a poor, loving but unacquainted couple, to come together, to be happy. While I am only just beginning, I will soon fathom each vibration of that precious statuette. It will spell out a name and then a place, and I will go there and claim her as my own. I have no fear that I will be turned away. Destiny will not be mocked. Fate will prevail.

"I am mastering an alphabet now; it will be regular notation, then all will be simple. 'Oh, dearer self, art thou like me astray?' I do believe if I had gone up to her in the car that afternoon, lady that she was, she would not have repulsed me, but Fate, in its moderation, wished otherwise. It must come through faith and struggle to be appreciated. Perhaps that afternoon, she could not have interpreted the vague longings that sent the color to her smooth, full cheeks when I surprised her watching me. Perhaps I considered my emotion idle curiosity and blushed at it when she turned around suddenly as I was sketching the upward yet round and well-molded end of her exquisite little nose—like the nose on that statuette.

"Earnest little bit of porcelain, it is striving hard to give me its message; then I can let it fall to break to pieces or put it in a cupboard to accumulate dust or cobwebs. When it tells its story, maybe its spark of personality will vanish, like a ghost that has delivered its message. Perhaps there is a reward for inanimate objects that do their duty well; theirs is a harder task than befalls any mortals; they must be doubly patient, triply long-suffering.

"But everything great or small is a symbol of a thought, an exponent of a higher value. Love, the force that has upheld the world from its inception until today, and will do so for ages to come, is the vastest power existing. To know love, one must catch a glimpse of the hidden motive behind material things. Finding it, we take on immortality, for it lies 'beyond the mountains of the moon,' its transit is the Lost Chord.

XVI

BALD EAGLE'S NEST

(Story of Milesburg Mountain)

O N ONE occasion, when the famous war chief Bald Eagle was crossing the Buffalo Valley, he stopped for the night along Beaver Run on a farm tenanted by a certain Mordecai Wolford. Wolford, a courageous man of Quaker stock, came out of his cabin and shook the Indian warmly by the hand, bidding him be welcome. Later he presented him with some tobacco, and his wife introduced the great warrior to the mysteries of four kinds of pie. Not to be outdone by her parents, Mary Wolford, a tall, willowy slip of a girl, put into his hands the most welcome gift of all, a flagon of homemade wine. Even if she hadn't given him the wine, Bald Eagle would have become intoxicated at the sight of this rare young girl. At sixteen, she had far outgrown her years yet was as supple and lithe as a cat tail. She had simple and unaffected manners, which heightened her charm.

There was a look of genuine courtesy yet self-reliance in her pale blue limestone-colored eyes, which seemed a relief from the stolid glare of the squaws. Her face was a long oval, but her features preserved the mobility of youth. There was a suggestion of the aquiline in her well-defined nose, which, however, turned up just a trifle at the tip, giving vivacity to her otherwise classic countenance. Her abundant hair, which was worn in a thick braid hanging down her back, was the color known to hair-dressers as "medium light," but which really is the lightest shade of brown. Her white hands were tapering and smooth; there was a transparency to her skin that betokened innate cleanliness rather than delicate health.

There was generally a rather hard smile on her thin curved lips, lips that never had any color in them but were indescribably lovely. She seemed to fancy the burly chieftain, who was all smiles after the maiden had condescended to treat him to the spirits. She had done this without first consulting her parents, and they cast angry glances at her when they saw that she had made the impression of the evening. There was hardly any alcohol in the wine, but to the elder Wolfords, at least, the conduct of the great chief became most unseemly. He followed the couple and their daughter up the hill as far as their cabin door, reiterating his thanks for his kindly reception in grandiose but badly phrased sentences.

After he had gone, the mother turned on the girl churlishly, saying, "If that Indian goes crazy drunk tonight and burns down the house, you alone are to blame. I've a good mind, big as you are, to pound a little common sense into you when we get inside."

But Mary merely smiled superciliously; she was big enough to take care of herself, her father always interceded for her at the critical moment. She always was her father's idol, but she constantly quarreled with her mother. Sometimes the two did not speak for weeks.

As the Indian returned to his campfire, he began singing one of Heckewelder's German hymns, he had the tune correct, if not the words, and this was taken as proof positive of his intoxication. But a little thing like this would not have been noticed in a white man. All was soon quiet in the encampment, and before daybreak, the Indians had departed. Bald Eagle had passed a restless night. Young, handsome, powerful fellow that he was, he had fallen in love, and his passion seemed a hopeless one. If the year had been 1764 instead of 1774, he would have bound and gagged the parental Wolfords and taken Mary away with him, and she would not have bemoaned her fate overmuch. But now settlers were a-plenty, and every act of the natives watched with jealous reprisal. He could not have gotten twenty miles with his fair prize without being apprehended. The girl might run away and join him if she really cared for him, but even then, his death would be the penalty for her voluntary elopement. He felt the barrier of race hatred, the knowledge that the settlers regarded him, king though he was, as belonging to an inferior race.

If she was older, he might win her more easily. Maybe he would meet her later; both were young and could wait. But despite all these considerations, Bald Eagle was still a warrior. He would have run the risk of carrying the girl away had he been sure of her sentiments towards him. In an earlier day, that would have mattered little, but now she would have to be an accessory to a runaway. He would have tarried longer in the meadows of Beaver Run and found out how matters stood, but that he was hurrying westward to get some of his braves, who were accused of a highway robbery, out of the danger zone. It was afterward proved that two white men disguised as Indians committed the crime, which occurred on Lower Mahantango Creek, but at the present moment, this was not known, and popular feeling ran high against his tribesmen.

If Mary Wolford felt any interest in the burly chieftain, it was confined to when she feasted her eyes upon his superb dimensions. It was always that way with her. She liked best the man she was with, provided he was good-looking. She was a true woman in that she could not tolerate a homely or ill-formed man and made no effort to dissemble. She went to bed infatuated with her Indian admirer, dreaming all night long that they were crossing broad rivers and high mountains together. The next morning, when she was routed out of bed by her mother and told to go out in the damp fog and "clean up the mess left by the Indians," she forgot all the romantic and sentimental incidents.

That night, a handsome young Scotch-Irish trader with coal black hair and eyes stopped at the house on the trail to Middle Creek Valley and the valleys to the north and west, and she further forgot her infatuation of the night before. She sat up so long with him that she looked like a ghost when she got up to bid him goodbye the following morning. To her expanding consciousness, the world seemed a passing pageant of attractive men; it was hard to tell which one she could like best.

Once in a while, homely men applied for lodgings, but if Mary came to the door, she always told them that the house was full. Sometimes, undaunted, they camped in the lush grass by the run, near where Bald Eagle spent the night, but they received scant courtesy. She even hated to have to carry a pail of milk to them. More than one undersized, bearded frontiersman passed the word on to his kind that she was a "very snippy girl." But Mary did not care; it was her chief delight to snub the unattractive. All this while she was growing in beauty and height. On her eighteenth birthday, in September of the memorable year of 1776, she stood against the jam of the door at the cabin while one of her admirers measured her height as five feet, eight and a half inches.

In the late summer of that year, her father, having quarreled with the cantankerous Scotch-Irishman who owned the farm, besides having tired several years before of working for somebody else when there was so much wild land to be had for the asking, decided to move further west. In the Bald Eagle Valley, along the foothills, were numerous tracts that could be "taken up" and the Wolford family started in this direction.

The household goods were loaded in a heavy wagon drawn by two yoke of red and white spotted bulls. Mordecai Wolford himself walked by the animals as the driver while his wife and five young children rode on the box seat of the wagon. Mary, clad in a buckskin riding habit with red bead trimmings mounted on a handsome black-grey colt, was the vanguard of the procession. In the rear, her older brother, Thaddeus, assisted by four savage dogs, drove the cows, hogs, and sheep. Mary had her usual quota of adventures on the way. Wherever the party stopped for the night, some young man who had seen her dashing equestrienne figure would make pretense to come to the camp and get acquainted. She left a trail of promises from the mouth of White Deer Creek clear to the mammoth spring at Bellefonte.

No one so beautiful, no one so arch or coquettish, or so brave and light-hearted had passed up the valleys before; she was the ideal of half a hundred young mountaineers. But she had no intention of marrying just yet, although she was perfectly sincere "at the moment" in each flirtation.

The caravan was moving along famously and nearly at its destination when Mary's spirited mount took fright at a blind grey squirrel that ran between his prancing feet. The poor little animal's eyes had both been shot out; consequently, he did not notice the approaching horse as he scurried across the road to a cornfield. The colt became unmanageable and started to run away. There was a heavy curb on the bit, and Mary, perhaps losing her presence of mind for a second, reined him in too sharply. The animal fell over backward, throwing the girl off, rolling on her, badly bruising one of her thighs. It was a narrow escape; she might at least have had a broken leg or been made a cripple for life. It was decided to pitch camp on the scene of the accident and remain there for several

A PICNIC IN THE WOODS
Photo by W. T. Clarke, Conrad, Pa.

days until she was all right again. The scene of the mishap was on the south bank of Bald Eagle Creek, half a mile below the present town of Milesburg. It was a pleasant place, a glade wooded with gigantic white oaks, through whose topmost lace-like branches, the sun was ever sending bright, vivid shafts of light while flickers and pileated woodpeckers and parrots echoed the chorus of the breezes.

In the early fall, the woodbine and the shinhopple had turned to red; the blue-wood asters were everywhere. By the water's edge bloomed the bright-hued cardinal flowers. A little further upstream and on the opposite bank was the "Nest" of the famous Indian warrior, Bald Eagle. It consisted of a giant hollowed-out buttonwood tree, inside of which the chieftain used to sleep, according to his boast, in a standing position. There was plenty of room for him to have reclined full length, even though he was over six feet tall. An old Indian named Whistle-town was always on hand as a sort of sentinel. When the Wolfords pitched camp across the creek, the chief was said to be absent on a hunting trip. The spot was interesting to Mary as she well recollected the Indian and how interested he had been in her two years before. Instinctively she felt that he would like her better now. Already she had been loved by several young men of consequence, and a noted Indian chief was a decided *divertissement*.

She was disappointed that Bald Eagle was away; she said she would give almost anything to see him again.

"You didn't feel that way," snapped her mother, "when you had to clean up that pile of bones and entrails he left at our place two years ago."

Mary made no reply. She had forgotten everything except her conquest of the Indian's heart. A couple of mornings after their arrival, Thaddeus appeared with the news that Bald Eagle had returned. Whether old Whistle-town had slipped away and informed his chief that there was a party of white people in the neighborhood or he had come back unintentionally was never explained. When he found that it was the Wolford family who were camping at his very door, his joy knew no bounds. He at once crossed the stream, looking like a conquering Viking as he stepped from his canoe. He presented them with a saddle of venison and a string of water birds. He seemed delighted to meet Mary once more, commenting volubly upon her increased height and general attractiveness.

He opened a package of beaver skins, carefully saved from the winter before, bestowing them upon her with much *éclat*.

Temporarily Mary was smitten again by the charms of the stalwart chief. All other loves were for the nonce forgotten. For the two succeeding days, Bald Eagle was constantly at the Wolford camp. He was always bearing gifts or having his henchmen appear with unexpected presents or "surprises." Mary's parents did not know how to take his conduct but concluded to make the best of matters until they could move on to their ultimate destination. For this reason, an early date was set for departure.

When the great chief learned this, he said he would like to entertain the family at a supper at the "Nest" the evening before they left. He wanted to give them an idea of how well an Indian could live in the wilderness and entertain. Colonel Samuel Hunter had been pleased by his hospitality, as had other dignitaries. The invitation was cheerfully accepted, as the entire family wished to wind up their stay as pleasant as possible. Besides, there was no telling when the great war chief's friendship might stand them in good stead. Mary had confided to her father that she did not love Bald Eagle, so he was reassured that there was no danger of his having a dusky son-in-law. The supper was scheduled to commence an hour before sundown, which meant about five o'clock.

Bald Eagle sent out hunters and fishermen to provide the season's delicacies for the repast while he himself built a bower garlanded with wildflowers and woodbine over the spot where it was to take place. On the morning of the promised festival, a visitor in a chestnut-bark canoe appeared at Wolford's camp in the person of young James Brady, the second son of John Brady, the pioneer. He was eighteen years of age at this time and a sergeant in the militia. He was traveling on military business to the western part of the province. In personal appearance, he was easily the most handsome youth of his age and generation. He stood six feet, one inch, in height, with clear-cut aquiline features, and had a shock of red-gold hair. No countenance can be as attractive as a Scotch-Irish face, so brimming over with intelligence and wit. His brother, Hugh Brady, speaking of him many years later, said, "My brother James was a remarkable man; his mind was as well-finished as his body. I have ever placed him by the side of Jonathan, son of Saul, for beauty of person and nobleness of soul, and like him, he fell by the hands of the Philistines." But we will touch on the sad fate of the "Young Captain of the Susquehanna" later. Like drops of quicksilver run together, the handsome James Brady was attracted to the fair Mary Wolford, and she, of course, reciprocated.

There is no stopping an attachment based on mutual physical charm. Mary had seen the young soldier once before and, despite her other "loves," always cherished a secret admiration for him. Her father had taken her to the horse races at Derrstown, now called Lewisburg, where instead of watching the sport, she followed James Brady with her pale, limestone-colored eyes all afternoon. Before the first race, there had been an impromptu horse sale, and her father, for twenty pounds, had bought the black-grey colt, then a two-year-old. Ordinarily, this would have excited her greatly as she was devoted to horses, but she had no eyes nor thoughts for anything after she saw young James. She was especially enamored after her father told her his name, that he was a noted shot and hunter even at the tender age of sixteen. She never saw him again in the interval but kept her interest alive by calling the colt James. She liked the animal, she declared, because of his name and for his having been bought the day that she had seen his namesake.

Now when the "Young Captain of the Susquehanna" appeared at the camp, whether by accident or design, it was as hard to clear this up as Bald Eagle's sudden appearance; she could indulge her romantic fancy to the utmost. James seemed happiness personified to be with her and, after dinner, proposed they take a canoeing trip upstream towards the site of the present town of Bellefonte. Spring Creek, which flows from that direction, joins with the Bald Eagle a short distance above the "Nest." It was an enticing invitation, especially as he promised to have her back at camp in a couple of hours. He was informed of the party and said he would attend if invited. Just as the pair were starting away, Bald Eagle, who had been watching them from the opposite bank, hurried across in his skiff, arriving in time to extend a cordial invitation to the young pathfinder. Brady accepted smilingly, showing his white teeth, his Irish blue eyes dancing with health and pleasure.

But Mordecai Wolford declared afterward that he noticed an ugly scowl on the war chief's face as he re-entered his canoe. He watched the young couple until they were out of sight and then resumed his superintendence of preparing for the feast. Piles of rich pine were stacked at regular intervals, which meant that by the light of the campfire, a spectacular ghost dance, a rare honor to white guests, was to be enacted. All the Indians from miles around were drawn to the scene by the extraordinary preparations and stood about in groups with awe and interest written in their generally listless faces. It was one o'clock when the canoeists left, three o'clock rolled around, and they had not hove in sight. Bald Eagle, keeping count of the time by the sun, began to get uneasy and paced up and down the bank, seemingly forgetful of his horde of observers. Four o'clock came, then five, and soon after, the sun set with all its autumnal splendor behind the Alleghanies. By the savory odors rising from the fires, supper was ready to be served, but absent was the fair guest of honor.

At six-thirty Bald Eagle paddled across the creek and told Mary's parents that the repast would begin as soon as she returned. He said he was certain there had been some mistake, that she would be back before dark. It seemed that darkness set in with extra alacrity that night, though it was clear and moonlit. As Bald Eagle, disconsolate and gaunt, stood by the shore, gazing up the stream into the impenetrable gloom, the very katydids seemed to mock him with their metallic singing. It was the only thing that broke the rapt silence of the camp that night. The spirit dancers, as they waited, shifted uneasily from foot to foot, but they made no comment.

Sometime towards midnight Bald Eagle, humbled and mortified to the quick, slunk into his Nest, and the retainers dropped out of sight among the logs and vines. Probably an hour after his disappearance, a canoe drifted into view; it contained Mary Wolford and James Brady. Sheepishly the young girl got out of it and slipped into her lean-to for the remainder of the night. The young man drew his boat on dry land and slept in it. In the morning, he heard violent quarreling among the Wolfords and hastened to the scene. He arrived in time to help explain that three miles upstream, they had run into a submerged rock, which drove a big hole in the canoe. He had difficulty in getting Mary to shore in safety; it took until long past dark to repair the leak. They had returned as quickly as they could; none regretted more than he that Mary had been forced to miss Chief Bald Eagle's supper and ghost dance. They could see where he had put the patch in the canoe if they wanted further proof. This silenced the elder Wolfords, although Mary looked very pale and penitent. To clinch the matter, young Brady, who was every inch a gentleman, crossed the creek and visited Bald Eagle at his Nest, expressing his heartfelt apologies for keeping the guest of honor from his party and for his own unavoidable absence. The thief took the apology with apparent goodwill, but there rankled hate in his heart, which he cherished to his dying day.

The Wolford party went their way, and Brady, abandoning his canoe as he intended, continued his mission on foot across the Alleghanies. The only outward sign of pique was that Bald Eagle did not come across the creek to bid Mary goodbye, although he signaled to her in Indian fashion as the caravan moved along the trail on the southern shore. For some reason, young Brady never visited Mary again, though she did not want for lovers.

Two years later, during harvest, James Brady, then a Captain, was guarding some cradlers who were at work in a field near the mouth of Loyalsock Creek. A party of Indians fired on him, wounding him, and in the struggle which ensued, he was knocked down with a blow from a tomahawk, stabbed by a spear, and scalped. After scalping him, one of the Indians, with hate on his face, drove a tomahawk four times into his skull. Despite all these tortures, his spirit held steadfast to the body, and he lived five days. Just before he expired, he regained consciousness and described the attack with great minuteness. The Indians were of the Seneca tribe, he said, and one of them whom he personally knew was the great chief Bald Eagle. Why this celebrated Indian had taken such an active part in the horrible mutilation of this splendid young patriot would seem a mystery, but for this story of Mary Wolford.

Perhaps it was the humiliation that he felt when she absented herself from his party in company with the "Young Captain" that caused him to brood and repine until nothing but revenge "long and deep" would suffice.

But one death meant another; others must have revenge. Captain Samuel Brady, James' older brother, several years later, noticed a large party of Senecas marching along the Alleghany River on their way to Bald Eagle's Nest. Brady recognized Bald Eagle, who was in the lead and fired at him, killing him instantly, the bullet having pierced his heart. But that member had been sorely wounded long before; it was his vulnerable point ever since he first looked into the pale blue eyes, cold as limestone, of Mary Wolford.

XVII

THE RUNNING RACE

(Story of Lookout Mountain)

"YOU MUST meet Agnes Letort." These were almost the first words that greeted Martin Fryer upon his arrival at his uncle's home in Philadelphia. They were addressed to him in a chorus by his three cousins, girls ranging in age from fifteen to twenty. Martin was nearly twenty-one and already was quite experienced with girls, the simple country maids of Earlysburg. Agnes, it was explained to him, was a very beautiful girl of sixteen who had moved into the house directly across the street. Martin Fryer's uncle was the proprietor of a large livery and sales stable; his home was next door to the big brick repository.

The afternoon of the young man's arrival, he went for a stroll with his cousins. They had gone hardly half a square when Agnes Letort, dressed all in white, hove in sight across the way. When she was opposite, the girls called to her to wait until they brought their cousin, who had come on a visit, over to meet her. But Agnes motioned with her hand as if she was in too great a hurry. So the first attempt at "getting acquainted" ended in failure.

Just before supper, one of the girls ran across to Agnes's house and asked her to come and spend the evening meeting the young stranger. Agnes, it was said, was gracious at the time and replied that she would be delighted to come over, only too happy to meet him. It was a warm evening, so the family sat on the front steps until dark but saw no signs of Agnes. At about eight-thirty, one of the girls telephoned but was told that Agnes had gone out with a girlfriend. The next morning the girls met her on the street, and she apologized for not keeping her promise but said she had an earlier engagement with a girlfriend, about which she had forgotten. She promised to come to call that evening if they would permit her. She was so very pretty that she was instantly forgiven and her promised visit welcomed. She did put in an appearance that night, bright and early. She made quite a contrast to the youth whom she was expected to charm. Of medium height, slight, and shapely, with an oval face, pale rather than pink, she had full grey eyes, with black lashes and brows, a nose which, but for the fine, straight line of the bridge, might have been called *retrousse*, rather full lips, and a wealth of ash-brown hair, which curled and crinkled like spun- sugar. She exhibited a genial friendly manner when she wanted to, a manner which would disarm the most hostile critic. She was in a word chic and up-to-date, a *belle bourgeoise*.

On the other hand, Martin Fryer was tall, gawky, and stoop-shoul-dered; his nose was long and beaked, his pale blue eyes were small, and his red hair hung down on his coat collar. But there was a look of intelli-gence on his face, showing the latent power that makes every backwoods youth a possible Judge, Congressman, or multi-millionaire.

He was ill at ease with Agnes, and she made no effort to interest him. Her general conversation was witty and bubbling over with the exuberance of youth, but she had few words for the young man. He was actually glad when she left. The door was scarcely closed when the girls, all three at once, began asking him how he liked her. He had a veneration for truth but, on this occasion, said he liked her very much. Secretly he was angry at her for her indifference, but it piqued him to the extent of arousing a permanent interest.

During the remainder of his visit, he saw her perhaps half a dozen times, always when others were present. He probably liked her less when he left than he did the night she called; her indifference was mortifying. She was so very pretty that it made him feel worse. He would rather have had one kind word from her than a deluge of kisses from all the belles of Earlysburg. He put her down as "pert and snippy" but secretly wished that she had cared for him.

After he got home, he used to lie awake at nights, imagining that he had met her again and her manner had changed. He dreamed of her occasionally that she was in his arms and telling him that she loved him. Between waking fancies and dreams, she was a hard proposition to forget. Once, he made bold to send her a card with a picture of a Thanksgiving turkey on it. He went to the post office every day for two weeks, pestering the old postmaster with inquiries for "mail," a thing he had never done before.

During the winter, his father, a prosperous farmer and stockman, fell through a silo and was seriously injured. This put the management of the farm on young Martin, which developed him quicker in a few months than ever before in his life. In the spring, the old man said he would like the racehorses campaigned just the same as usual; Martin must handle them, must take them on the fair circuit.

Old Jacob Fryer had loved the "runners" ever since the days when as a lad of twelve, he had run away from home and become an exercise boy at the historic course at Monmouth Park in New Jersey. He was very proud of a photograph that had been taken of him, perched on the back of the mighty Longfellow, with the venerable John Harper holding the bridle. Later he had gone back to the farm in Central Pennsylvania but again yielded to the old desire and, for a season, campaigned an attenuated sprinter named Guy Grey at Gloucester. Then after a lapse of nearly a decade, he bought three yearlings at one of the Rancocas sales in West Philadelphia. One of them, a son of the gallant Locahatchee and Bow Bells, he named Lights o' London, a combination of the dam's name and a melodrama that he had witnessed one night in the Quaker City. The colt never grew to be tall but was nicely turned, and, save for a white face and two white hind feet, was black as ink.

"If I had time, I'd take him to the big tracks," the old man continually said.

With the two others, Quaker Girl and Creole, he followed the county fair tracks for several years. Creole was a good half-mile and repeat horse, but Lights o' London excelled in distance races. Quaker Girl was good to get a place in the half-mile events but seldom came in a winner.

Jacob Fryer was proud of Lights o' London and, contrary to his hidebound custom, kept him entire. This gave him a dash and brilliancy and a luster to his coat that would not have been his as a gelding. It seems a hideous confession of man's weakness to seek to control animals by depriving them of sex. He was at his best as a five-year-old, winning eleven out of fourteen starts, going several miles better than 1.45.

This was the season before the old man met with his accident. Lights o' London as a six-year-old was to be campaigned by the son. The young man felt the responsibility thrust upon him; he was determined to do his best by his father's horses. He had watched his training methods, so he knew some of the tricks of the game. Besides, the horses were not hard to manage; they knew what was expected of them almost as much as if they were humans.

The first start was made at the mid-summer fair at Milton. Lights o' London was victorious, beating out his old-time rival Matador, in a driving finish, on a heavy track in 1.52. Quaker Girl and Creole finished second and third to Little Christmas in the half-mile heat race. Old man Fryer was in the grandstand and tried to leap for joy when he saw how well the horses performed. He could have stood a total crop failure better than the downfall of his beloved colors, *green cap, green shirt, dark green and white check sleeves*. After Milton, they raced at Hughesville, Bloomsburg, Lewisburg, Carlisle, York, and Altoona. Out of seven starts. Lights o' London was first five times, Matador beating him once, and Lois Cavanaugh once. Quaker Girl and Creole did not do so well.

The season was to be ended, almost on home ground, at the fair held at the picturesque track at the base of the towering Lookout Mountain, one of the landmarks of the Bald Eagle range. Running races were all the vogue that year; interest in them was fitful in Central Pennsylvania, although they were the earliest form of sport of the better class of settlers. Penn's Valley still rankles over the defeat two-thirds of a century ago of the Kentucky thoroughbred owned by the Potter boys of Potter's Fort, which was "taken into camp" by the pride of the West Branch Valley owned by "Johnny" Myers, on the famous course which extended from one end to the other of the Big Island, below Lock Haven. The old people still remember the victory of Sea Turtle, a Jersey Shore flyer, in a twelve-mile race over the champions of Williamsport and Shamokin.

The fair at Lookout Mountain was scheduled to last four days, with one running race each day. The mile dash, in which Lights o' London was entered, was to take place on the opening day.

Martin Fryer, riding in the box-car with his charges, never forgot the sight which greeted his eyes that bright October morning as he was being shunted into the fairgrounds from Milesburg. The Indian Summer haze was in the air; a dense fog still rested in the more inaccessible hollows and over the pinnacles of the mountains. The gums and hickories were vividly tinted, and as if to keep the oaks in fashion, the Virginia creeper was garlanding them with scarlet. A hoar-frost was on the grass, which sparkled when the sun rays touched it. There was a tang to the atmosphere, an invigorating odor of the frost-bitten leaves. Along the fence corners bloomed the blue-wood asters; the golden rod was paling, like blonde beauties growing grey. A pair of crows, strutting across the infield, cawed loudly as they took to leisurely flight upon the near approach of the freight train. Once or twice the not-disagreeable smell of soft-coal smoke wafted into the car from the engine. The train moved quite a distance past the fairgrounds in order to back into the switch, going by a line of workmen's houses on the outskirts of the town.

On the back porch of one of these cottages, so near to the car that he could almost have shaken hands with her, Martin saw a young girl bending over a washtub, for it was Monday morning. The steam from the hot suds was rising up about her like the fog on Lookout Mountain. Her sleeves were rolled up, her pretty arms and hands were "turkey red." There was something in the texture of her ash-brown, kinky hair and her round face, which seemed familiar. Suddenly recollecting her, he called out, "Hello there, Miss Le-tort; what are you doing in this part of the country?"

Before she could answer, the car had moved on, but he was sure she recognized him. When they backed past the house, she was on the watch and waved to him, calling, "Hello, Mister Fryer, I'm living here now, come to see me."

She seemed so genuinely pleased to greet him that Martin muttered to himself, "a new Agnes, my dreams maybe are coming true."

He could hardly wait to get his string unloaded and ensconced in their boxes and get his dinner before brushing himself up to call on the fair charmer. What had brought her to this part of Pennsylvania? Could it be that, after all, she was married, and his visit would be that much time wasted? He was not sufficiently *evolved* to understand such an unnatural state of affairs as being attentive to a married woman. He was sincere, and if he went to see her, it was because he was genuinely fond of her. He could forgive the past.

When he reached the humble home, a very differently attired young woman came to the door. Evidently, like himself, she had been preparing for the visit almost from the moment of their unconventional encounter. She wore a neatly fitting suit of some pale brown material; there were traces of powder on her young face, her frizzy hair was neatly parted in the middle, her hands were white, her fingernails polished. Her attitude was so changed that, for an instant, he imagined he must be calling on the wrong girl. It was the suddenness of their meeting, or perhaps an improvement in his appearance, that was responsible for the genial welcome. There were no "secondary" or "underlying" motives in a nature as frank as Agnes's. Her greatest fault was that she was totally lacking in dissembling. She would almost tell a homely man to his face that he was homely; therefore, she did not like him. She explained that her father had secured a good position in the iron furnace, hence her new place of residence.

It was two o'clock when Martin arrived at the Letort cottage; supper was announced when he started to leave. He had been invited to remain but thought it best not to extend his "first call" too long. When he left, he arranged to return and spend the following evening.

His brain was in a whirl that night as he walked along the ties to his lodgings near the stables.

All the next day was spent preparing Lights o' London for Wednesday's running race. His most dangerous adversary Matador, a game old stag, was also out on the track. He was a chocolate-colored animal, technically a "dark chestnut," and had raced his way across the continent from San Francisco to Fort Erie, finding his "ultimate islands" on the fair circuit. The wiseacres predicted it would be a "toss-up"' between Lights o' London and Matador; there was a rumor of as many as four other entries, but they didn't count.

In the early evening, when Martin was on his way to the boarding house for supper, he noticed a running horse being unloaded from a box car. The animal was blanketed and hooded, but from the long, light-colored tail which trailed the ground, it was either a sorrel or a light bay. There were handlers on each side of his head leading him down the incline, but this indicated his value rather than fractiousness. The young man watched the proceeding for a few minutes, trying to identify the horse, but it seemed a complete stranger.

After supper, he hurried to Agnes's home, spending a most delightful evening. He literally "made up for lost time" as he held her in his arms for a full fifteen minutes inside the closed door before he departed. The couple had come to an understanding. Coquettish to the last, Agnes said she would marry him if his horse won the race. She would get her father to take her to the track. Her parents were violently opposed to her marrying so young; besides, she was an only child. But she could wed clandestinely.

After the race, if the right horse was winner, she would slip away and meet her lover on the flat rock on the summit of Lookout Mountain. From there, they could climb down to Snow Shoe Intersection and board a train that would soon have them in Clearfield County. There they could "take out license" and get married. It sounded very romantic, so much so that Martin forgot the many insuperable difficulties. There probably was no night train from the Intersection to Snow Shoe. If there was, they could not get a Beech Creek train for Clearfield until the next morning; by that time, the whole country would be aroused. Central Pennsylvania is hardly adapted for a Gretna Green.

Martin returned to his lodgings, feeling really happy for the first time in his life. At daybreak, Lights o' London breezed over the course in fine fettle; Martin secretly felt that the horse had never gone so well. Matador looked peaked and hide-bound; there seemed an almost rheumatic stiffness to his joints.

As Lights o' London was being put in his box, the "strange" horse was brought out for his gallop. Martin had a good look at him. First of all, he was not a big horse; he was built on rather fine lines. He was a light-bay or fulvous color; his tail was very long, trailing the dust when he spread out for action. There were black tips on his ears and a black streak running from the top of his nose to the tip of his tail. He was ridden by a small, sandy-haired white boy whom the other lads called

Crackers. One of the boys led the horse through the gate into the track, and from there, he broke into an easy canter, sweeping along the course with much the sliding movement of a fox. Martin asked the lad who the unknown horse might be.

"Why, that's a Kentucky horse, mister, his name is Indian Fields, he's by the old champion Falsetto, dam Indian Apple by old Shiloh. He ain't never raced before; he's only a four-year-old and a stud."

Martin, encouraged by such a flow of particulars, inquired the name of the owner.

"Why, that's Mister Will Buckler's horse; he's a young Kentucky gentleman who holds down a big job in Pittsburgh; Andy Essenwine's trainin' him."

None of the names were familiar, and Martin had a "sneaking notion" that this colt, and not Matador, was the competitor to be afraid of.

The day was sunshiny and cool; there was an enormous attendance at the fair. Early in the afternoon, Martin saw Agnes and her father at one of the side shows; she was on the grounds, true to her promise. She whispered to her lover that she was ready to climb old Lookout in case his colors flashed in front. She wished they would. He was so hopeful of victory that he arranged with his exercise boy, Linn McGrady, to ship back to Earlysburg that evening "in case he should be called away on urgent business."

It was four o'clock when the gong sounded, calling out the entries for the mile running race. It was a pretty sight to see them parade to the post, the bright colors gleaming in the waning sunlight. From a far corner of the grounds came the strains of an automatic piano. First came Matador, dark chestnut, sixteen hands, lank, rangy; he was ridden by a white boy, the colors were straw and white. Second came Cold Deck, a small, pudgy light chestnut; a white boy rode him, decked out in black and white polka dots. Third came Little Christmas, a dark brown entire horse with roached mane and tail, a white boy astride him, colors pink and brown. Fourth came General Coxey, a lean fly-bitten white; a tiny Black boy rode him; his colors were "green above the red," the same colors that "Father Bill" Daly sported. Fifth came Cheerful Mary, a golden chestnut, full of life and fury, buck-jumping, prancing, every foot of the way, ridden by a colored lad, colors mauve and cerise. Sixth came Lights o' London, entire, shiny black, with white face, pink nose, two white hind feet, ridden by a husky white boy, colors green and white. Seventh came Indian Fields, jogging along at a cavalry trot, his sandy-haired rider, posting in the saddle; an oddly marked entire horse, a throw-back clearly to some ancient type, with a tail like a street-sweeper; jockey colors red and blue. The handsome horses and gay colors fascinated the rural spectators; there were many "ohs" and "ahs" as each horse passed the stand.

Contrary to the custom of most running races at the fairs, there was a good start, a quick start. In fact, they were "off" at the first break. All broke about even, except Cheerful Mary, who got much the worst of it. The boy on Matador kept watching Lights o' London as if there was nothing else in the race. Martin's instructions had been to take his horse out in front and keep him there. He was going to take no chances against the possible prowess of Indian Fields.

As they passed the grandstand the first time around, Matador and Lights o' London ran side by side.

"Hitch the sprinklin' cart behind 'em," shouted a facetious onlooker.

Little Christmas, under a terrific pull, was running third, five lengths behind, with Indian Fields, at his withers, a good fourth. Rounding the turn, Indian Fields moved forward, and the rider of Little Christmas went to the whip, pounding him all along the backstretch. Turning into the straightaway Little Christmas having stood a drive for three-eighths of a mile, quit while Indian Fields was breezing along unconcerned, a fair test of his endurance.

The "hippodrome" between Matador and Lights o' London continued past the stand. It promised to be a tame race.

"Say, them guys has got it fixed between 'em", said the same facetious onlooker.

Few watched Indian Fields make his run after they had rounded the next turn. He had "killed off" Little Christmas; his eye was now on the pair in front. His rider leaned forward; it was a signal, and the fulvous-colored bay shot forward like a driving rod. In a bound or two, he closed up the five-length gap which had separated him from the leaders, and all along the backstretch, the three raced side by side:

Indian Fields on the far outside. Near the last turn, Matador's rider began his effort with whip and spur. The old stag responded gamely, his long chocolate-colored muzzle shot out in front of Lights o' London's pinkish nose. Then the rider of the gallant Lights o' London "put his nose to the grindstone," and it was nip and tuck between the two old-time rivals. Far on the outside, his jockey sitting far back in the saddle to steady himself, Indian Fields swung around the turn. The black streak down his face stood out like an arrow; his ample mane and tail were flying in the wind like gonfalons. Onward he came, with an irresistible rush, striking the track with terrific hoof beats as he lengthened out for home.

"Hey there, boy, see that striped horse," yelled a score of Matador's or Lights o' London's partisans.

Both jockeys looked quickly at their unreckoned foe and dug their spurs deeper. A lull fell on the stand; it was to be one race in a thousand. The distance down the stretch was short; Lights o' London's jockey pulled his mount across the track to avoid a possible bumping match with Matador to give him freer action. This lost him a second at least, but he caught his stride, rushing ahead with a notable display of courage. At the far end of the stand, Indian Fields passed his two competitors and romped under the wire an easy winner by five lengths. A spontaneous cheer went up from the stand; it was a well-won struggle. Lights o' London beat out Matador by a length. Behind them, jaded and worn, trailed in General Coxey, Cold Deck, Cheerful Mary, and Little Christmas, in the order named. Little Christmas, it must be said, was more of a sprinter than a distance horse.

The timers hung up 1:46 as the time, beating the track record by six seconds. A great crowd assembled around the winner; his mysterious antecedents and odd markings made him an object of curiosity. In the crowd, there was one sad-hearted youth; Martin Fryer refused to believe that the best horse had won, the jockey in driving Lights o' London across the track at a time when every leap counted was the cause of his defeat—and the loss of Agnes.

After cooling off the doughty black horse, he made arrangements to ship home the next morning; he wanted no more racing. As he walked to the freight house, he gazed up sadly at the dusk-encompassed height of Lookout Mountain, which was to have been the opening scene of his happiness, had only Lights o' London won. He felt too sick at heart to go to see Agnes that night. The next morning, after he had loaded his string, he wended his way to her modest cottage. The house was closed, and several stout women, with their sleeves rolled up, stood outside the gate talking loudly and gesticulating. Martin started to enter when one of the women stopped him.

"There's no use going in, mister man; they're all away. That pretty girl Agnes disappeared at the fair after the running race last night. They think she's gone off with a horseman; why those fellows are worse on the girls than the picture show men."

Martin, overcome with a cowardly fear, the inward form of his loneliness turned about and returned to his box car.

In another half an hour, the car was on its way, shunting out past Lookout Mountain. The autumnal tints were even more distinct than on Monday in the clear light, the yellows now predominating. As he gazed from the open door of the car at the pine-tipped summit, the thought flashed through his mind:

"Maybe Agnes climbed to the top of the mountain last night, even though Lights o' London didn't win; she might be there now; I ought to go back and see."

Then the narrow, cowardly streak mingled with a thought of her ill-treatment of him in the past, and images of ease and home got the mastery.

"Even if she is up there, I'd not climb that mountain for any girl; let her come after me," he said as he pulled to the sliding door.

XVIII

TWO ROSES

(Story of Mount Julian)

"WALTER PATER," said the antiquarian, "in his chapter in Marius called 'White Nights,' speaks of 'The mystery of so-called white things.' They are, according to a German authority whom he quotes, 'ever an after-thought; the doubles or seconds, of real things,' the red rose came; first, the white rose afterward."

That was the reason, apparently, why my love for the beautiful blue-eyed Cleise seemed only a reflected counterpart of my romantic episode with the black-eyed Hermionie. And that was why after an association that bid fair to end in matrimony, it reached the "high water mark" by sending a birthday card to Hermionie telling her of an intended marriage, which never took place. And that was why, when I posted the card, m the presence of Cleise, I felt a sudden pang of sorrow that, through a marriage, I would belong to Hermionie no longer.

As long as I was single, I still was hers in spirit; a marriage would sever the tie. And yet Cleise was so much like Hermionie that at times I was startled, like her in everything except in coloring. I had been first attracted to her for that reason; she was a veritable double, or second, or counterpart, in blonde coloring. Hermionie had never been mine; our romance had been so delightfully vague that I had never asked her how much she cared for me; it was continued to the point of love-making and declarations with Cleise, but the finale was as nebulous as my last evening with Hermionie. It was predestined that Cleise was to hear what Hermionie had never heard, the words of a love that lasted unchanged for years but were to sink into oblivion unrecorded. Cleise was the mirror in which was reflected every detail of my ill-starred affection.

Can it be that we love a dark person more intensely and lastingly than a blonde? Surely we do if the fair person is only the reflected image of a black-eyed ideal. When I shut my eyes for inward contemplation, Hermionie, I always see more clearly than Cleise. And yet, in life, I had never mentioned a word of love to the dark girl, while to the blonde, I had made clear my passion, not only in speech but in letters and almost daily verses. However, I have liked more blondes than brunettes. By the way, I wonder where those verses are now, as her wedding day approaches? She bought a Japanese silver jewel case to put them in, but that was in the days before she had yielded to her Fate. Discarded verses suffer a worse ending than discarded photographs. I got my faded tintype back from Hermionie and Cleise, but I never asked for the verses. They have gone to that borne of oblivion which swallows up old race-horses, old show-girls, old bric-a-brac. I will always believe that Cleise came into my life to continue my soul's fealty to Hermionie. It might have wavered were it not for her—but now it is over its giddy period and is as solid as a concrete light-house on a rock.

I will never forget the first time I saw Hermionie. It was the first epoch of my love-life. I was at a railway station, waiting for the Northern Express. Why is it that our sweetest moments come before a separation? It seems to emphasize that losing is loving. It was in the clear light of a June afternoon; the intense radiance of the summer sun was upon us, intensifying the deep green of the maple trees, the rose bushes, the sparks of humidity glistening from the rails. I had been driven to the depot half an hour before train time, and I was nervous—at the delay, I thought. I know now that it was the nervous apprehension that comes to a person before some important event. Presently I saw three very young girls approaching; the oldest was less than sixteen, and I was five years older than the youngest. As they drew near, I observed that while all three had very dark hair, only one had thick eyes. They were all pretty and dainty enough, but only one could be called beautiful. That one was the girl with the darkest hair and black eyes. A description of her appearance at that time is a description of her as she is today, for she hasn't changed a particle in all these eleven years. God was pleased with her and ordained that she should never be different. Besides, a changing person cannot be the bulwark of a love that lingers in the innermost depths of the spirit, which is unchangeable.

I remember first of all that her figure was very slim and very straight; hers was the most erect, yet the most graceful form that I have ever seen, excepting Cleise, her golden shadow. Her thick hair was black, a brown-black, not a blue-black, but her eyes were the blackest of ivory black that ever sparkled from between two pairs of shadowy lashes. She had dark eyebrows, prettily arched. Hers was the most beautiful nose I have ever seen on a human face; it must have been the nose of the dryads, the wood-nymphs, the Nereida—I must admit it was prettier than Cleise, which is saying a good deal, as everyone is aware. There was a slight arch to the bridge of Hermionie's nose, but it was saved from Quaker severity by turning up just a trifle at the tip, giving a vivacity to her expression, the secret of eternal youth. Yet the nostrils turned downward, which is a sign of mental excellence. I am a great believer in noses; a nose is either a bridge or a barrier. And, Hermionie has the most beautiful nose I have ever seen. Her upper lip was short, of Grecian shortness, but her exquisitely curved lips were pitifully thin. It was the visible expression, surely, of some spiritual bitterness if we concede anything to the science of Lavater. I have always been partial to full lips, as I have been to blondes, yet I prefer Hermionie's to any girl's mouth I have ever seen. I do not mean that I would prefer to kiss it, for I never have except in dreams; I mean, I prefer to look at it as a triumph of Nature's art. It was the most expressive feature of an uncommonly expressive face. There was a good outline to her chin and throat; her little pink ears had a peculiar formation; instead of being pendulous, the lobes grew to the sides of the face, like in certain statues of fauns. This gave a quaint archness to her expression. Even at fifteen Hermionie was extremely pale, not the waxy pallor of ill-health, but the rugged whiteness of intellectuality. Just as there are blondes and blondes, there are various textures of paleness. This was the mental picture I absorbed as I watched her with her young friends walking about on the platform that summer afternoon. Twenty minutes of contemplation did not reveal to me all her charms; I seemed to be just beginning when the whistle of the approaching train brought all the travelers, baggage handlers, cabmen, and idlers to attention.

Our eyes had met several times, and they met again as I climbed into the day coach. I looked back from the car window; I could see the three girls laughing and chatting with the older sister of one of them, a blonde whom they had come to the station to meet. As I knew one of the young girls by sight, there was a chance I could become acquainted with Hermionie. I felt that I had seen the rarest being who had ever crossed my path; she seemed most harmonious to my spiritual faculties, and surely we would meet again. Through the hours, while the Northern Express thundered along, I sat rapt in a dream world with Hermionie. I thought of the past; I had seen no one anyways like her; I strained my spiritual sight to look into the future; I never would see a being quite the same. Boy-like, I must have found a loophole in the canvas of the infinite, as the years never did bring her counterpart, except her fair shadow, Cleise.

Months rolled around before I was able to revisit the abode of Hermionie. At times it seemed as if I would never get there—the time passed slower, the task more difficult of accomplishment because its realization meant so much to me. If I had understood the driving orders of destiny—do it now, or not at all—I would have waited over another day and met her—but as a boy, 'tomorrow' seemed nearer and more positive than it does at present. The difficulties in returning to Hermionie's locality taught me I was becoming a man, a dweller in a real and less accommodating universe. But I returned nevertheless, in September, when the trees were just beginning to change color. I was introduced to the older sister of one of the girls, the one whom Hermionie and her friends had gone to meet, and through her became acquainted with my rare ideal's companion.

The first thing she asked me was if I remembered that day at the station; we had a pleasant chat concerning it. They knew who I was, it seemed, and were wondering whether I recognized them. The next afternoon after this pleasant introduction, I met this young girl just as she was coming from her home on a shady street that ran along the river bank. I stopped for a few moments to converse, and when I turned to go my way, I saw, to my surprise, standing beside us, Hermionie and her other young girlfriend. I don't know to this day what became of the other two girls; Hermionie and I were left together amid the deepening shadows that September afternoon.

I suggested that we take a walk, and she acquiesced; when two people like one another, one never refuses a wish of the other. There were many maple leaves on the sidewalk, and we kicked them as we walked; they sounded like the roar of some miniature ocean. We passed the Judge's mansion, and that grand, kindly old gentleman was sitting on his favorite rocker, talking to some political henchman; he recognized us and smiled merrily. At the far end of his shady yard stood an ancient fountain separated from the sidewalk only by a low iron fence. In its plashy bowls, in the late afternoon, robins were bathing. We stopped to admire the pretty creatures, dashing the water about with their nut-brown wings like tiny tritons. Our hands on the scroll-work of the fence, I was telling her how I always used to stop at midnight when returning from dances to listen to the music of the fountain, sometimes standing in that same place for fifteen minutes; how one night I thought I saw the ghost of a little man, with a forked beard, but that he turned out to be the reflection of the moon through the trees, on the fence and shrubbery. I told her about the fairy parks up on the Pike; if you visit them on a moonlight night with someone you love and who loves you as much in return, you will see the fairies; otherwise, you cannot. It is a true test of love. We got no further than the realm of the old fountain that afternoon; the Judge must have wondered what we found there that was so interesting.

It was nearly supper time, a pale gold sunset gleamed through the foliage, and the old jurist was leaving the porch as we passed by the mansion again. But at the fountain, I had gotten to know Hermionie, and an intimate congeniality was revealed that was destined to last through the years without often seeing or hearing of her. I recollect telling her, just as the last robin saucily shook his feathers to fly to the treetops, 'I feel as if I knew you so well that even if I never see you again, it will always be the same.' But we were destined to meet in the future but at wide intervals. Sometimes a year would pass, but I always felt unchanged.

When a more tangible romance came into my life, hers were the last letters I burned in the grate that May morning. And a year later, when that romance was no more, I found, to my joy, another packet of her letters in that scrawled, irregular hand in a filing case in my office. I had destroyed other letters from that same case; it was so miraculous that those must have taken on an invisible wrapper to escape the conflagration. They were to cheer me, simple, good-natured, girlish letters in the darkest of hours. Hermionie had married sometime before my romance culminated, and was happy in her new life. In the melancholy tide which beset me, I needed the kind consolation of her radiant memory.

One beautiful afternoon in the early springtime, I was traveling on a train. At a small station, a young girl wearing a fresh white tulip, accompanied by her mother, got in. She was above medium size, of the slender, very erect type that I admired; she was about the same age as Hermionie when our romance was at its height.

The more I looked at her, the more I marveled at the resemblance of her features and expression to those of my former sweetheart—except that she was an ash blonde, and Hermionie was dark as midnight. There may not have been as much aquilinity to the nose and a trifle more fullness to the lips, but these were fine distinctions; barring coloring, they were counterparts. I liked her, I wondered who she was, I wanted to meet her just as I had Hermionie, and because blonde though she was, she reminded me of Hermionie. She was her 'double or second' . . . 'half-real, half-material,' the golden reflection through the years of a long-absent love. I hoped that someday I would meet her, though I had no idea who she might be, mostly because she gave gratification to my soul's hunger that few could appease.

Months later, at a dinner party, who should appear in the drawing room, but the beautiful blonde girl herself. I couldn't have been more amazed if it had been Hermionie. I found that her name was Cleise, and I was to escort her to dinner. When the time came, and she spoke to me, I was further surprised to find that she talked with the same peculiar inflection so characteristic of Hermionie. It is hard to describe how Hermionie or Cleise talked. It was not a nasal twang, or a sectional dialect, for both were well-educated and used the best English. It was a tone of voice just their own, that's all. You who have heard them speak to know what I mean and how pleasing it is to listen to them. Cleise had the same enthusiasm, the unbridled exuberance of youth, of youth that has

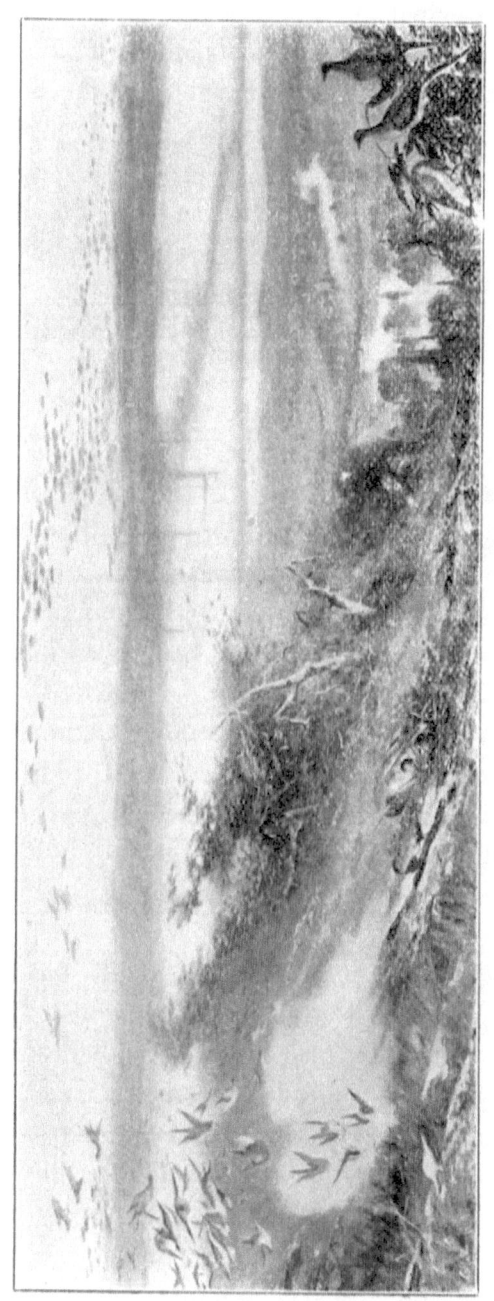

THE FLIGHT OF THE WILD PIGEONS
(From the painting by C. H. Shearer,)
in the possession of the Author

never had a crossed hope. Throughout the dinner, I sought to learn her point of view, it was original and clever, but it was Hermionie's, as well. And yet Cleise had never seen Hermionie; perhaps similar racial strains flowed in her veins; their ancestors may have lived in the same villages in the Highlands or the Pyrenees. But it was a delight to hear Cleise talk; it was also a delight to look at her. She was as if I had caused a sculptor to make a golden image of the unseen Hermionie. But I did not tell her she reminded me of someone I had known, for she didn't; she *was* Hermionie, her double, her second, her re-issue. I couldn't bear to part from her that night; I wanted to listen to more of her peculiarly intoned speech; it is the quaintest inflection of English that I have ever heard. When she left the room, I overheard several men say, 'She is the most beautiful young woman in town.'

I saw Cleise several times after that, but only at wide intervals. But I transgressed over the spiritual boundary; I told her how much I loved her; I literally began where I had left off with Hermionie. I found her as responsive a sweetheart as Hermionie had been as a friend, but she was more than that—Oh, what shall I call her, a more-than-friend, *an intimate companion, a dear associate.* We took little excursions together to spots of rare scenic beauty, historic localities, and the homes of congenial mutual friends. To the happy mental intercourse was added the thrill of acknowledged affection. With Hermionie, it had always been a word left unsaid, a sudden pause, a silence ever since regretted. But I have always been shy; it pains me now to utter a word of love, though I feel that my heart is full to overflowing.

On one of these pleasant little excursions to the old home of the immortal Bayard Taylor, I recollected that it was within a day of Hermionie's birthday. I always had sent her cards on this occasion, even from foreign lands; I did not want to break the sequence, even though I was with the fair Cleise. 'I am going to send a birthday card to someone I used to know and who reminds me very much of you.' After all, I had to make use of the old platitude. But in this case, I said it to satisfy myself that to Cleise, I was true in thought and deed. It was a poor-looking postcard, too, with only a view of the village church on it, but it had to suffice. I laid it on the writing shelf in the cozy little post office and wrote, 'I wish you a very happy birthday,' and signed my initials. I walked over to the letter drop to toss it in when something restrained me. I looked at the card to make sure I had addressed it right, that I had said nothing which might offend a happily married woman. I walked back to the shelf and wrote below the other words, 'I am thinking about getting married.' The spiritual restraint was satisfied, and I dropped the card through the slot unhampered.

Cleise, who was watching me all the while, said, "Oh, what a funny man you are; you give as much time to that card as if you were applying for a post in the diplomatic service."

She would have thought me funnier had she known what I had added to my greeting, expectations of matrimony without ever having proposed. Later that evening, on our homeward journey to the great city, I ought to have asked Cleise to marry me. She was just as responsive as she had ever been that night; if she cared for me enough, she would have said 'yes.' But I always had a feeling when with a girl that translated into language would be 'perhaps she doesn't care for me.' It had given me many heartaches before; this night, I feared to go ahead. How awful to confess such cowardice! I should have realized that if a girl cared enough to go with me on these little outings, she would be liable to stand me as a permanent companion, *perhaps*. But the cars ran swifter than usual that night; there were other subjects to discuss.

I remember how Cleise shuddered when we got out of the hot train at midnight and drew her neck-scarf of fisher's fur tightly about her face. I would have loved to have taken her in my arms then; I was always courageous at the wrong time. But I hoped someday I would marry her; she was so beautiful, so congenial. But the wish without the word is far from the accomplishment. I never got any nearer to a marriage than sending that card. Two weeks later, Cleise departed for Europe. I should have dropped everything and followed her, but I didn't. I contented myself with going to the steamer to see her off. But as I look back on it now, I had a presentiment that morning I would never see her again. We were talking in the gloomy passageway near her stateroom; no one was about; the thought came to me, 'Why not ask her for a kiss? I may never see her again.' I stifled the soul's cry, and we parted in a conventional manner,

I and the companion of so many little spiritual adventures. Then for weeks, I engrossed myself with various occupations, so much so that I did not notice the matter-of-fact tone of Cleise's letters. Nor did I pay much attention to the fact that a new photograph of herself which she promised to send me as soon as she reached the other side, never came.

One bright May afternoon, when I should have been out-of-doors mingling with the happiness of awakening nature, a letter was handed to me. It was from Paris, from Cleise, addressed in her scratchy, uneven hand, so reminiscent of Hermionie. I dropped the scientific problem, the theory of conic sections, on which I was working and set to reading it. To my dismay, it told of her engagement to a young man whom she had known anterior to meeting me. He had come back from India and won her with a fiery, impetuous wooing. I was heartbroken at first; an awful pall sank down upon me, which I could not reason away. To ease the pain, I hurried out into the sunshine and wandered under the budding trees. I had not gone far before I saw in a front yard a small bed of white tulips, typical of Cleise's fair loveliness. It was her symbol as a golden shadow, a distant echo, a light imprint of my mental photograph of Hermionie. Now the shadow was gone; I was face to face with reality. Like there is an end to every afternoon, there is an end to every shadow. But there are certain fixed verities that always remain; Hermionie was one. I judged her more clearly, now that the shadow of Cleise was dissipated. I was alone with the specter of what might have been. All I could see in the past was the miserable botch I had made out of my life. And the future loomed dark and uncertain as a torrent at night below an unsteady bridge.

These were terrible thoughts on a May afternoon when the orioles and the larks were in such good humor. I had lost reality and could not lay my hands on the shadow. Someone else had plucked the red rose; now I found the white rose transplanted in another person's garden. If neither Hermionie nor Cleise cared for me, my disappointment was like an armistice after a bloodless war. To have had either turn me away would have left an unhealable wound in my heart of hearts. But each had passed gently out of my life. Yet, what is the difference between a red and a white rose? Each waked the noblest sentiments in me and aroused the worthiest ambitions, but the result was the same, of reality and shadow. When a man grieves for a woman he has never asked to marry, it is the thought of what might have been that tortures him; when it is over a woman who refused him, it is for an actuality. Each grief has its own particular poignancy, *I suppose.*

I came back from my walk, resigned to fate, and turned again to my scientific research. But my soul must have been unquiet as I had to read Cleise's letter again before I retired at midnight. And now the invitations to her wedding have been issued; the happy date is drawing near. This clear afternoon, while seated on the summit of Mount Julian, gazing over the beautiful Bald Eagle Valley, the fairest valley in the world to those who love it best, my thoughts turned to Cleise and how different this scene with its foliage "a blaze of scarlet and gold" from that foggy, muggy morning, so confined and stifled, when I talked with her in the passageway of the *Mauritania.* Here I noted a jaybird's shrilling, there the raucous droning of the hoists. I wished she were here with me; the thought was as if a shadow had swept across my path, and the smile vanished from my lips. Love is a very choice emotion; it is a pity that we cannot grasp it when it comes our way, but who ever heard tell of grasping a shadow? I looked down the valley; I could see ridge after ridge of the Bald Eagle Mountains on one side, the great, cumbersome hump-backed mass of the Alleghanies on the other. In the far distance, from the ochre-hued valley between, rose the thin blue veil of autumnal haze, where valley blended with sky and infinity, where fact was one with fancy, for the glory of Indian summer.

It was back there, where the ideal and the real were so closely interwoven, where sunlight and haze gave out harmonious light in vanished years, that I had loved a tangible reality, Hermionie. She had, then and now, burned deeper and stronger and truer into my soul than the fair and spectacular Cleise. She had been my chance of happiness which comes only once to every man—God makes as many signals as He can to "go ahead," if we fail to take heed, we are eternally lost; the best we can find thereafter is only shadow, rainbow, the white rose.

XIX

THE SORCERESS
(Story of Warrior's Mountain)

T HE GYPSIES were camping in Warrior's Gap. They were not the genial, blue-eyed tribe that Bill Stanley led, but foreign Gypsies of a darker and swarthier type. They had a string of six wagons and the usual collection of horses, ponies, and dogs. All were a pretty tired lot when they selected an abandoned pasture lot, near the bubbling spring, as the best place for a twenty-four hours' rest.

They were traveling a full day behind schedule, as one of their number, a young woman, had been arrested for flimflamming a "simp" who had come to have his fortune told. Bond was given, and the party permitted to move on, but it was putting them a day late to all their points, and the season was well on the wane.

After tying the perspiring horses to trees, they sat about on the grass, in the lea of their mural-decorated wagons, smoking and discussing the incidents of the day. Their brief repose at an end, they began building fires and foraging. They were a picturesque lot, take them all in all, much more so than Bill Stanley's bigger and fairer complexioned aggregation.

The sun set clear that night, its colors markedly similar to the blaze of the Gypsy campfires.

Dusk softened into night, and above the Bald Eagle mountain, a full moon rose in all its effulgent glory. It was when the moon shone down on them that the strange nomads seemed most alive. There is said to be some mystic connection between moonlight and witches; there is even a more intimate bond between moonlight and Gypsies. They were all animated by its silvery light; some gathered into groups of two or three and chanted weird melodies.

It was in the midst of their celebrating that a two-horse buggy containing a couple of travelers appeared in sight of the camp. They had been in Spruce Creek Valley and, after taking supper in Warrior's Mark, were on their way to some village in the valley of the Bald Eagles. They had made a quick trip across the mountain, the chill, frosty air stimulating the horses more than words or whip.

When they met the Gypsies, sitting about their cheery fires, the temptation was too great; they stopped and entered into conversation with them. They had heard of the Gypsy caravan in the southern valleys, of the young girl's arrest for filching a pocketbook from a too trustful youth. They vowed, when they stopped, that they would allow no fortune-telling. A girl of such low caliber as to rob a patron could not very well be gifted with any such thing as second sight.

"She would have foretold her own downfall," said one of the travelers, an antiquarian.

"But she may have felt that a legal complication would do her good; one can never tell what cosmic wisdom figures out," replied the other.

The Gypsies proved entertaining hosts, and the antiquarian sought to extract from them some memories of their past to form an opinion as to their origin. They looked like such pure descendants of the Hindoo famine sufferers who wandered into Europe hunting food nine or ten centuries ago and have been wandering ever since that they might have proved valuable "historical landmarks." But the best they could do was to recollect traditions of fifty years before when they were trailing through Assyria.

While the travelers were talking with the oldest man in the party, who said he was "about sixty-three," a well-developed young woman, who looked to be about twenty-one, approached and sat down beside them. There was a curliness to her dark hair, a whiteness to the eyeballs of her dark blue eyes, that gave her a certain individuality. She listened intently to all they had to say, keeping track of every sentence with her lips and not with her eyes, as is the case with more highly civilized persons.

When the old man relapsed into silence, she leaned over on her elbow and asked the antiquarian if she could tell his fortune. He had a habit of saying "no" at first to everything and then changing his mind, but he changed the *no* into a *yes* before she noticed it. His friend looked at him dismayed; all his ridicule of these wayward soothsayers had come to naught. The young woman looked at him intently.

"Say," she said, "I like to tell your future; you have some of the same power that I have."

From that, she went on predicting many things, including a serious illness, which was not very cheerful to hear. Then she delved a short distance into the past.

"You were married once, you have a little son, whom you have never held in your arms, but you will never marry again."

The antiquarian pressed her for a reason, although matrimony did not appeal to him very much at the time.

"I cannot tell you myself why that will be, but I know this much; it will all be revealed to you some night this coming November one year."

Further than that, she could tell nothing; she could divine that the explanation would be given but said there was an impenetrable cloud between her and the whys and wherefores. After she had finished, a curious smile played over her full red lips an instant, but she made no remark.

"What makes you smile like that?" inquired the antiquarian, who was quite won over.

"Oh, nothing—yes, of course, I will tell you—won't you please look in your coat pocket and see if your money wallet is there, I have just been released from jail for taking one."

"Oh, I know that story, it is all over the valleys," the antiquarian answered, "but I don't believe it."

"Very well, look in your pocket," said the sorceress. The young man did as requested but found the pocketbook missing.

"That's very funny," he said, "after all my travels and experiences, I fall as easily as any common garden simp."

The girl laughed out loud and rose to her feet. As she did so, she extracted the wallet from the bosom of her shirtwaist, handing it to him. "When you were driving across the mountain," she resumed, "you were saying that you didn't believe in Gypsy fortune-tellers, that anyone was a fool to bother with them, that the Nittany Valley farmer in question deserved all he got, now didn't you say that?"

The antiquarian was glad to admit the truth but claimed that he now thought otherwise.

"I don't know whether you do or not, in your heart," said the young woman, "you say you do because you have 'taken a shine' to me personally, but secretly you think I am only a shrewd guesser. You will believe in my powers after next November one year."

The hour was late, so the travelers bade goodbye to their unconventional acquaintances and started for the little village across the valley. All the rest of the way, the antiquarian kept thinking of the bizarre Gypsy girl and wondering how much she had penetrated into the workshops of destiny. Some folks have been behind the scenes; surely, perhaps she was one of them. It was Balzac who remarked that the Creator poured his messages into some very frail vessels. One has only to think of Henry VIII, Joe Smith, Brigham Young, the Fox sisters, and the founder of Christian Science, with her many names and occupations.

Time rolled on; one by one, the predictions of the Gypsy came to pass. Most of them were very minor details of life, but one or two were events of some importance. The serious illness took place, and for weeks the antiquarian's life was despaired of. Oft-times he thought of the Gypsy's words that he would get well; it could not be otherwise. They proved a beacon of hope to his sick room.

The months moved along as rapidly as a flowing tide that no one could stem. The harvest moon, the drying leaves, the hoar frost, the chilly nights, all indicated the passing of summer. September swept by like some gorgeous pageant, as did October. November was ushered in with one of the most impressive days in the life of this young man. He had hardly expected any revelation of his destiny, but the events of that day could never be forgotten. He had heard that a panther, killed by one Lewis Dorman in the late sixties, was stuffed and on exhibition in the old academy in the quaint old town of New Berlin. He was engaged in some natural history research at the time. He had visited this abandoned county seat seven or eight years before and wandered, hat in hand, under the shade trees surrounding the then-deserted academy. He had sat on the porch at the ancient tavern stand beneath the swinging sign of the Golden Swan, listening to the reminiscences of the greybeards of Indians, ghosts, and panthers. None of them had mentioned that there was a stuffed panther in the schoolhouse, the famous Dorman panther, at that, about which so much had been written, so he had doubts as to the correctness of the legend.

But accompanied by the same congenial friend who was with him the night of the meeting with the sorceress at Warrior's Gap, he started for the old settlement beyond Shamokin Mountain. It was a buoyant, blowy, cloud-swept afternoon when they left the livery barn in Lewisburg. Their first objective point was the hilltop, or "New" cemetery, on the outskirts of the town. A cemetery, especially one on high ground, always is at its best when high winds shake the Norway spruces and bend the arborvitaes almost double; when the distant mountains are a purple-brown, and the sun a golden disc in the whirling mass of smoky clouds, when the gold-fish in the fountain feel too congealed to swim about freely, when dry leaves and bits of hydrangea blooms chase one another along the pebbled paths, when the old gravedigger turns up the collar of his faded military coat, when an occasional shaft of pale sunlight throws into bold relief some crumbling inscription. No cemetery was ever better fitted as the resting place of the glorious dead than the hilltop "God's acre" in old Lewisburg.

Perhaps the grave which impressed the antiquarian and his friend the most was the simple marble slab above all that is mortal of one of the bravest and noblest of mothers, Mary Q. Brady, who died in 1783, wife of Captain John Brady, the pioneer and mother of the ill-fated Captain James Brady. "All tears are wiped from her eyes," is the modest epitaph. Her illustrious progeny are buried in many different localities, but though she sleeps far from most of her descendants, she is tended by a host of precious memories. Not far distant is the tomb of Colonel John Kelly, one of the heroic figures of the Revolutionary War and a pioneer of Buffalo Valley, who is also remembered as having killed, in 1801, the last buffalo in Pennsylvania. On higher ground is the neatly-fenced plot of the old Slifer family, the most notable member being Colonel Eli Slifer, whose name is familiar to all who cherish in their families Civil War Commissions; he was Governor Curtin's Secretary of the Commonwealth. Nearby is the classic marbled enclosure of the Cameron Clan.

Colonel James Cameron, who was killed while leading his regiment, the immortal 79th New York Highlanders, at the Battle of Bull Run, in 1861, lies near the imposing shaft, and Captain William Cameron, his brother, not far away.

There is also a tottering stone that marks the last resting place of Eliza Pfonts, an aged aunt of all the older Camerons. Nearer to the main entrance is a smooth marble upright marking the grave of Lieutenant Andrew Gregg Tucker, nephew of the War Governor, who died in his nineteenth year, on July 5, 1863, from wounds received at Gettysburg. Facing the iron gates and not far from the fishpond is a slab of weather-beaten brownstone, the tomb of George Derr, the son of Lewis Derr, the famous founder of "Tarrstown," or Lewisburg.

Had it not been for the lessening of the pale gold disc of the sun as it retreated towards the White Deer Mountain pinnacles and the fiercer sweeping of the gale, the two sympathetic pilgrims might have tarried longer. As it was, they bade *au re voir* to the kindly, well-informed superintendent, who is a war veteran, and started out the broad pike for the road leading across the mountains to New Berlin. They passed the deserted Lochiel Tavern, once the scene of great activity and hilarity, in the days before the building of the L. & T. snatched the trade from the teamsters and stage drivers. In the far distance, on the brow of a hill, rose the graceful spire of Dreisbach Church, the "church of the three streams." Beside it, as grey and cold as the autumnal sky, probably as himself, was the granite shaft erected in memory of the deeds of Samuel Maclay, an obscure United States Senator, by a state which has left unmarked the tomb of Colonel Conrad Weiser at Womelsdorf. Maclay's bones must tremble, his ghost must stalk and gibber on All Souls' Night, as he gave instructions that he await the "last trump" with Presbyterian exclusiveness in a private plot on his farm, on the opposite hill. Despite this, nearly a hundred years later, he was dug up and reinterred in Dreisbach churchyard, among the Germans, "because the monument would look better there."

Dark looms the level ridge of Shamokin Mountain over which the travelers must pass before reaching the tree-bowered precincts of New Berlin. The drive is long; the horses tug with might and main to cross the ridge. On the very summit, they encountered a snowstorm that hid everything in its downy mantle. At length, the ruddy village lights are seen, shining eye-like through the leaf-bared maples. The horses, when they reach the level street beneath the double row of giant trees, strike a nimbler gait and soon reach the snug tavern stand with the swinging sign of the Golden Swan.

All is brightness, good nature, and warmth that beams out on the frosty twilight. The travelers alight, an ancient hostler with only one eye and a patriarchal grey beard climbs into the rig and drives it back to the stable yard. Supper is just on the table; they have time to register and wash and then take their seats in the cozy lamp-lit dining room. Once, this room entertained bands of laughing, roistering rivermen homeward bound from Safe Harbor. Tonight there is only one other guest besides themselves, a tired-looking country lawyer, in town to claim an inheritance for a client in Iowa.

The waitress, a buxom, good-natured Pennsylvania German girl, flounces in and out through the swinging door, serving neatly and quickly. Roast goose and apple sauce is the principal dish; it is very good. A plate of freshly roasted chestnuts that had been in their burrs on the trees a couple of hours before and, as a special compliment, some cider with just the right tang to it are the relishes; pumpkin pie nicely spiced is the dessert.

But the air of cheer, the atmosphere of the Halloween just passed, sweetest and purest of all our holidays, pleases most; the travelers are loathe to leave the soothing lamp-glow. After supper, they sat and talked awhile in the parlor, but there was a dampness and a melancholy reflected even in the family portraits in their oval frames, which brought thoughts of bed earlier than usual. All three travelers carrying lighted candles and pitchers of ice water ascended the stairs just as the tall clock on the landing struck nine. As the antiquarian was locking his door, he recollected that his mind had been so engrossed on the big events of history, the picturesqueness of the inn, that he had omitted to ask the landlord about the Dorman panther.[2] But he recalled that this was All Souls' Night. The room he was assigned to was in the front of the house, on the sec-

2. See Appendix B.

ond floor. It was cold and damp but possessed the delicious odor of an old-fashioned room. The single window, eight-paned, and slow of locomotion, looked out on the park-like street. There was a kerosene street lamp directly across the way in front of the former courthouse, but most of its unsteady gleams were lost through the heavy branches of the trees. The huge four-poster took up most of the room, but there was space for two small chairs and a walnut, marble-topped washstand. A mirror, gilt-framed, hung above it. On the wall, at the side of the bed, so that the occupant could touch the walnut frame with his hand, was an ancient frame containing some wax flowers.

The antiquarian laughed and thought of his experience with the Gypsy fortune-teller over a year before when he proved himself wax in her hands by letting her get his wallet so easily. But she was a wonderful woman; would all her predictions come true? Later on, he was sorry he had thought of her at all before he fell asleep. What subsequently happened had to undergo the suspicion of being a dream caused by his waking thoughts. But he consoled himself with the belief that if he had not thought of her at bedtime, the events could be charged to subconscious memories. No one could rob him of his belief that there is a supernatural world of some kind. He was feeling at peace with existence; its turmoil and strife bothered him not as he sank into repose.

This is invariably the time when tragedy or tumult stalks into our midst. During the hours from nine-thirty until twelve, the sleeper's dreams, if any, dwelt on the glorious past, the historic panorama called up by the visit to the New Cemetery, the drive through Buffalo Valley. At the witching hour of twelve, sleep became less intense; consciousness was slowly returning. When wakefulness finally mastered, he opened his eyes; the room was inky black, and the street lamp had been extinguished an hour earlier.

He placed his hands behind his head, which was a custom he had, and determined to think for half an hour before returning to dreamland. As he roused himself, he became aware that he could see about the room, though no *light* was visible. He counted the chairs, two; the washstand, one; the frame containing the wax flowers, one; the mirror, one; the bed was surely there, yes, all the fixtures of the room were in their places.

He began noticing a strange vapor sweeping in the half-opened window. Did it arise from Penn's Creek, or was it generated in the dense forests on Montour's Ridge? There was a sparkle to the mist that seemed unfamiliar; it kept swirling and coiling about as if impelled by an unseen force. It began assembling itself by the bedside, assuming the shape of a spiral, gradually solidifying. As it turned and twisted, it seemed to take on human form, the outlines of a woman in a silver-spangled ball costume. Natural colors were faintly apparent, the features preternaturally distinct. From a formless mass, it became a ravishingly beautiful young girl of perhaps twenty years of age. Her heavy wavy hair was ash-blonde, the most exquisite of all colors; the brows and lashes were dark, the eyes full and grey. There was a slight upward tilt at the end of the aquiline nose; the upper lip was short, an "Austrian lip," both were full and clearly cut. The chin was beautifully rounded, the throat smooth and white.

She was above medium height; her slender, erect figure showed off in bold relief in her spangled gown. Her arms were gloved, but the gloves were pushed back from the shapely white hands. She stood by the bedside a full minute, irresolute, her lips moving as if she wished to speak. The antiquarian rose up, his lips twitching but fearing to speak lest it dissolve her into thin air. The thought of the sorceress flashed through his mind. This was the month when she declared his destiny would reveal itself, and All Souls' Night. But why was this cold little bedroom at the Golden Swan chosen as the place? He mustered his courage and spoke to the apparition,

"It is a pleasure to see you here tonight", he said in a tone of voice that was not his own. "How did you find me in this remote corner of the world?" He took for granted that one so elegant as she belonged to the "big world."

The wraith found it difficult to articulate. Her lips twitched and twisted; the words would not shape themselves. At last, in a voice slightly above a whisper and with the most conscious effort, she unfolded her story.

"I was to have been your destiny, that was decided years ago, we were to have met this coming January in Philadelphia, and every fortuitous circumstance was to have worked towards our happiness. I was the one

woman who would have understood you, your love of music, art, literature, and science, who could have made the most out of your tempera-
mentally acute life. Ours was to have been a love that would have existed
unchanged through the years; it would have lasted even into the world
beyond, for there really is such a world. But alas, it is very different from
what any of us ever imagined. You had heard of me, but I knew nothing
of you until the day we were to meet, and then all would have conspired
to make you the happiest of men and me the happiest of women.

"But did you know that destiny has a habit of revoking its decrees?
In the mortal world, we are taught that fate and destiny are irrevocable,
inexorable. But nothing of the sort; destiny is most capricious. A week
ago, the cosmic forces veered about; I was not to be for you after all. I
met someone at a ball, and my heart or something was overcome; I will
marry him in April.

"Yet I do love you, but don't tell a soul."

The antiquarian leaned forward and took one of the hands of the
gorgeous apparition in his; he pressed it tight; it felt like a gardenia in
his grasp. He put his lips to it and kissed it long and deeply. The sense
of something in his hold suddenly left; he looked up; the lovely form
had gone. Over by the window, he saw a mist trailing out like a spangled
scarf; he thought he heard the word "farewell." Then came an ominous,
doleful silence. The room became black as the proverbial midnight. From
a shed in one of the alleys came the strident crowing of a chanticleer. The
night wind sent a shudder through the maple trees; he heard the swish of
occasional leaves falling on the flagstones. The odor of the old-fashioned
room became more distinct.

Was it true, or had it been all a dream; he had no token to prove the
visitation, only the memory of the Gypsy woman's prophecy. Why hadn't
he asked her if she had ever known of the voluptuous pocketbook-filch-
ing witch? Perhaps she could have established in him a firmer belief in
her powers.

The sight of this fair creature who was to have loved and understood
him was indeed enough to keep a man single for the rest of his life. How
could he contemplate marrying an average woman when he thought of
how a radiant and responsive creature might have been his own? But

was he worthy of her? Probably not; that may have been the reason why destiny canceled its fiat, or it may have been caprice. But worthy or unworthy, he could *go on* worshipping her; perhaps in some distant future year, she would revisit him in the night.

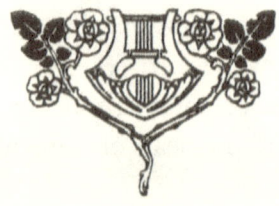

XX

UNREQUITED

(Story of Vail Mountain)

O UT IN the mountain pass, where the old-time furnace was located, is the badly shrunken remnant of an artificial pond, which once covered a dozen acres. It had been used in the days when the furnace was at "full blast," but now, its usefulness over, leaks were allowed to go unmended, it was fast dwindling back to its original size as a mountain rivulet.

In a semi-circle, around the steep banks of slag, which lined the pond, stood the deserted and decaying barracks of the vanished workmen. They were solidly built structures of yellow stone, two-storied, slate-roofed, and diamond-paned. Most of the doors were unhinged, many of the panes were broken, and the bats scurried in and out in full possession. Hosts of swifts flitted into the gaping chimneys; a pair of barn owls had a nest in one of them that was particularly dilapidated.

Across the pond rose the crumbling walls, the tumble-down chimneys of what had once been the furnace. Sumac, red-leaved in autumn, vied with the woodbine's scarlet tints to give artistic harmony to the ruins. In the background spread the dark branches of several large white pines, in contrast to the paler tints of the sapling-massed, coaled-over mountain. It was a desolate-looking area, one fitted for the habitation of a ghost. It seems a pity that acts of violence, which produce wandering shades, often occur in such lonesome spots. A ghost would find more comfort in a habitable sphere.

Where once had been the breast of the dam which created the pond, quite a little water still remained. It had once been the "deep hole" of the pond; even now, it was five feet deep in the dry season. But in the old days, the water was clear; now, it was almost boggy, the abode of newts, frogs, and skippers.

At sunset, a lone great blue heron, that bird the old settlers not inappropriately called the "gander snipe," was a regular visitor, finding the crop of tadpoles much to her liking. Her mate had long since been crucified on a barn door down in the valley, yet this one lingered on as she could not resist the rich pickings in the stagnant tarn. It was a comical sight to watch her chasing a lizard on the bank, looking all the world like a skirt-less woman running about in her corset cover. Persecuted as an "arch enemy" of the fish, she ate enough snakes, toads, lizards, and bugs to make her immune from the farmers' rapacity if they but understood. There were few persons crossing the mountain road these days, at least compared to the travel in the past. Even the farmhouses in the foothills were "going down." Nobody cared, and nobody wanted to stay; the big cities down the valley were too alluring.

The ghost that haunted the pool at the furnace was in grave danger of having no one to appear to after a while. Deserted houses lined the road beyond the empty barracks; even the farmers, further on, showed signs of dissatisfaction. But a ghost in such an unregenerate, unappreciative neighborhood must need be a poor, puny specimen of its kind. It was such a small, distorted ghost that the majority of those who saw it never credited it with being one. It, therefore, lost the only satisfaction that a ghost can have, the ability to impress or startle folks. Flitting about the pond after night, it was frequently mistaken by travelers for a belated "gander snipe." Time and time again, they made that hackneyed wish for a gun "to blow the top of its head off." But while a gander snipe would have small chance, no load of buckshot could damage the anatomy of a ghost.

Did you ever see a ghost assemble itself? First of all, you will notice a few tiny globules of transparent water floating in the dusky atmosphere. These will increase in numbers, dancing and shimmering like quicksilver. They will become more numerous, seemingly materializing from the gloom. As soon as there are a sufficient number, they will begin drawing together, and as the mass solidifies, assuming human proportions. Sometimes if there is enough cohesion or vitality in the particles, the natural colors of life will be reproduced. If it isn't a vigorous spirit, it will remain the color of water, or quicksilver, until it dissolves again. A spirit that can take on the colors of life will persist longer than a vale ghost, but the pale ghosts are much more plentiful. The ghost in natural colors is usually a silent specter; it attempts to deliver no message, and there is nothing to shock it into nothingness unless the destruction of its environment. The pale ghost generally has something to tell; when this is done, it disintegrates forever, even though its environment remains undisturbed.

The ghost at the furnace pool was pale and very indistinct, although it probably had no message to impart. But it was frail and filmy because, in life, it was only a wisp, a mite of humanity, a little red-haired hunchback girl. She was born when all was prosperity about the furnace. In fact, with her advent, the tide of ill luck, which later engulfed it, first appeared. Her father was a foreman in one of the departments and lived in a comfortable stone cottage a quarter of a mile down the road from the pond and the barracks. He was a steady, good-natured Englishman, highly respected by his friends and employers. He had married a good-looking German girl from Half Moon Valley, over somewhere near Gatesburg, and life started out auspiciously. The coming of a baby was a great event, as both were fond of children. When the little girl was born, she was said to be a most beautiful child and was idolized not only by her parents but by the entire settlement. She was a bright little thing, fond of pranks and full of activity.

When she grew to be three years old, she developed a habit of running to meet her father on his return from work. At first, this was considered "real cute," but when she came up the path, almost as far as the breast of the dam, it seemed as if she was running too big a risk. Her mother tried to watch her, but she would elude the indulgent parent. The mother could not talk cross to her, and neither could the father, so it was difficult to control her. When she ran out to meet her father, he always took her on his shoulder and carried her home. These were her proudest moments and his. It was an ideally happy home of the kind which ought to be met with more frequently. When the young people went to church on Sundays, they gave thanks for manifold blessings. It was a beautiful world; all was sunshine while things went their way.

One bright summer evening, when the young father was on his homeward way, he was surprised to see the little girl running towards him across the breast of the dam. It was a dangerous thing to do; on one side was the pool, twenty feet deep; on the other, the swift running spillway, with the sharp rocks below. He was so terrified that he shouted to the child to stop running at once. The loud voice bewildered her, and she stopped short, in so doing, losing her balance. She tripped over her feet and tumbled headlong down to the rocky gorge below the spillway. The father screamed in terror and ran to the scene of the disaster. He saw the child lying motionless on the rocks, with the spray from the overshoot just missing her face. A little more, and she would have drowned. He laid down his dinner bucket and clambered after his unfortunate darling. She was unconscious when he picked her up, and she hung over his arm as limp as a broken doll. He laid her on the breast of the dam and ran up to the workmen's barracks for assistance.

Among those who came forth was an old English woman, a modern prototype of Mother Shipton, who had some reputation as a practitioner of the black art. She was a kind old soul and knew as much about surgery and doctoring as some practicing physicians. She picked up the unconscious child, and as she did so, it bent over double, like a jack-knife. With a groan, the old woman called out "Oh, Mercy, the little dear has her back broken!"

The agitated father, who was standing nearby, fell in a faint on the ground. His wife, who was hurrying to the spot as fast as her legs could carry her, heard the awful diagnosis and also swooned.

The superintendent of the furnace appeared on the scene and scoffed at the old woman's ominous pronouncement. He sent one of his clerks on horseback for the nearest doctor. The child was carried to her parents' cottage, where she was laid on the bed. When the doctor arrived an hour later, he stated that it was only too true; the backbone was broken; in most probabilities, she would be a hunchback if she lived.

The child got well, but she was a hunchback, as predicted.

The whole affair was so horrible that the father took to drink, in which he was joined by his wife. When well-meaning friends urged them to brace up and have another child, they said they wanted no more; one had been curse enough to them. When the child was about ten years old, the furnace shut down for good; her father was thrown out of employment. Most of his fellow employees, who had rented sections in the barracks, moved away to more flourishing localities.

The Englishman did not care to move, as, after years of struggle, he had lately made the final payment on his house and three acres of ground. This added disappointment set him to drinking more heavily, but as he had a good constitution, he held out until a week before his hunchback daughter's fifteenth birthday, when he died in Milesburg on one of his drunken sprees.

The crippled child was diminutive to a degree, but she looked smaller than ever in the mourning garb that she donned. On the way to the graveyard, a young man on horseback passed the cortege, tipping his hat as he rode by the hearse. He appeared to be about twenty years of age, dark, and good-looking. The preacher, who had peered out at him from under the drawn curtains of the hack, said he was the only son of the wealthy man who owned the furnace.

"His country estate is on the other side of the valley, but he comes here very seldom since the furnace is no more." Then he went on to say how the boy, who had been educated in France, had failed to get into West Point on account of his eyes.

A thrill shot through the sorrow-laden little hunchback, the handsome youth like herself was afflicted. During the brief services, she forgot her grief over the deceased and kept thinking of the young hero, of her chances of seeing him again.

After that, she took walks in the afternoons, about the same hour she had seen him pass. Within a week, she saw him again; he rode by gaily and unconcerned. All through the summer, they met every few days, but neither made an effort to speak. The girl did not dare; the boy did not care, that was why. In the autumn, she ceased seeing him; he had gone back to school in Philadelphia, so the preacher told her. But all through the long dreary months, she cherished his image in her heart. The snow ceased being formidable; the nights did not seem as cold as formerly now that she had this ideal to "warm the cockles of her heart."

It was an idyllic winter, for she often forgot she was a hunchback. In her dreams, she always saw herself as perfect, and the handsome boy smiled at her in that land where everything was run to suit even the most afflicted.

The springtime was one sweet paean waiting for him to return. Often she sat on the slag-piles singing old-fashioned hymns in her cracked, prematurely-old voice. On the first day of June, when the air was sweet and the sky a cloudless blue, her wait was rewarded. The young boy looking more vigorous and handsome than ever rode by on his slashing bay charger. To her surprise, he tipped his cap; it was the happiest moment of her poor starved life. After that, every time he passed, he bowed, and she smiled in return, but he never made an effort to stop and talk. If she had been content to let well enough alone and keep her hero in the dream world, all would have been better. At first, she felt a thrill merely to look at him; then, he had to speak to satisfy her. After a while, this seemed insufficient; she must have a meeting with him, perhaps tell him of her love. She puzzled for a long while as to the best way to go about it.

One afternoon when the preacher called, she asked him in the course of the conversation which was the nearest post office to the furnace owner's country estate. He told her, so she resolved to write to her "prince charming" and arrange to meet him in the pass. She wrote and tore up a dozen letters before she composed one which suited her. The completed version ran:

> My very dear sir:
>   I have been meeting you almost weekly on the mountain road
> for now nearly two summers, and I would like to know you better. I
> will be out on the road, where I usually walk, on Saturday afternoon,
> after three o'clock; if you are out, please stop and talk to me. It would
> make me most truly happy. I hope you are feeling well and happy.
> From a friend.

It was a simple statement, but from the heart, even if it did show a poverty of phrase and vocabulary. She tramped three miles to the post office, affixed the stamp carefully, and dropped it in the box with heart a-tremble.

AMONG THE GIANT PINES
(Courtesy of Pennsylvania Department of Forestry)

Poor little wretch, it was her ambitious effort for a little happiness, a vain moment when she burst the bounds of conscious affliction, imagining herself like other girls. She actually believed he would take notice of the epistle. Why; merely because the preacher had told her that his eyes had kept him out of West Point; an afflicted man must have gentleness and humility like herself. She posted the letter on Wednesday night; he ought to get it by Thursday. He would surely have it in time to meet her in the glen on Saturday afternoon. Poor little soul, she even dressed for the occasion! She put some white insertion into the neck, bosom, and sleeves of her black dress; she tied a big bow of white satin ribbon in her wiry red hair. She slipped out of the front door, so her mother wouldn't see her. When she returned, she would tell her fond parent all about "the prince," but not now.

She sauntered up the road towards the gap, trying to look unconcerned. Her hands felt icy cold; would the grand young man notice it if he shook hands; her heart was thumping audibly. She was so nervous that she kept walking, except when she stopped to gather an early laurel cluster to give to him. It seemed a long time for him to get there; it was long past his usual hour when she heard the familiar hoofbeats in the distance. She almost died of joy when he came into view. As he neared her, instead of his genial smile, he dug his spurs fiercely into his horse's sides and focused his eyes on the top of the mountain. The hunchback, unprepared for such a slight, dropped her laurel cluster and sank down on a large flat rock as if she had been run over by the juggernaut. Her heart ceased beating fast; it almost came to a standstill. She almost died of humiliation and grief then and there. Death might have claimed her had not a flood of hot tears saved her life. With the tears came a fuller and more galling sense of her physical disproportions, the certain knowledge that she would never, never be loved; at best, she would be barely tolerated.

She thought of her poverty, her shiftless, unhappy mother, who secretly wished she was dead, of her father's grief over her affliction, which sent him to a drunkard's grave in an effort to forget. She knew she could never be anything better than she was at present or have anything more. What was life anyway, a system which made gods out of some, mockeries out of others? And she was one of the mockeries. Why was it so, oh God? Perhaps the cripple and the monstrosity have a part to play, which most of us are too dense to perceive, and even the afflicted ones are unaware of it themselves. They may be living on a higher plane than the beings who are "close to the type of the race" and find nothing to hinder their whims and passions, while the afflicted must carry on life's duties on a calm level of loveless mediocrity. These, and an angry host of other thoughts, surged through the poor little brain of the wretched girl. She had touched the high-water mark of her life, in her hopes which had just been shattered; why want to live longer? She felt she owed no one a duty, better exchange the ever-present image of her affliction for the impenetrable gloom of eternal night.

The heavy shadows were falling fast; even a June day must have its end. She waited until she heard the last cowbell tinkle its way down the ravine, then she turned and followed slowly after. She looked up at the tall pines, the lace-like tracery of the dusk-embraced mountains; she smelt the odors of fern and laurel, a night hawk darting past her face squeaked like a mouse on wings. It was a beautiful world, after all, but she would leave it; she was too inharmonious to match its perfections.

It was dark, all but the starlight, when she reached the breast of the dam.

She looked around to see if she was alone; a screech-owl chattering long and dolefully on one of the big pines back of the furnace was evidently her nearest neighbor. She did not hesitate an instant; her resolve was made to end all, she plunged into the "deep hole" head foremost. Twice she came to the surface, but she swallowed water to choke herself, to hasten the end. The struggle was soon over; she went down among the frog spawn, newts, and eels, her injured spirit found release from its contracted shell. It was a glorious sensation to be a disembodied spirit, especially after quitting such a body as hers.

The next day the poor little corpse was dragged from the pond, all decked out in the black dress with white insertion and trimmings.

"One would think she was dressing to get married," said an unsympathetic bystander.

It was literally true, but the bridegroom was the grim angel. That afternoon the handsome youth rode by; he saw a crowd around the cottage, but he spurred his horse on to greater speed. He disliked crowds, especially gatherings of common people. He never knew that a poor little girl had ended her life because he had disciplined her for being "beastly forward" in writing to him. Had she been a beautiful girl, he would have encouraged her, regardless of class.

But the poor, puny little ghost, about the size of a gander snipe, haunts the pond at the old furnace. Perhaps in her silvery, celestial raiment, she imagines that "prince charming," if he would ever come that way by night, would deign to notice her now.

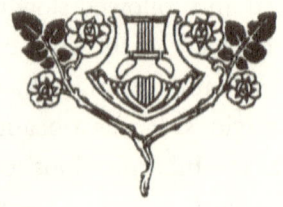

XXI

BEFORE THE FIRE

(Story of Tyrone Mountain)

AFTER MANY years, the Carothers tract of original white pine, on Bald Eagle Mountain, near Tyrone, was invaded by the lumbermen. Containing as it did, something under five hundred acres, a portable mill was selected as the speediest means to destroy it. Most of the biggest trees stood on a level park on the summit, but trail roads could be easily constructed close to them. The mammoth trees, many of which were a hundred and seventy-five feet in height and "straight as gun barrels," were well worth traveling miles to see. Their smooth, golden-brown boles rose from a cover of maple sprouts and shin-hopple; their feathery tops leaned to touch the sun. Most of them were the true "mountain pines," but there were a few Michigan or cork pines among them, trees with a lighter-colored bark and bluer and more upturned tufts of needles. It seemed a pity to cut the trees; they seemed so much alive, so happy in their communal life. They were inherently musical; they always churned the winds into their mystic harmonies. How impressive were the symphonies they created!

The tiniest breeze stirring the fragile tuft-like pinnacles would be sent along, swelling and growing, until it increased in volume and tone like a mighty chorus. It extended to the larger and lower branches, roaring and rolling with majesty and melody. Finally, the massive trunks themselves would sway and creak, like the bows of overworked titanic 'cellists, as the great climatic crash was neared. With a detonation like thunder, the whole forest would resound, then, the next instant, all would be calm. Where a moment before there had been tumult and blare, one could hear the faintest chirping of the wood peewees.

At the mouth of the ravine, which ran halfway up the mountain's side, right into the heart of the timber, was a log farmhouse with barns and sheds similarly constructed. Here resided a hardworking farmer named Terence McManus, whose lifetime of work showed but a score of acres of stump-dotted hillside lands. He was an Irishman by birth and not used to landowning; consequently considered himself lucky to have any kind of sod which he could call all his own. Besides, he acted as a caretaker for the Philadelphia family who owned the big timber. For preventing the Algerines, he was given the right to cut all dead or diseased trees, and he never abused the privilege. These he sledded, in winter, to a mill several miles up the valley, making a nice income thereby.

He had married a sister of this modest sawyer, who was of Scotch-Irish descent. Despite his wife's Protestantism, Terence had his way, and their nine children were all brought up Catholics. They weren't what might be called "good Catholics," but if they had lived nearer to churches of their persuasion, they would have been very devout. When they went to work or to visit in Tyrone, they took to Catholicism "as a duck does to water," which showed it to be the natural and instinctive religion.

But there was one thing that the children could not do, and that was to make a convert out of their mother. Many times she promised to "come over" but always kept putting it off as the date approached. This had been most disappointing to the eldest daughter, Mary Belle, who was at one time the most devout Catholic in the family. In addition to being the best Catholic, she was the brightest and also the best-looking. She apparently inherited all the desirable qualities of her father's and mother's races. There were few girls prettier than she, so it was acknowledged in Tyrone and in other big towns where she visited. She was full of life and, for this reason, left the ravine quite often, spending quite a little time with various relatives along the "main line."

When Daniel Caldwell bought the timber on the Carothers tract, he looked about for a suitable spot to erect his mill. It must be on level or gradually sloping ground, near the timber and the public road. One of Terence McManus's stump-dotted fields suited his purpose, so he made a deal with the Irishman to erect it there. In addition to paying a rental, he agreed to stable his horses in the McManus barns, to give the boys and the old man work whenever possible. A couple of the head men were to be boarded in the farmhouse. This was the best stroke of luck that had happened to the overworked farmer in many years.

"If it had come earlier, I could have enjoyed it better," was the comment that he made to his faithful wife.

James Ewing and Daniel Billman, two of the young men in charge of the operation, were the fortunate ones to be accepted as boarders at the McManus home.

Mary Belle had happened to be home when the crew first appeared on the scene, and every unmarried man among them wished he was boarding under the same roof with her. The two who were given the opportunity were tall, slim, good-looking lads, just a trifle over twenty-one years of age, and might have made favorable impressions on most girls. They could not imagine why Mary Belle, whom a local busybody had told them was twenty-five years old, could have gone that long without having a lover. She didn't look like an old maid; that was the strangest part of it. Most mountain spinsters who reached the age of twenty-five without being deceived wore spectacles and looked peaked around the nose. Mary Belle though not stout, had voluptuous curves to face and figure which belied her cloistered existence. And yet the local busybody, a grouchy German, could not be induced to say that she ever had a lover, let alone been deceived by one.

"I knows all about her," he kept saying, "she haint hat no lover, dats all."

"There must be some mistake about her age," said Ewing to Billman as they went to bed on their first night in the farmhouse.

The evening had passed pleasantly before the fire; Mary Belle had been polite and genial but drew herself up a bit when Billman sought to become somewhat personal in his talk. When they saw that it was time to retire, they left her by the fire, staring abstractedly into the glowing embers.

"She looks too healthy to be worrying over a lover, but when a woman wants to sit alone by the fire, there must be something inside that's bothering." These were Billman's last words as he blew out the lamp.

There were two younger McManus girls, Katie and Susie, who seemed anxious enough to win the good graces of the youthful boarders. They were pretty girls, or else the young fellows would have "pumped" them regarding Mary Belle's heart secrets. But their code was never to impose on a good-looking girl, so Katie and Susie did not guess they were only makeshifts for their older and more attractive sister.

There were other young men on the lumber job, including David Caldwell's two sons, who visited the camps occasionally, and all of them tried to make up to Mary Belle. Always civil and smiling, she kept a certain reserve, which was positively tantalizing. The more she kept them at a distance, the prettier she seemed; each day added a fresh luster to her round blue eyes, an apple-like curve to her smooth cheeks, her firm, well-molded chin, her generously molded nose. But she was acting a part, and it sent her to bed each night sick at heart; an unhappy love story was killing her by inches. If she thought that the camp could find it out, she would have run away, never to return, but luckily no Nemesis appeared to unmask her. Her parents often chided her for her melancholy demeanor when no strangers were present.

"Oh Mary Belle," her frank Irish father would say, "how can you be so two-faced, all gloom when you're with us, all smiles when with outsiders."

But Mary Belle never answered; she shunned arguments on a subject that dared not be discussed.

Somehow she did not care to visit on the "mainline" anymore; all the old towns and old friends had lost their charms. Invitations, even social letters, remained unanswered.

"Mary Belle's buried herself alive in the mountains" was her friends' version of her strange reticence.

Indeed she was buried alive, for she could not be induced to attend social gatherings; she even would not go any more to church at Tyrone.

A test came in the form of a dance given in the main lumber camp on New Year's Eve. All the girls of the neighborhood, including her sisters, were glad to attend, but she remained at home like a Cinderella before the fire. Her parents were positively angry with her that night. At the last minute, they hoped she would change her mind. Ewing and Billman pleaded hard—one of them whispering to her that it would be a shame if the beauty of the mountain remained away.

When the boys escorting her two sisters had gone, she burst out crying and sank into her easy chair before the fire. Her mother laid her hand on her shoulder, trying to rouse her from her melancholy.

"It is all a case of hysterics; girls sometimes get that way when they don't marry", she said.

But Mary Belle was indifferent, even when her parents scolded her for her mysterious and unsociable conduct.

"If you sit around like this, you'll go out of your mind; better get out of here and go to work at dressmaking in Altoona," was her mother's next thrust.

Mary Belle was a spirited girl, but she did not answer back; she merely wiped the tears from her big blue eyes. Her parents grew tired of prodding, so they went to bed.

In the "wee small hours," when the boys and Katie and Susie returned from the dance, they found her sitting alone, with the lamp burned out, by the dying embers, crying as if her heart would break. With the passing of time, she masked her feelings less from the two young boarders than at first. They saw her cry many times; it stirred them deeply, and they would have given anything to have comforted her. For a time, they imagined that her sisters knew her secret, but they disliked appearing inquisitive. But this was dispelled when the girls asked them one evening if they had the slightest idea what ailed poor Mary Belle.

"She came back from a visit to an aunt in West Virginia over five years ago, and she's never been the same since. We wrote to our aunt, but she said everything had been pleasant during the visit; there was no man in the case."

"Beg your pardon," said Ewing, "but there must be a man somewhere; no girl ever acts like that for any other reason."

The sight of such a beautiful woman so often in tears stirred a deep-seated passion in James Ewing. Her tear-reddened eyes were ever before him; he longed to kiss them into brightness and joy. He would marry her to make her happy. He knew she did not love him, but she might someday. No woman's love is impossible to a good-looking man. But to a homely man, her indifference is final. But the difficult task was to get her alone, where he could declare himself. Like a hunted roe, she seemed to divine his purpose. He could not catch her any place except in the cold upstairs halls of the farmhouse where love-making was unthinkable. She even gave up her siestas before the fire; she stuck close to her mother in the kitchen.

Terence McManus was not born an Irishman for nothing. He sized up the situation and, fearing the future of his daughter, and liking young Ewing, concocted a plot to leave them together. On the next Sunday morning, all were to go to church except Mary Belle, who would "keep house." Ewing, without being consulted, guessed the situation, so accompanied by Billman, went for a walk immediately after breakfast. He had not gone far when he found that he had forgotten his barometer, which he was fond of carrying: he returned, finding Mary Belle seated before the fire.

"You must feel pretty lonely today," he remarked in his cheeriest manner.

Mary Belle, who could not be rude if she tried, looked up at him and almost smiled. He fancied that he was going to have at least a hearing, so he began talking pleasantly, standing beside her easy chair. He would have given everything he possessed if he could have laid his hand on hers, so white and shapely, as it rested on the arm of the chair. Mary Belle's politeness induced her to ask him to sit down, so he drew up a rocker close to her. He tried his best to touch upon the story of his love, but she did not give him an opening.

When he persisted, she said, "Oh, Mr. Ewing, you know me too well for that; please let us discuss some other subject."

Here the tears began to flow; she seemed unable to stifle them. So he excused himself, fetched his barometer, and departed.

When the family returned from church at noon, they found a very pitiable object seated before the fire. The tears had burnt furrows in her smooth cheeks, her lips and eyes were swollen, and her golden-brown hair was disheveled.

"Come, come, help get dinner," said Mrs. McManus sharply.

Mary Belle arose mechanically and started across the floor. At the kitchen door, everything became black before her eyes; she reached out wildly, tumbled, and fell in a heap on the wooden floor. Just at that moment, Ewing and Billman came in and helped to pick her up. They dashed cold water in her face; she soon revived; she had only swooned. But her mother put her to bed, and there she lay all afternoon, her pretty face staring out from her mass of matted hair and the pillows, for all the world like a Lady of Sorrows.

As she lay inert and helpless in the dim light of the cold cheerless bedroom, the story of her sad young life, her stubborn loyalty, her hopeless misery, rose up afresh. She thought of her happy girlhood, of the host of friends she had known and lost. She thought of many men who had admired her, of the friendly feeling she had for them, of how her love always withheld itself. She pictured to herself how happy she felt when she started away from home five years before to pay her first visit at a distance with an aunt in a West Virginia mining town. Everyone there seemed to be glad to meet her; her visit was like a great round of pleasure. Boys and girls alike had vied to make her stay enjoyable. She remembered, oh, so well, the wintry night when she went to the church fair. All her young friends were present, and the parish priest was so whole-souled, genial, and genuinely good. She had noticed the tall, dark, foreign priest, who was with the good father, and who kept staring at her with his lustrous eyes. She admired him more than any man she had ever seen at first glance; he felt the same towards her. It was easy for him to be introduced; the good priest who performed the offices, little dreamed of the consequences entailed.

The foreign priest, whose church, also in the mining town, was attended by the families of the poor wretches who toiled their lives away underground, had always borne a spotless reputation. He was beloved by his congregation, his deeds of goodness were legion. Tall, dark-eyed, firm-lipped, he was a personality bound to command respect, to win love anywhere. Despite his physical charms, no woman had ever stirred him until he saw Mary Belle. An electric shock shot through his body and set his brain to reeling; he was subjugated by a force that he did not know existed, the unconscious witchery of a woman.

The young girl herself was shocked to feel that a priest could stir her blood, could make her feel as she had thought she would if she fell in love. Her conscience suddenly became dormant; she found herself talking most of the evening with the handsome "father." He turned out to be as engaging in manner as in looks. He said he was a great believer in destiny, in the divine science of mathematical probabilities. He asked her the date of her birth—she told him that it was October 30. He said that his was January 24.

"It is a sign that we are suited to one another; let me show you. You know that two persons to be congenial must have their birthdays on dates which are multiples of the same number. Three goes into thirty, your birthday, ten times. Three goes into twenty-four, my birthday, eight times. Add ten and eight together; it gives you eighteen. Put three into eighteen, and you have six. Divide six by three, our multiple, and you have two, which means two souls in perfect harmony."

Accompanying a small party of her friends, he escorted her to her aunt's home that night; they parted without making any arrangements to meet again.

But some unseen force was dictating their progress; she met him on a lonely hill the next afternoon, on her way to visit a sick woman, quite by accident. They walked in an opposite direction from the town; both declared their love before they parted just at dusk. They met every afternoon for a week, and then the young priest begged her to marry him; he felt that she, rather than the church, was his ultimate goal. She loved him too much to interpose a word of objection; it was how and when, nothing else. She could go ostensibly to another aunt's home in Pittsburgh; he would meet her in the B&O station and then proceed to some city in Ohio where marriages were quick and easy. He would then write to his flock and his bishop, telling everything; by the time they got the letters, the happy couple would be on their way to the Canadian Northwest, perhaps to the Orient.

He spoke in such impassioned tones it seemed as if the future had been revealed to him, that he was acting out a divine injunction. It was very easy to explain about a promised visit to Pittsburgh "for a few days," and one foggy morning Mary Belle and her renegade lover met in the dingy B&O station as arranged. He wore a plain business suit, had a check cap drawn well down on his head, and on his upper lip was a two-day's growth of dark mustache. He carried a large omnibus suitcase; it looked as if they might be going around the world.

At the Ohio town chosen for the ill-omened ceremony, the railway platform was thronged with noisy cabmen, on the alert for eloping couples, who shouted, as the train came to a halt, "Courthouse and preacher. Courthouse and preacher."

They chose the most villainous-looking barker as probably the most reliable for their purpose. A license under assumed names was easily obtained; she was twenty, he was thirty-two; a foreign clergyman, almost as despicable looking as the cabman, tied the knot.

They were man and wife in the eyes of the law, but not to an outraged God. Their first wedded hours were blissful. They managed to catch a train for Cleveland, where they had planned to spend the bridal night. From there, they were to go by boat to Duluth, their "jumping off place" into the Canadian wilderness.

Cleveland was reached without delay or inconvenience. In order that no one could recognize them, they put up at a small European or Italian-kept hotel on the lakefront. They had eaten supper in the "rathskeller car" on the train, so they asked to be shown to their room immediately after registering as "J. W. Reilly and wife, New York City." They had seen the name on a laundry wagon in one of the towns they had passed through on their journey. When they got to the ill-kept room, they asked the low-browed Italian who acted as bell boy to bring some writing materials. The momentous letters to the bishop and the congregation were to be written before retiring. The sulky Italian, hating an extra trip upstairs, having as a precaution against this, carried a half-filled pitcher of ice water along with the suitcase and slammed the door after him. The priestly bridegroom and his fair beloved were together for "weal or woe."

The young churchman stood by the door while Mary Belle, who was feeling a trifle tired, was sitting on the bed, leaning against the pillows. As he looked at her, another electric shock, more blinding than the one he had felt at the church fair, swept through his frame. It was the victory of his conscience, of his sense of moral responsibility, his religious convictions. He clenched his fists and backed into the furthest corner of the room. His eyes and lips twitched nervously; his whole being shook with emotion. Mary Belle, who had been watching him with eyes of love, and marveling at his sudden coldness, was now aware that something had snapped. Yet he dared not speak; he would go to his rain first before unmasking his change of heart.

The young girl, when the truth had dawned on her, spoke out boldly. "You find you love your vows to your church more than your promises to me, speak out quickly, isn't it so?"

The priest was silent a full minute and then simply nodded his head in affirmation. The pallor in Mary Belle's face turned to a crimson flush; her temple of happiness was a house of cards. The priest leaned against the wall, speechless and trembling. Just at that minute, they heard a heavy shuffling of feet on the stairs and in the hall, then a loud knock at the door. It was the Italian back with the writing materials. When he came in, Mary Belle ordered him to lay the articles on the bed, to go downstairs at once, and order a cab. The Italian looked at her in blank amazement; the class who usually stopped at this hotel would consider it a luxury to take a trolley ride. When he had gone, the girl jumped up from the bed and, among her bundles, extracted a timetable. By the light of the electric globe, which hung from a cord, she located a train leaving for Pittsburgh at midnight.

"You will have time to get that train if you hurry. You can be back in your parish without anyone even guessing at the cause of your absence. I will remain here until tomorrow and then go home. I could not feel happy to ruin your chance of Paradise just because we happened to fall in love."

The priest took his cap, which he had hung on a peg on the door, and came over to where she stood under the electric light. Her golden-brown hair seemed an aureole of sanctity above her exquisite, loving face in the reflected light. His decision wavered again as the time came to leave her. Holding out his arms, he said, "May I kiss you just once before I go?"

For a minute, she hesitated; she thought she would turn her back, but the hot fire of passion conquered her scruples, and she fell into his arms. He had kissed her many times and squeezed her to his capacious breast as often when the same dull, shuffling feet were heard in the hall. Then came the knock for him to go. He got as far as the door and ran back for one more kiss and a pressure of the hand, and he was gone.

Mary Belle's bridal night was spent with a specter bridegroom, sure enough. She was too dazed to cry, too unnerved to sleep. She ached nervously from head to foot; her spirit pained as much as her body. She turned off and turned on the light a score of times. When the light was out, she heard rats scampering across the musty carpet; the noise of snoring guests echoed louder from adjoining transoms. She heard the whistles on the lake, the creak of hoisting chains along the docks, the distant clang of trolley bells, of sodden voices in the streets. She had forgotten to pull down one of the shades; it let the first streaks of dawn into the narrow room, it looked even more sordid and modern by daylight. It was the signal for her to get up and dress; she did not want to wash her face; it might quicker erase the impress of her husband's kisses.

She gathered together her traps and made her way to the railway station as best she could. She got home somehow; it was a painful battle with self all the way, yet none of her family could see the marks of her soul's conflict. But her manner had changed; she lost all interest in life. Her mother shrewdly wrote to the aunt in West Virginia, but no, she knew of no unhappy love affair there.

"It must be her general health," they argued, "she's in a decline."

Life was a blank to her; it could never be anything else. Now, as she lay in the cheerless bedroom in the little mountain home, she felt as desolate as she did that dreadful night in Cleveland. Once, the thought came up within her, "That marriage is nothing; I will tell all; I will be free."

But another voice answered, the voice of love and duty, making her call out, "I will never tell, I will die first, I love him, I will never cause him trouble."

Then exhausted from the flood of unhappy memories, she turned over on her face and fell asleep.

XXII

SIMPLER'S JOY

(Story of Altoona Mountain)

HOW MANY persons remember the aged simpler Caspar Jaudon, whose log-cabin home was at the base of the Bald Eagle Mountain, not so very far from Altoona? Only sixteen years have passed since he went to his reward, yet his personality has been forgotten to such an extent that he seems almost a myth.

He was a striking-looking figure in his latter days, with his shock of snow-white hair, his heavy, irregular features, thickish lips, and rough, shaven face. His eyes, which he generally kept focused on the ground, were light blue, as pale, clear, and deep as Lincoln's. It was an unusual face but not an altogether attractive one. There was something about him that fascinated yet repelled; that was probably why he became a simpler, a hermit. In Europe, he would have been said to possess the "evil eye."

When an animal varies to any considerable extent from the "type of the race," it is shunned by the other members of its kind, and becomes a hermit animal. Some hunters in Wyoming, in the fall of 1867, came upon a buffalo with a single foreleg that grew from the breastbone, leading a solitary existence miles from the millions which composed the herds. Caspar Jaudon was just different enough from his fellows to have them feel the unlikeness and for himself to be aware of it, hence his lonely life in the foothills.

His mother, the widow of a Mexican War veteran, kept house for him until her death, but that sad event occurred shortly after he was mustered out after gallant service in the 7th Pennsylvania Cavalry in the Civil War while he was yet a young man. As a soldier, there was nothing retiring or hermit-like about him; he was always in the thickest of the

PENNSYLVANIA PINE FOREST
(Courtesy of Pennsylvania Department of Forestry)

fight. But his fellow mountaineers, always ready to look upon him as odd and eccentric, were quick to forget his military record, and he was seldom counted among the "old soldiers" of the neighborhood. As a simpler or herb doctor, his chief glamor rested, and if there were good herb doctors and bad herb doctors, he was a good one. His cures were legion, often after the regular practitioners had failed. His knowledge of the efficacy of herbs and roots came to him in an "apostolic succession" from the days of the Indian medicine men.

Old Johnny Halftown, from the Allegheny River country, who had wandered among the Bald Eagle Mountains as far south as the Juniata, had fancied Caspar as a boy and taught him all he knew. Halftown, who wore a long white beard, claimed to have been born the year the Declaration of Independence was signed, had learned the almost magic art of simpling from no less a personage than Joe Pye himself, that most famous of Indian healers. It was Joe Pye who cured a whole section of New England from an attack of typhus fever with a decoction made from the tall, graceful plant with "crushed raspberry" blossoms that still bears his name.

Caspar's humble cabin was a veritable storehouse of relics as well as herbs. He never took money for his efforts at healing, but in the summer, when he hunted ginseng, he earned a little, sharpening the mountaineers' razors. His grateful patients often made him many odd presents. These more than filled the one ground-floor room where he worked and slept. There still remained the huge open chimney; old Caspar declared it was more healthful than a stove, with the crane hanging in it just as in pioneer days. Above the fireplace was nailed, upside down, a much-faded pair of Moose-antlers. What a story they could tell of some poor, half-starved wretch hunting in Canadian wilds, maybe from the sheer need for food and contracting then the scurvy that caused him to donate his most precious trophy upon the simpler who cured him! Below the horns were hanging a cavalry saber, the sole memento of soldier days.

On the shelf in a fly-specked gilt frame and under a cracked glass was a colored lithograph of a French steeplechaser, with the inspiriting name of Vive-la-Chasse, with the date "1855" beneath. One could imagine some sad Gallic wanderer presenting this picture, probably of some horse he had tended on a better and happier day, as his supreme gift for restoration to health. At one corner of the fireplace hung a soiled and armless doll-baby, the gift, it was said, of a heartbroken mother whose child he had patiently tried to save from a snakebite, but without success. On the other side hung a violin, much stained, and cracked. Inside the case, burnt into the wood, were these words: "Antonius Stradivarius, Cremona, 1729." In a small frame of crossed twigs was an old-time photograph of the simpler in the garb of a cavalryman. It showed the rugged, irregular face, then adorned with the blackest of mustaches, the shock of heavy black hair, but there was the same downcast glance of the deep-set eyes.

Suspended from the ceiling were large bunches of Joe Pye weed, wild ginger, verbena, yarrow, tansy, sweet fern, liver leaf, mallow, mandrake, catnip, Blue Mountain tea, elder-berries, Pennsylvania tea, poke-berries, spearmint, ginseng, boneset, Indian pipe, sage, thyme, chamomile, as well as other plants and berries not as well-known. These were the components of the simpler's herbarium.

There was a footstool made of buckhorns in front of the fire. On one side of the room was an immense couch covered with a buffalo robe; age had made it almost destitute of hair. There were only two windows, and at each of these stood a rocking chair; one had been his mother's favorite. In these, mother and son had probably sat for hours, on the long winter afternoons, looking out at the narrow snow-bound road, with the great forest of oaks and the skyline of the mountains beyond; lucky if even a fox passed to vary the monotony.

It is a pity that the ghosts of the good and the devoted don't return, as they might cheer many a lonely heart. It is only the shadow of a lost cause, a lost opportunity, a lost love that comes back to keep us company. That accounts for the unpopularity of ghosts. Despite his trafficking in past agencies, in mystic formulas, his solitude, his silence, Jaspar Jaudon could never be induced to say that he had seen a ghost. His mother was a good woman; she had no reason to return. He had fought on the winning side in the war; it brought no lingering regrets. He had made the most of limited opportunities; his lost love was still alive. If he lived long enough, he might yet hold her spectral essence in his enfolding arms, but Fate, inscrutable as always, decreed that she must survive him.

The story of his one love story dates its beginning to the years just previous to the war. Then the fair vision first began her horseback rides, accompanied by a groom, along the woody road which led by Caspar's cabin. He was about twenty years old when he first noticed her; he had been born in 1840. On summer evenings, the old woman and her son brought their rockers outside the door, and both sat smoking, watching the distant hills assuming the distinct outlines and purple-blue tones of approaching dusk.

The beautiful young blonde girl, dressed in her black habit, and wearing a three-cornered colonial hat of velvet, with an eagle's feather in it, would gallop past like an apparition. After she was gone, the night seemed to fall faster; she was a spirit of light and life. When he dreamed of her, the whole room illuminated; she was the color to his colorless existence. When he played his violin, her image was the impetus, the motive, which brought out melodies sweeter than he knew before, or the bow seemed capable of. When he walked through the summer and autumn woods, gathering herbs or roots, thoughts of her endued with greater potency these natural panaceas. At first, he did not have even a bowing acquaintance with her—after a while, when they saw one another almost daily for months at a time, reserve was discarded; she made the first break by touching her hat with her little ivory-handled whip. Caspar bowed in return; from that day on, there was always the mutual salute in which the attending footman joined, tipping his cockaded hat.

The old woman and her son knew very well the young girl's identity; she was Elsie Chamberlin from the manor house. In fact, they were squatters on her father's land, the ex-judge; a word from this august personage would have turned them off homeless. The young girl was an only daughter, but she had several brothers, dressy, exclusive chaps, very different from her in disposition, it was said.

Then came the war, beginning with a long line of Confederate victories. It was a patriotic neighborhood, every time the Union's cause seemed darkest, more young men volunteered. Caspar wanted to enlist from the very first day, but his aged, helpless mother was reason enough to make him hesitate.

When patriotism reached a fever-heat in the inspiring happenings culminating in the Loyal War Governors' Conference at Altoona, he could stand it no longer. His mother read his thoughts; she told him to go by all means. She had a brother in Centre County who would keep her if he never returned. He enlisted haphazardly but got a lucky transfer to the cavalry, which determined the success of his military career. By re-enlistments, he served until the middle of June 1865, participating in sixty battles and skirmishes, being mustered out as a First Sergeant.

His mother met him at the Logan House on his return; it was an affecting greeting. She had aged while he was gone, but her heart was glad at his brave, unsullied record. A neighbor, who brought her to town, drove them back to the little cabin by the mountainside in the cooling twilight.

"Very little's happened since you went away," she said by way of carrying on the conversation. "Jacob Stineman killed a black wolf in his sheep pen; Abe Arbogast sold all his white pine timber, Elsie Chamberlin's married, and gone to Europe to live; guess we won't see her riding here anymore."

Caspar's pale face turned a ghastly white; he let fall the saber that was resting between his knees, they shook noticeably, and his teeth chattered. In an instant, he was composed again, feeling ashamed of himself at this spiritual insubordination. What should it mean to him that she had married? Surely she could never be anything to him, a girl in her exalted station. He began asking after another girl on the mountain, Tillie Quinn, and how her toppy chickens were coming along.

When he reached the little home, he hung his saber above the fireplace; they say he took it down only once until the day of his death. The neighbors remarked he was much more serious-minded than when he had enlisted.

"He saw so much bloodshed," said his mother, "it isn't to be wondered at."

He applied himself to his herb doctoring more assiduously than ever, and this, coupled with the temporary *reclame* of his war record, brought him more patients than he could handle.

In the autumn, a candidate for some county office stopped at the shanty, a sort of political protege of ex-Judge Chamberlin. From him, he learned the story of Elsie's marriage, which had occurred the previous April. The bridegroom was a wealthy young Philadelphian, and the new President, as a wedding gift, had appointed him Consul at St. Petersburg, he probably meant Secretary of Legation, but such positions were beyond the mental scope of the candidate and the unhappy simpler. The young couple sailed for Russia two weeks after the ceremony and, from last accounts, were very contented in their foreign home.

Elsie had always seemed to be a thing unreal to Caspar; in this new role, she was in a still higher sphere of celestial living. There were moments, though, when he drew himself up with pride to think she spoke to him and had been the first to speak. She had been an illumination in the darkness; from her, he had learned to live more keenly than before.

He continued collecting herbs, selling ginseng, and in the winter, trapped many valuable animals, including otters and pine martens. Apart from his spiritual sadness at the removal from his gaze of the ex-judge's daughter, he had a real grief in the rapidly failing health of his mother. The blustery month of March was hardly spent when she passed away from an acute attack of pneumonia. There was a simple funeral attended by a few neighbors, and the body was laid to rest in the little apple orchard near the cabin alongside her husband, sons, and daughters. An old comrade once planted a tiny American flag upon the Mexican War veteran's grave; it was the only marker in this family burial plot.

Caspar's loneliness settled down like a pall of blackness; occasionally, there was a golden gleam when he thought of Elsie. It was like an angelic visitation. Evidently, his mother was the popular member of the family. After her death, few came to the cabin; the oddity of the simpler's nature impressed itself more strongly upon the mountaineers now. With mid-April came many birds to cheer his loneliness. The Jays had been with him most of the winter, as had a pair of snowy owls, visitors from the arctic circle which fluttered about the oaks at the rear of the cabin. But now came the flickers of emphatic song and flight, the mourning doves, woodpeckers, thrashers, tanagers, robins, bluebirds, martins. High above the mountain tops soared the hawks and buzzards. At rare intervals, he heard the plaintive utterance of the meadowlarks. The roads were still muddy, but wagons were beginning to plow through them with safety.

Late one clear afternoon, he was sitting on his buck-horn stool outside the cabin door, his mortar on a wooden bench, pounding herbs. He was mixing a special compound for a typhoid sufferer in a lumber camp five miles up in the mountains. The flickers were calling to one another from the bare branches of the walnut trees; a cricket was tuning up his violin-like music. He thought he heard the "slush, slop, slip, slop" of a horse's hooves struggling through the juicy mud.

The sounds grew nearer and nearer; he looked up and saw a big sorrel horse—on its back was the former Elsie Chamberlin. No servant was with her. At first, he thought she was a ghost; he couldn't grasp the idea of her being able to return from Russia in the flesh. He was certain she was no ghost when she reined her horse by the paling fence, wishing him a cheery "good evening."

He laid aside his tools and walked to the gate, holding out his hand, saying, "I'm very glad to see you back again."

The girl blushed, a guilty red; evidently, she had some secret thoughts concerning him.

Then and there, he had a really good look at her for the first time in his life. She was more beautiful at close range than from a distance. She was a blonde, not a yellow blonde, but an ash blonde, *cheveux de cidre*, they call it. Her deep-set grey eyes were rather small but were adorned by delicately rounded black brows and long black lashes. Her face was rather broad, denoting some Norse blood, but the high coloring was emphatically English. Her lips had much color to them; her chin was round and dimpled. Her black three-cornered hat had forced her profuse hair down over her eyes.

"What were you doing with those things ?" she said, pointing to the bench on which rested the mortar and pestle.

Caspar explained to her that he was a simpler by occupation, not a very remunerative calling, but one wherein he could do much good. He made bold to ask her to tie her horse, and dismount, to come in and see his collection of relics. He had a ginseng root that was shaped like a human body, with head, arms, and legs. Some day it would be owned by the Emperor of China.

She let him tie the horse and assist her dismount, going smilingly with him to the humble home. Inside, the first thing she noticed was the cavalry saber—she must know its history. She seemed interested to learn that he was a veteran of the late war, urging him to tell her of some of his battles. She asked after the old lady, expressing regret that she was no more. She kept eyeing the young man steadily; it was a gaze caused by his rather unusual face, a gaze of passion aroused by his very oddity.

When he helped her on the horse, and she wheeled about and rode away, he watched down the road long after she had disappeared from sight. As he returned to his work, he kept muttering to himself, "Oh, if a woman like that could only care for me."

He put her visit down to idle curiosity or a desire to pass the time, nothing more.

He did not see her again for a week; in fact, he had never expected her to come again. But exactly a week later, at the same hour, she appeared and spent a couple of hours chatting with him in the curious little house. Before she left, she asked for his photograph in the soldier suit. He had recently made the frame for it out of twigs of sassafras; it presented a neat appearance. She wanted a glass on it, so she loaned him one of her diamond rings to cut a piece from a window pane.

When she had gone, he sat musing, supperless, until he went to bed. "Why would she want my picture", was the drift of his mental ramblings. Like all human beings who are odd looking, he was painfully aware of his peculiarities. In another two days, she was back, arriving earlier, leaving late. She condescended to remain for supper; she said it was the happiest meal of her life. Words like these sunk deep into the reflective, introspective nature of the simpler. He pondered upon them, turning them over and over in his mind. But he would always conclude his arguments with the corollary, "How could a woman like her ever care for me?"

The next time she came, he allowed the passion that had been consuming him ever since her first visit to assert itself a little. She was sitting by the fire in one of the rocking chairs as the day was dying, pensively gazing into the embers. Caspar put his hand on her warm cheek; she placed her hand over his; he knew his anguish was reciprocated. He sat on the arm of the chair and put his arm around her waist, drawing her very close to him, kissing her flushed face. To his surprise, she whispered, "I love you."

He poured out on her the pent-up love of years. From that time on, these visits were an Elysium to the eccentric simpler. There was enough good in him, of common sense, of honor, to appreciate her infatuation, to try and make her happy. He was a manly chap and never once asked her why she preferred him to her distinguished husband.

Her visits kept up at intervals of a few days apart, all through the glorious springtime. The birds and breezes sung every inch of her blonde, buoyant personality into his soul. She became a part of the humble room, as much a part of it as the cavalry saber, the inverted moose-antlers, the lithograph of Vive-la-Chasse, the strings of Joe Pye weed, verbena, and Culver's root. She was the simpler's joy—something too good to be true—but real nevertheless.

But despite this, on account of their different positions in life, she was an enigma to him, for why should she have chosen to care for him? But we must take what Fate sends and never question: Its gifts are really only loans. But no humble man ever strayed further upon life's exalted heights than Caspar Jaudon, perhaps because he was wise enough to be grateful.

One May evening, while he was leaning against the Acacia tree in the yard, inhaling the odor of the sweet-scented blooms, listening to the wood notes of a Blackburnian warbler, he heard the noise of a horse and wagon coming up the rocky road. It couldn't be his fair visitor; she always traveled on horseback. When the vehicle drew in sight, he perceived it was Elsie's servant whom he had not seen in several years, driving her favorite saddler, harnessed to a high Stanhope. The teamster guided the vehicle close to the gate, beckoning Caspar to come near. When he did so, he handed him a small package, then he turned the horse quickly, striking it several sharp cuts with the whip, and drove out of sight at a high rate of speed.

Caspar was sorry afterward that he did not ask the man a few questions, but at the moment, he was dumb. He opened the package; it contained a cardboard box. Inside was the little photograph of himself in cavalry accouterments and a letter; he did not know if it was Elsie's hand or not; he never had anything in writing from her. The envelope was unsealed, and he opened it nervously. On a single sheet of note paper of the commonest sort—the kind that has a picture of the capitol at Washington embossed in the upper left-hand corner—flimsy and blue-lined, was scratched the following:

Mr. Caspar Jaudon,
Dear Sir:
    When you read this, I will be far out on the Atlantic Ocean, never to return. I have come to the conclusion that it was a mistake ever to have visited you. I do not see what I meant by so doing. I return your photograph, as I have no further use for it.
                    I remain. Yours truly,
                    E. C. M.

M. was the initial of the last name of her diplomatist husband, the simpler recollected. It might have been well to have preserved the letter, but in his wounded pride and collapsed romance, he tore it into little bits, letting the evening zephyr blow them about the yard. He went into the humble home, now doubly desolate, and placed the photograph on the mantel shelf. As he did so, he whispered to himself, "A woman like that could never care for me."

He made no effort to find out what had happened, whether her husband had learned everything or whether she tired of him through feminine caprice. He could hardly write; besides, getting a letter off to Europe would be a task almost like sending one to "The Home Beyond the Sky."

He accepted his sorrow with silent resignation. Whenever the beautiful vision rose in his mind while he worked over his herbs or lay sleepless under the buffalo robe, he would calm his burning disappointment by repeating over and over again, "How could a woman like that be expected to care for me."

Of course, he could not analyze the passionate vagary which brought her to him in the first place, the magnetic charm of his repulsive but compelling face. It was to him much like a person who has seen an apparition yet cannot ask the "whys" and "wherefores." Months became years; he worked on, and he suffered uncomplainingly, becoming more and more like a hermit or "old man of the woods" in appearance. His black hair became full of grey streaks even when he was well under thirty.

Two years after he had received his crushing blow, a chance came to him to learn a gleam of the truth. The self-same candidate, the ex-judge's protégé, appeared at the humble cottage to enlist Caspar's support for "a second term." The candidate was a talkative fellow; he liked to gossip.

"Elsie Chamberlin went back to Russia awful sudden," he remarked, "she didn't write her husband very regular, so he came home unexpected and found that she had been meeting some man; I could never find out who he was, on the sly, at least that's what they say. At any rate, he made her pack up bag and baggage and go back to Europe with him. That's where she is now, but the Judge's folks don't hear from her often. They tell it around that she's having a very gay time over there with all the high mucky-mucks."

This speech opened a vista of comfort to the heart-stung simpler. He closed his eyes; he folded his hands. Perhaps, after all, she had not tired of him; it was force rather than choice that tore her from his side. Their romance had progressed as far as was possible; there was no future to it; they could never have married. Yet she had whispered to him many times, "I love you, I love you." He had held her very close; he could feel her flushed cheek by his, his fingers running through the electric meshes of her ash-gold hair. That was equivalent to reaching the threshold of the divine. The candidate noticed that he was acting rather strangely; evidently, this talk about the aristocracy was disquieting. He started to go, but Caspar offered to accompany him, to introduce him to some good people on the mountain who might help him. He was delighted; he had long wanted the "right" introduction to these people. The simpler felt that this man had done him the greatest favor of his life; he had shown him a gleam of hope that Elsie's love was probably real, that at worst, she had merely turned back when Fate and Circumstance commanded.

"Besides," he whispered to himself as he climbed into the politician's buggy, "How could a woman like that be expected to care for me."

XXIII

IRONCUTTER'S CABIN

(Story of the Last Mountain)

WHERE THE Bald Eagle Mountain comes to an abrupt end north of Hollidaysburg and looks down upon the fertile plain, then forms a coalition with the Shade Mountain, rolling away to the east, there once stood a lowly one-roomed log cabin. It was destitute of windows, and the door was not half a door; it was kept shut so much. The most noticeable feature of the shack was a huge mud chimney which was nearly as wide and twice as high as the house itself. This chimney saved the house from being dubbed "deserted" for once in a while, a thin trail of blue-grey smoke issued from it, smoke about the color of Indian summer haze. Back of the house rose the steep face of the big mountain, its lower levels covered with gnarled rock oaks and chestnuts and higher up a dense network of stunted pitch pines. Below the cabin was a broad clearing, fast growing up with scrub oaks, despite the efforts of a small flock of sheep to pasture it bare. Beyond stretched the fertile valleys, with their fields of brown, and red, and yellow, interspersed with dark green woodlots.

The growing town was plainly apparent; here and there could be seen the red roofs of barns and farmsteads and an occasional church spire. Far in the distance ran the faint blue outline of the South Mountains. All in front of the cabin seemed smiling, thrifty, cultivated; behind it loomed the end of the Central Pennsylvania wilderness, which stretched a hundred miles or more, clear to the rock caverns of the panther and the wolf, to the swamps of the elk and deer, to the inaccessible pathways of the bison, to the areas where the sun for days would be darkened by the incessant flight of wild pigeons.

There the Indians made their final stand, retreating only after the disappearance of the last buffalo, the last white-spotted bee. But they remained in song and story and in a troop of melancholy ghosts that lingered among the rocks and waterfalls. But when John Ironcutter moved into his little shack near the base of the Last Mountain, wildlife, Indians, and settlers were still embroiled far off in the fastnesses of the Bald Eagles. The spirit of primitive days was still uppermost. You can sometimes feel that vague sensation still if you gaze long enough upon some particularly wild bit of scenery. Ironcutter felt it in his veins; it echoed and reverberated in the stunted pines on the rugged heights of the Last Mountain.

Fifty years of hermit-like existence at the foot of this eminence had passed over his head. He had been there so long that he had outlived all the other settlers who were in the neighborhood when he arrived. He had outlived the thrilling story of his youth. It was just old enough to be in shape to be forgotten and not sufficiently in the long ago to make history. Apart from his hermit characteristics, his earliest neighbors had shunned him, calling him "the Indian killer." He had outlived that name, not that he cared, but it was an unpleasant appellation to carry about.

After half a century, there was an air of dignity about the old man, a halo of romance and mystery. Age gives a glamor to the most commonplace; the John Ironcutter, of eighty-odd years, commanded respect, whereas the John Ironcutter, a rough German peasant of nineteen, had not. His ponderous form and face, the heavy, aquiline features, his sluggish walk, his impenetrable silence, all gave him an atmosphere that was hard to forget. He never once told his life's story. Consequently, there was a score of hazards. Had he told it once, the secret out would not be worth repeating or speculating about. Then all at once, he cast aside the habiliments of the hermit, becoming actually sociable, genial, and frank. The children whom he formerly shunned, he made his warmest friends. But some said that the change had come too late, he could not survive it long, that the real Ironcutter had died, and a fresher and younger spirit had crawled into the crumbling tenement just as the faded soul was departing.

But the old man continued to defy all precedents, living on to his ninety-first year. When he died, it was from old age, a clear conscience;

issued from the tumbledown shell, a mild spirit sought glory. John Iron-cutter's history was a most unusual one. His name now appears in history in connection with a bloodthirsty episode, but many say that here like in divers other cases, history errs.

Ironcutter's beginnings were humble and sordid enough. He had run away from his German home as a boy of fifteen and somehow got to Rotterdam. There he sold himself for his passage to Pennsylvania, fall-ing into the hands of a wealthy landowner, Frederick Stump, of Middle Creek Valley, upon his arrival in the province. Stump picked him out of a crowd of a hundred low-browed ruffians on the Front Street wharves in Philadelphia as being the most likely of the lot. The choice was a good one, as the lad early displayed intelligence as well as fidelity, a rare trait for the ill-born, of no mean order. He became his employer's right-hand man and, when he was nineteen, was appointed overseer of one of his farms. He was treated on terms of equality by his master, who, although a graduate of the University of Bonn, and a man of some breeding, was of plain and democratic manners.

His future seemed a bright one, leading perhaps to a marriage with some niece or dependent of the landed proprietor and a prosperous old age. Then occurred the catastrophe, which brought his bright hopes tumbling about his feet like so many pieces of broken glass. Then came ten years of hiding and wandering, followed by a half-century in the hermitage. Out of this musty chrysalis emerged the regenerated old man, who bloomed like a crop of fall clover for a while and then stumbled off to his reward.

Frederick Stump was a liberal-minded man and possessed a broad spirit of tolerance towards the Indians. He fed them in winter and gave them sound advice, as well as innumerable gifts. There were always three or four natives hanging around his commodious mansion. It was the finest house of its day in Middle Creek Valley. Built of limestone, of herring-bone construction, with a broad chimney, and the Stump coat-of-arms carved out of a block of sandstone embedded below the gable, it was a conspicuous landmark. Inside was a wide hall with a winding stairway; there were spacious rooms, along whose walls gaped great clos-ets running from floor to ceiling with curved walnut doors and frescoed lintels. It was a home fitted to start a dynasty, yet Stump was driven from it suddenly, never to see it again to his dying day.

He died at a very advanced age in Miller-Stadt, afterward called Woodstock, in Virginia. Stump had a favorite nephew, Balzer Minnich, whose wife was kidnapped in broad daylight by a roving band of drunken Indians. Stump, Minnich, and the servant Ironcutter found it out none too soon and trailed the Indians to their camp. They rescued the young woman, but in the battle, they killed six Indians. Three Indian women belonging to the party committed suicide for fear that they would be imprisoned, and one squaw, who had an infant, butchered it. To get them out of the way, all the bodies were dumped into Middle Creek through a hole in the ice. At least this is the story that Stump's relatives and partisans told at the time; it was pretty generally believed, even if it never got into history.

Minnich and his wife opportunely left the country, but Stump and Ironcutter, after the bodies had appeared in the Susquehanna near the Isle of Que, were arrested. Sympathy waxed strong for them, as it was considered a Quaker plot to curry favor with the Indians at the expense of two obscure Germans. The prisoners were lodged in the jail at Carlisle, but a determined mob led by James and John Morrow, two noted pioneers, rescued the prisoners, and they were never recaptured. Stump, as stated previously, drifted to Virginia, while Ironcutter became a wanderer in the Pennsylvania Mountains. The shock of the butchery had unsettled his mind, it was said; he suffered from delusions and hallucinations. Many of his sympathizers harbored him, trying to give him work, but his familiar ghost urged him ever onward like the wandering Jew.

During the massacre, he had singled out a young Indian named White Feather, of about his own age and size, whom he determined to kill. It was a bitter struggle as the youths were evenly matched, but finally, Ironcutter dashed his knife into the Indian's throat. It was a mortal wound, and the young man sank down on his knees. "Oh brother white man," he sobbed in his dying breath, "my loved one is waiting for me tonight, over on Shreiner's Knob; please go tell her that I will never meet her in this world, but I will surely keep my tryst in the next."

Tears were running down the dying lover's cheeks; he made a pitiable spectacle, all blood and tears. But Ironcutter was in an ugly mood; he mimicked his expiring foe, saying to him just as his eyes were glazing, "Let your cursed sweetheart wait; I will not go a step to tell her, let her think you have gone off with someone else."

He would have said more, but the poor young warrior was dead. He kicked the rigid face a couple of times and then dragged the corpse by the heels and threw it on the pile with the other victims of Stump's fury. He helped cut the hole in the ice and push the bloody mess into Middle Creek. He was too proud of his achievement to notice such a thing as an angry wraith until after his delivery from Carlisle Jail. He had parted from Stump, and a settler named McCaslin, who lived in a remote glen in the North Mountains, hid him in his barn. It was in this structure, built of rough logs, and in the haymow that occurred the nativity of his conscience. It was on a chilly midnight, starless and still, that he heard a voice speaking to him from the rafters above. He thought at first it was a bevy of barn owls quarreling as to which controlled the beam. "Oh brother white man," in tones measured and low, came to his ears, "my loved one is waiting for me tonight, over on Shreiner's Knob; please go tell her that I will never meet her in this world, but I will surely keep my tryst in the next."

The words of this disembodied voice sounded familiar; he was about to answer with uncouth jest when he felt a pressure at his throat. He could not articulate; at the same time, arose in him for the first time a pang of regret for the Indian lover he had slain on Middle Creek. A haunting sense of fear overcame him; he climbed out of the mow as best he could, tripping over joists and beams and cutting his shins badly on a Dutch scythe. Just as he emerged from the barn door, he beheld the figure of the murdered Indian not twenty paces in front of him, with one hand held across the angry gash in his throat. Ironcutter uttered a piercing yell; the specter vanished instantly.

The next morning McCaslin's family found the German lying unconscious in the barnyard. It was a week before he came out of his trance, or unconscious state. When he did, he said he had seen a ghost; he refused to remain longer at a haunted plantation. With the ingratitude inherent to ill-bred men, he departed without a word of thanks. For ten weary years, he moved from place to place through the mountains. He was always waked by the voice of the unhappy lover; he always ran from bunk or mow into the open, there to see the avenging wraith. He passed through Dry Valley, Buffalo Valley, White Deer Valley, and into the mazes of the Bald Eagle Mountains. There seemed to be no peace on earth for him; he wished every day that he might die. Once he shot himself, once he leaped into a mill race, once a copperhead bit him, but somehow it was ordained he must live and suffer. As he followed the chain of the Bald Eagle Mountains, he always imagined that the next peak further on would give him relief. But each one seemed to house the torment, keener and more horrible. He feared to turn back; like the Wandering Jew, he must go on. His story preceded him. The sympathetic mountaineers were ever ready to receive "John Ironcutter, the Indian killer." Frederick Stump and Minnich were overlooked; the story was told that Ironcutter killed ten Indians, sometimes it was twenty, it did not matter much. Perhaps the best friend that the tormented man-killer met in his wanderings was a certain Roan McCann, who occupied a neat little clearing not far from the present site of Port Matilda.

And strangely enough, he was a bosom friend of Old Frank, the celebrated Indian chief from whom Frankstown received its name. Some whispered that Old Frank had told McCann that a spell had been put on Ironcutter and that he had suffered enough; at any rate, he was merciful. He advised the German to cease his errant habits, to go live by himself, offering him lifelong use of his hunting cabin at the foot of the Last Mountain. And it was here that he sought refuge and ultimate peace. He understood that if he tilled a small garden patch and subsisted partly on wild roots and berries or killed a deer occasionally, he could get along all right. He was of stalwart build, on the sunny side of thirty; life would have been no problem if he could rest at night. Even if he worked himself into a state of exhaustion, the pleading voice would echo through his tired consciousness. The old desire to rush out into the open would overcome him. Once outside, he would see the ghost holding the gaping wound on the neck with one lean, bony hand. He would run back to his bunk to hide his head beneath the buffalo robe until daylight.

He shunned everybody except for his latest benefactor, Roan McCann. Evidently, his moral nature was expanding; ten years, yes five years before, he would have turned his back on his best friend after getting all he could get out of him. McCann was somewhat of a philosopher. That was another new attribute that seemed to find fallow ground in him. He liked McCann's philosophy because he pointed out the possibility that the ghost would be laid someday; there was a chance of surviving it. But neither of them guessed how this would be accomplished. The laying of the ghost was the one ray of hope in the repentant murderer's dreary routine of existence.

What a long story of distorted, hideous nights it was, always followed by days marked by listlessness and exhaustion. Small wonder that he had no mood for visitors. Probably many hermits see ghosts, hence their exclusiveness.

One evening before the old man went to his bunk, he was sitting outside his cabin door on a small wooden milking stool presented to him by one of McCann's daughters, trying to count up the years since the vindictive ghost had rested on his soul. Sixty-two years it was to the best of his calculation, fifty of which years had been spent in solitary retreat at the cabin at the base of the Last Mountain. Below him, several miles away, he could make out a light or two in the small village called Hollidaysburg; it was the year 1830, and there were then but seventy-two souls in this afterward prosperous community.

"What a wasted time," he muttered to himself, "I were far better dead than buried alive here."

Then the chilling fear ran through him that he might have to live forever, that might be the full extent of the curse upon him. He reached up with the fingers of his left hand and felt the deep scar on his neck where he had shot himself over half a century before. And he thought of how he had been rescued, and of all strange fates, by an Indian, from the mill race at William McElhattan's mill; of how he just didn't die after the savage bite from the copperhead.

He waited until the last light was extinguished in the distant village; then, he was ready to retire. He was in a particularly melancholy frame of mind that night. A bat chasing a mosquito rushed into the open door ahead of him; he struck at it savagely with his ironwood cane as it darted past his head. Despite his gloomy reminiscences, he fell asleep quickly.

It must have been midnight when he was awakened by pressure on one of his hands. He rose up, rubbing his eyes. Moonlight was filtering in through chinks in the roof and from under the door. He heard a voice. It said in distinct, measured tones, "'Oh white brother, I have met my loved one over on Shreiner's Knob tonight. I am very happy. I have found that this is the next world. It was near to me all the time, please come outside, and all will be forgiven."

John Ironcutter could hardly believe his senses; he got up slower this time; he rubbed his hands over the buffalo robe to make sure that he was not dreaming. He pushed open the door and looked out. On the sward before him, white with dew, stood two figures, arm in arm.

One was the Indian youth, the White Feather, whom he had slain, but the gaping wound was gone. The other was the frail, beautiful figure of a maiden. When White Feather saw his old foe, he raised his right hand and made several antic passes above his head. Then he spoke. "My deliverance has come, after sixty weary years, my loved one crossed into our world, the spirit world, tonight. She had waited for me every evening, in moonlight or storm, since the night she expected me when you laid me low. She, too, wanted to die, but she never lost faith or believed I had gone off with another. Somehow, I could appear to you, to torture you, but I could not visit my loved one and tell her to cease her solitary vigil, that death would unite us. I suffered as you have suffered, above all as she has suffered. But now she has crossed over; we are one for such time as the Great Spirit may allow. We are happy. We forgive you. Farewell, white brother."

Then the two figures faded away into the white dew and the moon-beams. Instead of feeling frightened, the old German experienced a sense of calm and peace such as had not been his portion in sixty-two long years. He turned about, re-entering his cabin. Lying down on his bunk, he fell into a dreamless sleep, waking in the morning refreshed and reju-venated. It was as if he had bathed in the Fountain of Youth. He felt just as he had when he was a bright, ambitious lad of nineteen down in the valley of Middle Creek. During the morning, three small children passed his cabin, driving the sheep to their pastures on the mountainsides. Instead of turning his back, he called to them cheerily, and when they spoke to him, he chatted with them pleasantly. At noon two fox hunters chanced his way. He greeted them genially and asked them to partake of his simple meal.

In the afternoon, Roan McCann rode up on horseback; he was surprised to see the altered appearance of his dependent. "Oh John, you look fifty years younger," was his sincere exclamation.

Old John explained what had happened as quickly as he could. "Your prophecy was correct; the ghost has been laid; I can now spend my declining days in peace."

Roan drew a bottle of mountain-still whiskey from his saddle bag. "Let us celebrate this day; let there be many more of them."

Ironcutter passed an evening such as he had not known since youth, an evening of song, stories, and cheer. When he retired that night, his sleep was absolutely dreamless. A new era had come for him; he was spared ten years to enjoy it.

When he died, a goodly array of mountaineers followed his remains to the tomb.

"It must have been all a mistake about his having been the Indian killer," said the traveling preacher as he watched the last spade-fulls of dirt thrown in the grave, "the deceased was a grand old gentleman; he wouldn't have killed a fly."

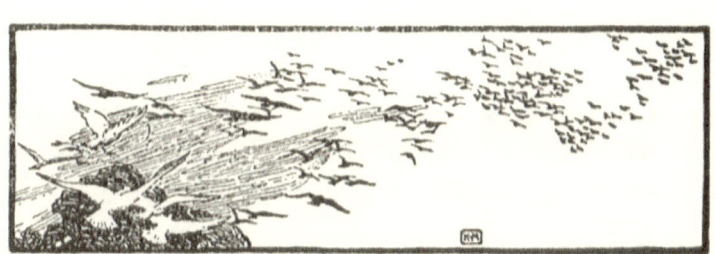

APPENDIX

Appendix A (see page 40)

A man named George A. Schmenk is said to have killed a genuine brown bear, weighing three hundred pounds, not a *color phase* of the black bear, as at first reported, near Carroll, Clinton County, Pa., on Nov. 31, 1912,

Appendix B (see page 182)

When a few days later, the author had a look at the Dorman panther in the natural history museum at the Albright College, Myerstown, Pa., the following lines shaped themselves in his mind:

At twilight, when the shadows flit,
Within the ancient museum, I sit,
Gazing through the dust-encrusted glass
(While hosts of native memories pass),
At your effigy, ludicrously stuffed
The fulvous color faded; the paws all puffed.
The bullet-holes in jowl and side
Tell where your lifeblood ebbed like some red tide;
A streak of light-the last of day
Gleams through a window on your muzzle gray.
And lights your glassy eyes with garnet fire
You almost stir those orbs in fretful ire
Which gape into the sunset's dying flame
Towards the old mountains whence you came:
Revives old images that dormant lie-
Outside the wind is raising to a sigh
Like oft you voiced in the primeval wood
In your life's pilgrimage. I'd trace it if I could
In white pine forests, tops trembling in the breeze,

Like restless sable-colored seas,

Beneath, in rhododendron thickets high.

You crouched until your prey came by.

Grouse, or startled fawn, or even fisher-fox

You rent, and then slunk hack into the rocks.

And on the wintry nights, lit by the cloud-swept moon

Your wailing to the music of the spheres atune.

Rose to a roar which echoed over all

Beside which wolves' lamenting to a treble fall.

And through the snows, your mate so slim draws nigh

Noiselessly, with strange love-light in her eye

You lick her coat and stroke her with your tail.

Whispering a love-song wearisome as the gale.

You leave her with a last long fond caress

Adown the glen you go in stealthiness,

. . . A loud report! another! how you leap.

With a resounding thud into the snow, you fall asleep.

Your blood-stained hide the hunter bears away.

The virile emblem of an ampler day.

Your enemy, the golden eagle picks your carcass dry,

Wild morning glories trellis on your ribs awry.

Your meaning is a deep one-while your kind live, men will rule.

There will be less of weakling, runt, or fool.

No enervation will our rugged courage sap,

We will not dawdle on plump luxury's lap.

But as your race declines, so dwindles man.

The painted cheek replaces coat of tan.

And marble halls, and beds of cloth of gold.

Succeed the log-cabins of the days of old.

When the last panther falls then woe betide.

Nature's retributive cataclysm is at our side.

Our boasted civilization, then will be no more,

Fresh forms must come from out the Celestial store.

Nov. 6, 1912.